Heart
of the
Goblin King

The Realm
Book One

Lisa Manifold

ISBN: 1943530052X

ISBN-13: 978-1943530052
OTI Press LLC

DEDICATION

To Rachel, Shannon, Monica, Corinne, and Wendy.

Between the five of you, I am becoming the writer I want to be.

To Sandy —
We all need more
Goblin King in
our lives!
Lisa Mantfold

Contents

ACKNOWLEDGMENTS

This is always a hard section for me to write, although it's one of my favorites. I love being able to publically acknowledge those who have a hand in making this book come to life.

I only worry that I'll forget someone.

First, to my critique groups. It's funny, I hear the complaint that no one ever sees the whole thing from start to finish. I'd never get a book out if you did. But I love that you all give me heartfelt and honest feedback. Even when it's what I don't really want to hear.

To my amazing, long-suffering editor, Rachel Millar. What would I do without you? Talk about hard home truths! I love them, though, and all that you give me. I love ya to the moon and back.

To the fantastic Aria at Resplendent Media. She does all of my covers. I may at times give her an idea, and in the case of Brennan, a cover model, but she makes a visual of what's in my head, and she gets better every time she does. Thank you for bringing Brennan to life.

To my parents: Mom, Dick, Dad, Liz, Sue and Don—your continued belief and support means the world.

To Sap and Big Easy, my sister and brother—you are my favorite cheerleaders, and future BBs.

To Rocky Mountain Fiction Writers for providing a place for me to learn and stretch my wings. The value of being part of such an organization is priceless.

My Darling Boys—just before this went to print, they wanted to help me edit, and read over what I'd written to make sure it was right. For always asking me how my writing is going, and telling me how proud they are of me. I only hope that my going for what I want can inspire you both one day.

To Jimmy, my wonderful husband. You support me in all I do. I love you.

Lisa Manifold

CHAPTER ONE

Brennan

After what seemed like an eternity, his mother let him go. Lessons were finished for the day, and the sun shone brightly on the afternoon. He could go and find the others, and forget about magic and all the drills his mother made him practice so many times. "You must always have control of your power," she said. As though he might forget it.

He put the thoughts of lessons out of his mind and raced into the garden. Hopefully the rest of the boys would be playing there rather than in the woods. Hopefully Cian would be in a good mood and let him play too.

He heard them before he saw them. They were playing *caman*, even though there weren't enough players for two full teams. Cian led them, as he always did. Brennan could hear his brother shouting to another player.

He moved around the hedge that opened up to a grassy area where the other boys were. He didn't speak, only watched them, struggling and laughing as each one tried to get the ball. Cian, as usual, spoke first.

"What are you doing here? Don't you have lessons?"

"I'm done," he said.

"And?" Cian stood up a little, letting his body lean on the *caman* stick, the snotty look Brennan hated on his face. "Why are you here?"

"I bet he wants to play," said Illion. His brother's closest friend.

"Is that true? You actually want to join us rather than becoming the greatest magical magician ever?" Cian snickered as he asked Brennan, looking to the other boys for support.

No matter what he said, there was no hope of escaping humiliation. May as well be honest. "Yes."

Cian laughed, and the others laughed with him.

"Weren't there any goblins you could play with?" Sneered Illion.

Ever since their father Jharak had announced that his younger son was the heir to the Goblin Realm, Cian and all his friends lost no chance to make fun of him. He didn't understand why it was a bad thing. He liked the goblins. They were funny and, although they were also funny looking, they were loyal, and kind, and caring in ways Brennan had never imagined they could be. Besides, just because he was the heir didn't mean he'd be the Goblin King. The current king had a lovely wife and would no doubt have sons of his own.

"Enough of this, Cian. Let's play," said one of the boys impatiently. Brennan couldn't tell who it was.

Cian faced Brennan. The mocking look had disappeared. "No one wants you here, Brennan. Go away! No one wants to play with you, nasty little *goblin*!"

Without waiting for a response, he gestured to Illion and the game resumed.

Brennan held back the tears and bit at his lip. He would not cry in front of them. Walking back to the hedge and around to the side away from the game, he tried to puzzle it out. Why did Cian hate him? He'd done nothing to him. In fact, Brennan did whatever Cian asked.

"When is your father going to send him to the Goblin Kingdom? I'm tired of him hanging around. He's starting to creep, just like a goblin." Illion had to know that Brennan could still hear them.

"Not soon enough." Cian's reply was bored, uncaring.

It stopped Brennan in his tracks. How could his own brother feel this way? Dismiss him like this to people who weren't even family?

Cian really did hate him, Brennan thought. It wouldn't matter what he did, Cian would always hate him. He could feel his face begin to burn as the blood rushed to it. His fists clenched, thinking of all the horrid things Cian had said and done since Father made the announcement. That's when everything changed. Brennan, not Cian, began receiving advanced lessons in magic. As the eldest, Cian felt he should be taught more of magic, but their parents hadn't agreed. Brennan's lessons had doubled, and Cian became a stranger to him. He didn't understand why anyone would want to be stuck learning magic all day long. Usually, Mother was very cross and scolded him a great deal. Nothing to be envious of.

Cian's voice came to him again. "The fewer sniveling goblins we have skulking about, the better. Enough of the little goblin scum. Let's play some more before Mother comes looking for me."

He could feel the rage that had been building ever since his father made the announcement and everything changed for him. It curled inside of him like a living thing, pounding on his insides like a prisoner trying to break free. That's what he was—a prisoner. How could Cian not see it? Because he didn't want to.

Stupid, mean, hateful, spiteful—his thoughts centered on Cian, everything he felt but that he hadn't been able to say. Just once, he'd like Cian to feel how his words hurt. To feel the pain he inflicted with no thought at all. Cian was going to be a terrible king, because Cian was mean. Brennan wanted his brother to feel the weight of his words and actions. He felt the anger rise from him, taking wing now that it was free from confinement.

A yell from the field behind the hedge where he struggled broke his thoughts.

"Cian? Cian!"

"What happened to him?"

"Go find the Queen!"

***

Brennan stood hunched next to his mother, trying to disappear. Even though the other boys had been sent away from the castle, talk flew like birds on the wind. Everyone knew that he'd been angry with Cian. Everyone knew that Cian had fallen, never to get up again after arguing with his younger brother.

Eyes followed him wherever he went. His parents looked at him with eyes deepened by sorrow.

His mother put an arm around him. He turned his face towards her robes, hoping to keep from crying in front of all these people. The warmth from his mother was the only thing decent on this gray, overcast day. In a rare moment of affection, Mother allowed him to stay close to her, and kept her arm around him. They stood together until he felt her grip on him loosen, and Brennan looked out from her robes.

The body of Cian, wrapped carefully with his face exposed, being carried out by the men of his household. As the heir to the Fae King, Cian had his own household, just as Brennan did. He could see the marks of tears on their faces. Maybe Cian wasn't mean to them as he'd been to his brother.

The small bier with its attendants reached the coach that stood waiting outside the gates. Brennan didn't understand why they weren't taking him to the place of kings, where all their ancestors were buried. He had been kept from everyone, even his parents, ever since Cian had fallen in the garden.

Brennan leaned into his mother again, trying to find some sense of this, to feel something other than overwhelming guilt.

It didn't come. Nerida now held herself stiff, and Brennan looked up at her to see why. He couldn't contain his shock when he saw a solitary tear slide down Nerida's cheek. Fae didn't cry, even in times of sorrow.

He hung his head, and stepped away from his mother. He didn't deserve any comfort. He'd killed his brother, and made his mother cry.

This is my fault. I let go of my magic. I lost control of my emotions. He felt like crying himself. He knew that wouldn't make things any better, not with his mother refusing to allow him close, and all these people watching. He took a breath, forcing himself to hold everything in. Had he not allowed himself to be angry, to let his anger and strong feelings out, Cian would still be here. No wonder he'd been alone. He could not be trusted.

I must never lose control like this again. Never again.

CHAPTER TWO

Iris

"So, um, Iris?"

Oh my god. He sounded nervous. Heath sounded nervous! It seemed an impossible thing to say about the tall, kind, ridiculously handsome captain of the lacrosse team who'd also been my crush since I'd first seen him. Nervous about talking to me, plain old Iris Mattingly.

"Yes?" Please sound calm! I turned to look up at him from where I sat in the student union. Please sound normal, and not as though I was about to scream like a little girl! He looked even taller than usual, leaning over me.

"You going to the game tonight?"

"I hadn't decided yet." I made myself stop there, not wanting to be foolish.

"Would you like to come with me?"

Would I? If I threw my arms around him and smothered his face in kisses, I'd bet the invitation would be off, so I only nodded, and smiled. "That would be great, Heath."

"It would?" I hoped I wasn't imagining the excitement in his voice. "Yeah, it would—I mean, it will be. So, I'll pick you up around six?"

I nodded again, trying to contain the grin that wanted to take over. "Okay. Let me give you my address."

He grinned then, the wide smile that made me fall for him in the first place. "It's okay, I know where you live! I'll see you tonight!" He leaned down and kissed my cheek, and then turned and sauntered off. It happened so fast that it didn't even seem real.

Heath *kissed* me. He'd kissed *me*!

I raised my hand to my cheek in wonder. How gross would it be if I didn't wash my cheek for…forever? I couldn't even contemplate why Heath, my crush, knew where I lived. The kiss distracted me from anything else.

Oh my god. What did I have to wear?

Out of habit, I glanced down at my watch. Oh, hell. I wouldn't have time to shop before, my eleven o'clock class. As I headed for class, I wondered how he knew where I lived, and whether or not I should be concerned. My concern faded each time I thought about him kissing me.

I couldn't tell what we talked about in English lit that morning. I didn't even care.

***

I looked out onto the football field, trying to contain my impatience and anger. This was not going as planned. Well, it wasn't as pleasant as I'd hoped it would be.

The night started well. Heath came to the house, and met my parents. I could tell they liked him. We'd talked easily on the ride to the game, and Heath had asked if I minded if we sat with his friends. All good to that point.

Most of his friends were nice. Some had girlfriends, and most of them were nice, too. But then things took an abrupt turn. One of the girls sitting with this group, Trista, I think her name was, obviously had designs on Heath. Because the moment we sat down, she leaned around him and started in on me. She looked at me intensely. "Are you new here?"

I nodded. I wanted to be friendly, but she didn't give

off the friendly vibe. "I am." I offered a smile.

She didn't smile back. She cut her eyes at Heath, and then looked at me. "Thought so," she said, and turned away.

That wasn't awkward or anything. A couple of the girls rolled their eyes at Trista, but none were brave enough to say anything to her. I thought I'd gotten lucky and missed out on all the mean girl stuff when I skipped high school by being home schooled. There's no other kind of school when you live on a boat full time. Apparently I didn't get to skip that part. College had the same mean girls, and Trista seemed proud to count herself among their ranks.

"Doesn't it totally suck when you have new people pushing their way in where they're not wanted?"

I heard a murmured response.

"Shut up, Trista."

Trista ignored that and continued. "I mean, if I went to school somewhere new, I would let people come to me, and not invite myself out and count on people just being nice."

Okay, really? Please. I glanced at Heath. He was glaring at Trista. "You're being really rude to my guest. The guest I invited."

Trista couldn't hide her shocked expression. She hadn't counted on Heath having manners. Or, apparently, the strength to call her on her behavior. I had to duck my head to hide a grin.

"Iris, I'm really sorry. Obviously, I'm too nice and give people more credit than they deserve. You want something to drink?" He stood up, not waiting for an answer, and took my hand. As he did, he glared around at the crowd of people we sat with. The way he looked dared anyone to speak up. No one did.

I stood with him. "A Coke would be great."

"Then let's go get one." He turned his back on his friends and led me to the stairs.

As we got further away, I could feel my shoulders relax. Sort of.

"I'm sorry," he said, the angry tone gone from his voice. "I can't believe she was such a…" He trailed off, looking down.

I could tell he wanted to call her a really rude name. I could afford to be nice. "It's fine, Heath. Sometimes people are just rude."

"No doubt." He still wouldn't look at me.

"Heath, it's okay."

That made him look up. "No, it's not!"

The fact that he felt defensive about me—protective, maybe—made me want to burst into song. "It is. I am new, and I'm out with the nicest guy in school. That's going to irritate people."

"What? Not the dreaded 'nice'! I sure as hell don't want to finish last! How about the most amazing guy in school?"

I started to laugh. The tension of moments ago dissipated. "Well of course you are! I have very exacting standards, you know."

"So do I. That's why I'm out with you."

I didn't know what to say to that. I squeezed his hand. Thankfully, I spotted the signs for the restroom, which would give me a little reprieve.

"Hey, I'll be right back." I let go of his hand, feeling the loss of its warmth.

"Okay. I'll grab your Coke."

I couldn't help the leap of happiness I felt when he said that. *Get a grip. It's a stupid Coke.* "Thanks," I said. "Wait for me here?"

"Right here. This very spot," he smiled at me.

I hurried to the bathroom. There wasn't much of a line, which is some kind of miracle for the women's restroom at a football game. I waited my turn, too keyed up to talk to anyone even if I weren't waiting in line in a bathroom, and hurried into the stall. When I closed and latched the door,

I heaved a sigh. Tonight was…wonderful, and overwhelming all at the same time. It felt good to have a moment alone and just *think*. Being with Heath had all my senses on overload. Add to that things were going even better than I expected, nasty girls named Trista notwithstanding. I knew his fraternity formal would be at the end of the month. Maybe he'd ask me…my mind swirled with happy possibilities.

When I opened the door again, I didn't even get one foot out of the stall before the bathroom exploded in a bright blue burst of light.

Brennan

He looked around, desperate to find Drake. The little clearing where they often stopped to let the horses rest and eat when out on business from the castle had exploded in goblins—all armed and coming straight for him. He'd lost sight of Drake in the angry, snarling mass of the enemy. Except the goblins weren't supposed to be *his* enemy. These were, however. They were doing their best to kill him.

He spotted a head above the rest, dark hair flying free of the helmet. Was that Drake? Just as he began to move towards the head, his vision was blocked by a bloody set of teeth. He slashed at the teeth and they disappeared. He didn't slow down to see what happened. Probably a good thing, as more teeth and swords rose to take the place of their fallen brethren.

He finally reached the place where he thought he'd seen Drake. If there were any more of the enemy about, they were hiding or pretending to be dead. Drake wasn't where Brennan thought he'd be—although he'd been there. The pile of goblins and trolls dead or dying attested to Drake's presence at one point. Looking down, he noticed his sword arm, covered in gore—the blood of goblins. His people.

How had it come to this? When he had time to think on this, Brennan knew his sense of loss would be overwhelming.

No time for such thoughts now. He needed to find Drake. Movement to his side made him turn his head. Drake strode towards him. Brennan guessed he probably looked as bad as Drake did.

"What happened?"

Drake shook his head. "I don't know. They pulled me away from you, and even though I kept fighting, the focus was to separate us. When there was only one particularly foul troll left, he turned and ran, dragging me along behind him."

"Did you kill him?"

Drake smiled, although there was no joy in it. "Yes. Just as suddenly as they came upon us, they were all gone." He shook his head again. "I don't understand, Brennan. What was the point of this?"

Brennan looked around where they'd been ambushed. "I have no answer for that. I wish I did. The only thing accomplished is more of my people dead."

Many fae wouldn't be sad. To most, the death of goblins and trolls meant nothing. But Brennan, as the Goblin King, had accepted his father's appointment to this realm hundreds of years before. He enjoyed the goblins, as funny and sometimes disgusting as they could be. They were nowhere near as serious or as pompous as his own kind, the fae.

To see goblins rise up against him—there was something dark and dangerous at work. There had not been such unrest in the kingdom since before Brennan came to the throne.

He studied all the dead, reigning in his temper and the nearly overwhelming anger and grief. There would be a reckoning for this. But he could not indulge in his emotions. Not now.

He turned to Drake. Whatever he'd been about to say died on his lips as a man appeared, walking through the bodies littered on the ground as though he walked through the palace gardens. Robed and hooded, he carried no weapon, but made straight for where Brennan and Drake stood. Once he got within ten feet of them, he stopped.

"Your Majesty," the voice was deep and dripped with scorn.

"You are?" Brennan drew himself up, keeping his sword at the ready. Beside him, he could feel the tension emanating from Drake. Every fiber of his being screamed that this man was an enemy and should be cut down immediately.

"It matters not who I am. What matters is that you now see what those you pretend to rule think of you. They hate you." Brennan could hear the satisfaction in the words. "They'd rather die than suffer your reign any longer. I'm here," the man threw back his hood, revealing himself to be a handsome fae with a long scar down the side of his face, "To offer you the terms of your surrender."

The man smiled, and Brennan was struck by how goblin-like his teeth seemed. Sharp, elongated by some form of magic. It almost looked like the scarred fae had deliberately sharpened the ends to the razor-like points. Nothing about the man before him made any sense. Brennan knew he didn't know the man, yet he had an air of the familiar.

"We shall not." His voice didn't waver. "I am the rightful ruler of this land, and while you might have stirred up and taken advantage of my people—"

"Your people? They are no more your people than I am."

"Are you not fae? What interest do you claim in this kingdom?" Drake interrupted.

Good question, Brennan thought. Most fae wanted nothing to do with his citizens.

"Again, I do not matter. The only question is whether you accept the terms of surrender?"

"Certainly not," Brennan answered. "I am committed to my kingdom and my people. I do not need to hear anything more from you."

"Very well," the man sighed. "You leave me no choice."

Before he or Drake could take a step, the man raised his hands and a blue light shot out of them. Brennan ran forward then, sword raised, but felt himself fall backwards as the light hit him as though a tangible weapon.

He landed flat on his back on a hard surface. He could hear screams around him. How was that possible, when everyone else had been dead?

He sat up, looking around. Wherever he was, it wasn't the clearing where he and Drake had been ambushed. A few feet from him, Drake also slowly sat up, looking as dazed as Brennan felt.

"Where are we?" Drake asked.

Brennan tried to take in the room. It had small boxes on one side, and mirrors and pedestals to the other.

"This doesn't seem to be one of the Fae Realms—I recognize nothing. If I had to guess, I'd say we're in the Human Realm," he said, standing.

"How did we end up here? Who was that fae? I didn't recognize him." Drake had gotten up and come to stand next to him.

"I don't know the answers to any of those questions, other than our scarred fae friend is obviously a sorcerer, and sent us here to—"

"Be a hindrance," Drake finished.

"Yes. We need to get back."

"How do you want...?" Drake stopped, his eyes on something over Brennan's shoulder.

Brennan turned his head and saw a girl standing in the doorway of one of the box stalls. Her mouth was open, one hand on either side of the door and looking as though she'd been frozen in place.

"Good day, madam," Brennan said, bowing. "I apologize for the inconvenience we have caused."

"Who…who…are you?" The girl finally got out. She looked terrified.

"He is called Brennan, and I'm Drake," Drake came forward. "How do we get out of here?"

She looked them up and down, her incredulity apparent. "Um…I'm sorry, I don't understand." Her gaze stopped at their swords, and her eyes widened even further. She had large, blue eyes, honey blond hair, and pink, full lips that currently were in the shape of an O. Brennan had the feeling that she wanted to scream but couldn't get the sound out.

"I think you need to speak something other than fae," He said quietly to Drake.

"That is Brennan, and I am Drake," Drake switched easily to the human tongue. "How do we get out of here?"

Her mouth moved, but words didn't come out right away. She seemed to be trying to herself against the edge of the door. When she managed to speak, her voice shook. "Where are you going?" Her eyes went back to the swords. Brennan could feel the fear coming off her.

"To the Goblin Realm," Brennan answered. "Where is the portal?" He directed this to Drake. While there were not many, he knew that there were portals to all the realms. Obviously, the girl was not a portal guardian. She was too frightened by their appearance.

What troubled him more was how the scarred fae knew of a portal between the realms. They were a closely guarded secret among the royal families. How—

"To the where?" Her voice rose to a squeak. "Look, I've obviously interrupted whatever this is—" her hand waved, taking in the cracked floor, and he and Drake, "So I'll just be leaving now." She took a step, sidling away from the stall door, clearly wanting to be far from them.

"Oh, no," said Drake, blocking her. "We must find the portal. Where is it?"

"I don't know what you're talking about!" She looked like she was about to cry. Brennan resisted the urge to sigh. Crying females. He found them completely disarming usually, and were to be avoided at all costs. Besides, when did crying ever help any situation?

"Drake, I don't think she is—" He began.

The girl wasn't finished. "I need to get out of here!" She made a dash to get around Drake.

Brennan reached out a hand, sending out the thought to *sleep*, and she dropped almost right in front of him. He leapt to catch her as she fell.

"Fabulous," Drake said, looking down at her with disgust. "Now we're scaring little girls. We must return, Brennan. The Human Realm is nowhere we want to be."

"I'm well aware of that," Brennan said dryly, looking at the girl in his arms. This close to her, he saw that her skin was pale, almost luminescent. The dark lashes against her cheeks were long. Without the barely restrained panic she'd given off before he put her to sleep, she was lovely.

For a human.

"Here, take her," he said, offering her to Drake. "I need to access a stone." Nor did he like the way holding her felt. It felt...dangerous.

"You know we're going to need to take her back. Even as good as you are, you can't manage her and a portal."

"You're mad," Brennan said, pulling a gleaming stone from the pouch on his belt. He wanted no part of this lovely, human girl, even if she'd seen them. "I will adjust her memories. She won't remember a thing."

"Oh, of course, your lordship. I'd forgotten you were the all-powerful Goblin King, capable of many feats all at once!" Sarcasm dripped from Drake's words.

"We cannot bring her back, Drake." He didn't take his gaze from the stone cupped in his hands. It began to glow.

"What if she's in league with the fae who sent us here? Don't you think it's suspicious that he sends us here, and the only person we see is a portal guardian who claims complete ignorance? Did you hit your head harder than I realized when we came through, Brennan? Think! We must bring her back, have the Court Mage look within her, and if he sees that she is harmless, then we can remove her memories and return her."

Drake's words made sense. His reaction to the girl did not. Normally, he'd toss her over his shoulder and be on his way. The thought of bringing her to his kingdom, to the Goblin Realm, filled him with dread. Which in and of itself was extremely irritating. He had nothing to fear from a human girl.

"I don't think she's a portal guardian. Now will you please give me a moment of peace? I need to concentrate. I have no idea where we are, and I have to get us back as close to the castle as possible."

Drake said something, but not loud enough to require any comment. Thankfully.

With moments, a glowing circle appeared in front of where Brennan stood with the stone. It grew wider and wider until it became the size of a tall fae. Once it held the shape, Brennan turned to Drake. "Put her down, and I'll address her memory. Get through the portal. We have no time to waste. Should it close, get to the castle. I will meet you there as soon as I may."

Drake tightened his grip on the sleeping girl. It made Brennan clench the stone tightly.

"No. We must be sure she's not in league with that scarred sorcerer. Stranger things have occurred," he protested, clearly seeing the look on Brennan's face. "Since when have we ever known a fae to keep a scar? On the face? It's better that we be sure, Brennan." He turned and still holding the girl, stepped through the portal before Brennan could get another word out.

He didn't want her there. She was too...lovely. Too...human. Too..something. He didn't know what. Whatever it was, she stirred something in him that made him want to put her away from him as quickly as possible. And now Drake had brought her back to Fae.

The threat from the sorcerer notwithstanding, regardless of whether she might yet be unmasked as a spy, he didn't want her there. Too late now, he thought. He sighed, and squaring his shoulders, taking a last look around the small room, he stepped into the portal. Just in time, as it snapped behind him and disappeared.

Drake stood, still holding the girl, looking around. He gave Brennan a look best described as annoyed.

"Where have you sent us, Brennan? This isn't anywhere near the castle."

As much as he hated to admit it, Drake was right. "I think we're on the edge of the kingdom. I'll just have to open another portal."

"No, let me. Something is off. You have not missed a portal in as long as I can remember. Here, take her."

Brennan reluctantly took the girl, not wanting to admit that he had the same fear. Had the sorcerer affected his magic? Was the presence of the girl affecting it? If she were in league with the scarred fae, it could be. He didn't want to give credence to Drake's worries.

Even with his suspicions, he couldn't help but note how right she felt in his arms. As though she had a right to be there. With him. The thought and the accompanying rush of emotion made him...unsettled.

Brennan didn't like unsettled. It led to mistakes. Mistakes on his part ended up with people being hurt.

"Hey, Bren, hello?" Drake peered at him.

"I'm sorry, I was—"

"Yeah, doesn't matter. I'll need—"

They both stopped as the girl in his arms stirred and woke.

CHAPTER THREE

Iris

"Where the hell am I?"

"An excellent question," a deep voice said.

I moved my head, but my eyes wouldn't—couldn't? see. "I can't see," I said, trying hard to keep the panic under control. I felt the arms holding me tighten briefly. The arms? Who held me?

"Who are you? Where am I?" I attempted to throw myself out of the arms of whoever it was holding me.

A puff of breath to my left, behind my head, told me there was at least one other person. An annoyed person. My fear increased, and I thrashed against the arms harder. They squeezed me, but I couldn't give up.

"Send her to sleep, Brennan. We are far from home, far even from the clearing we're—"

"I know," the man holding me sounded annoyed now as well. "I also have eyes, Drake. Young woman, will you hold still?" That last bit came out as a shout.

"No! Put me down, asshat! Help! Help! Kidnapping!"

"Wonderful. Announce our presence, stupid girl," exclaimed the voice next to me in disgust. "Shut her up, Brennan!"

"I'm…trying," the man holding me said, losing his grip on me somewhat as I struggled to get free.

Immediately, I took advantage of the slip to kick out. The arm holding my leg tightened again. It felt like a vise.

"Stop it!" He hissed near my head.

I screamed in what I hoped was the ear of the kidnapper holding me.

"Enough!" The other man snapped, and then I felt a hand on my forehead.

Suddenly, I wondered why I was fighting so hard. Everything would be all right. I relaxed, glad that someone held me and didn't let me fall. This man sounded nice...surely he'd be as nice as he sounded.

"Young woman, what is your name?"

"I'm...I'm Iris."

"What a lovely name," his voice warmed for a moment. Such a nice voice. I couldn't remember why he carried me but I felt sure everything would be okay. Then he spoke again.

"I am Brennan."

The name sent a delightful shiver through me.

"Yes, and I'm Drake, and we're lost and outside our borders, Brennan. Can we move this along? I dislike being dropped and stuck who knows where."

Drake must be the grumpy one.

"Drake, you need to focus." Now Brennan sounded stern. "Iris, please hold still."

"I'm okay," I interjected, wanting to be helpful. "You can put me down."

"Can you see?" Brennan sounded like he was trying not to laugh.

"Well, no."

"Then for the time being, I'll keep hold of you. I'll ask you to be silent. We need to concentrate. We're not in an ideal situation. If you can be patient, we will soon be in safe quarters, and then we can attend to your eyes and other needs."

The warmth of his—Brennan's—body felt good next to mine, and as he spoke, his arms tightened slightly around me. How nice of him to bring me along. But...oh, dear, I thought. My mom and dad would not be happy. This nice man Brennan would no doubt be able to explain everything to them. Then I remembered Heath. Oh, no. We hadn't bothered to tell him where we were going. Maybe Brennan could explain it to him too?

Another annoyed puff of breath, behind my head again. Drake. That's what he said his name was. Drake. Drake the grumpy, puffy dragon.

Drake muttered something I couldn't understand. It didn't sound like English. This Drake guy needed to relax. "Bren," he said. Even I could hear the warning in his tone. What was he so upset about?

"Drake, use this stone. This should get us there." Brennan's voice stayed calm, almost neutral.

"How can you be sure that it will get us home?"

"This one goes to my chambers."

"You didn't focus on that when we came through the first time?"

"Quiet, Drake. You must focus." Brennan didn't sound as pleasant as when he'd spoke to me.

Drake obviously didn't know when to shut up.

I could hear something. It sounded like skirts swishing. Were both these guys wearing skirts? They sounded older than me, which made the visual funnier. I held back a giggle.

"Shh," Brennan said, his breath warming my ear. His voice had lowered, giving me a funny feeling. It rolled over me, like a silk sheet being pulled up around me. "Mustn't disturb Drake. He needs absolute silence." He almost sounded like he wanted to laugh.

Apparently my giggling hadn't been quiet.

"Sarcasm will not improve anything," Drake said calmly. "What are you concerned about?"

"There is a dust cloud in the distance. The not-so-far distance, in case you were wondering."

I felt Drake walk past us. "Damn. I'd hoped to avoid detection. Is there a gong that announces your presence wherever you go?" Drake no longer sounded grumpy. I

could hear amusement in Drake's tone. He and Brennan
were close. But Brennan was obviously the nice one.

"Perhaps. If not, there should be. I do wish it was not
so prompt. What are you doing, Drake? Can you get a
better look at the dust cloud? Does it look like our friend
the scarred fae?"

The words hummed in my head. "Scarry McScarface,"
I giggled.

"What did you say?" I could tell Brennan spoke
because I felt the vibration in his chest next to my ear.

"Scarry McScarface. Our friend the scarred fae," I sang
the words a little.

Silence greeted my words, and then I heard both men
shout with laughter. Brennan leaned forward slightly, and I
felt myself dip. Kind of like flying.

"Well, at least she has a sense of humor." Drake
sounded almost nice for a moment. "I like that, Scarry
McScarface. No, I don't see McScarface but the cloud is
still some distance away. Hang onto the funny girl, Bren,
and let's get out of here."

Brennan's grip on me tightened, and I felt the hum of
his voice next to me again. "Let me stand back. No telling
what's going to happen. You and one of my crystals. I
think you're right. I did bump my head."

"Of course, lordship. Apologies." Now Drake was
laughing. "I'm hurrying. I know that holding the human
and fighting will be too much for you."

Brennan grumbled. "I am not sure why I put up with
you."

I felt Brennan tense up. Something was happening that
I could neither see nor hear. I strained, trying to get a read
on this. Then he exhaled, and I could feel his relief. It
flowed from his arms to me. Interesting how I could feel
his emotions. He walked forward, taking a large step.
"Finally. Now we need to find the Court Mage."

I couldn't hear the sounds of outside anymore. It felt
like we were inside. I really hoped that I'd be able to see

again soon. This pretty much sucked. Blind, I had no chance to get home, back to my mom and dad. And Heath. I felt a pang at the date that had just gone up in smoke. He'd think I ran out. Great! I doubted he'd ask me out again. How would I—

"Thank you, Drake. Well done. Good to see you remember something. Will you please bring Taranath to us?" Brennan's voice broke into my thoughts.

I heard footsteps and then the click of a door closing. Brennan still held me. Once the door closed, he turned and carefully set me onto what felt like a couch. I turned my head. Things didn't look quite as black. Could my vision be coming back? I could see a faint glow around the edges of the black.

Brennan's voice right next to my head made me jump. "I am sorry we had to drag you along, but Taranath will be here shortly, and then you'll be home and forget all about this. Is your vision improving?"

"It's getting a little bit lighter," I focused on the direction of his voice, which felt too close. It made my breath catch. I didn't feel so calm. If anything, my calm from only moments before was going away. "What? What the hell? Where am I, and why did you kidnap me?" I pushed myself up off the cushions. He'd laid me down? What was next? The panic rose like bile in my throat. Oh god. *Oh god!* I blinked, but my vision wouldn't clear. A small ring of light around the edge, but that was it! How would I get out of here if I couldn't see? And why had I been calm before? Did he drug me? Oh god, oh god!

I opened my mouth and screamed loudly, hoping to attract help.

Instantly a hand clamped over my mouth. I struggled, grabbing the hand to hold against me and bit down as hard as I could.

"Ow!" Brennan yelled. "What did you do that for, you insane human?"

I didn't answer, but screamed again, and again.

My mouth closed as though there was a zipper on it and someone had zipped it shut.

"Be quiet," Brennan said.

Rather unnecessary. Not like I could talk with my lips sealed shut. What the hell was this place? Blind as a bat, and now gagged. Oh my god. I'd been kidnapped by sex trade assholes.

"I must ask for your forgiveness, but not until later," Brennan said.

He certainly didn't sound sorry. Asshat.

"I cannot having you screaming down the castle. Just let my Court Mage have a look at you, and then we'll get you home."

That stopped me in my thoughts of escape, of getting my vision back, and finding the nearest weapon to brain him with.

He didn't want to sell me to the nearest sex ring? It was probably a lie. And how the hell had he gotten my mouth to shut?

Something wrong, very wrong, was going on here. I couldn't figure out how he'd done it, but my imagination supplied a number of fantastical ideas. None of which I really wanted to think about. None of which should be possible.

Of course, I'd been attacked by guys in skirts swinging swords around in a bathroom. That alone lent itself to falling right into crazy.

"If you'll hold still, and try to remain calm, I may be able to help your vision. Shall I try, or leave you as you are?"

He was still mad about me biting him. I could tell. After a moment, I nodded. Not the most gracious response, but my mouth wouldn't open.

"Don't move. You might want to keep your eyes closed."

At that, I actually rolled my sightless eyes at him. Really? Sarcastic and fairly mean?

I felt a touch on the top of my head, and I jumped, fearful of what was coming.

"Don't move, girl. This won't work if you don't hold yourself still!"

I wanted to ask what the hell he was doing, but...mouth still unable to open. Suddenly, that fact hit me like nothing else about this crazy whatever or wherever I found myself in, and I could feel the tears leaking from my eyes.

I'd been in a lot of scary situations living on a boat my entire life, and I'd never been as scared as I felt right this moment.

"Not tears!"

His voice sounded as though he'd stepped away. Figures. Big, bad kidnappers, falls apart when a girl cries. Asshole.

"Girl—Iris—listen. I won't hurt you. No one will hurt you while you're here. If you will please stop crying and let me help you with your vision, we can..." He stopped.

That sounded ominous.

He sighed. "We can get Taranath to meet with you, and then send you home. I realize it's a great deal to ask, but will you please trust me?"

I listened to his words, and the message behind what he said. He was worried, I could tell. Frustrated as well, although that might not have anything to do with me.

Not what I'd expect a kidnapper's mindset to be. Although I could be wrong. What the hell did I know about the criminal mastermind?

I would have laughed if my mouth worked. This guy didn't really seem to be much of a mastermind. Now his henchman, Drake—that one, maybe.

I crossed my arms in front of me. It made me feel safer. Stupid, I know. I nodded my head once.

He exhaled. "Good. This won't work if you're not being helpful."

Oh? What a bad kidnappee I was, being so *unhelpful*.

The light touch on the top of my head again, and I steeled myself not to jump. Then I could feel a warmth spreading from my head and down my face. It reminded me of having my hair done, and how much I enjoyed having someone else wash my hair.

"All right. You should be able to see again."

I opened my eyes, closing them again immediately as the colors and light overwhelmed my senses.

"Lean back. Breathe," I could tell that Brennan wanted to be comforting.

Right.

"I can't," I gasped, my eyes blinking fast, so fast that I could feel tears welling. Again. I didn't think the tears were only from regaining my vision suddenly. That one fact made me angry. I knew men saw tears as weak. I didn't want to look weak, but my damn eyes weren't with the program.

"How can I speak again? What did you do to me, you sick freak?" I pushed myself up off the couch—it was a couch, as I'd suspected—and tried to get up. He moved at the same time with arms out.

I smacked right into Brennan's head.

"Ow! God! Could your head be any harder?" My eyesight swam, threatening to leave again.

"Are you all right?"

That voice. I liked it, in spite of the fact he'd kidnapped me, and had some freaky stuff going on. I fell back into the couch and kept my eyes closed, rubbing my head. "I think so. I might be blind again, though." I opened my eyes a little, and allowed the light to seep back in. Then opened them a little wider.

To see Brennan standing in front of me, looking very guilty. He saw my glare.

Brennan held up his hands. "If you would please control yourself, I'd be happy to explain."

"Explain what? Are you a sex trafficker?"

The confusion I saw on his face didn't look faked. "What are you talking about?"

"Why'd you drag me here? How in the hell did you get into the ladies? Oh my god!" I clapped my hand to my mouth. I'd been on a date! Finally, Heath asked me out. How would I explain this? Worse, how would my parents take me disappearing like this? I looked around, feeling wild. I didn't even know where I was. "Where am I? And how fast can you get me home?"

An odd expression shifted across Brennan's face. Almost as though he didn't want to tell me something. A kidnapper with a conscience?

"We are not in the Human Realm at the moment, Iris. Once you meet with Taranath, I'll make sure you return there."

My mouth opened but no words came out. What? I must have lost my hearing as well.

I tried again. "What are you talking about, we're not in the human realm?"

Brennan sighed, and I could see so much in his sigh. For a moment, I felt empathy for him. Obviously he carried a great weight of some sort. It bothered me that I had feelings other than *run away fast* for this guy. That moment didn't last long.

Because I had my own great weight, and he wasn't helping it. I had to remember that. No matter how good looking he is, he still kidnapped me.

I looked him up and down, really looked at him, for the first time. My earlier impression of a skirt wasn't far off. He wore pants, but he had a long coat over his whole get-up. That must be what made all the noise.

His hair was cut close to his head, and his eyes. Oh, wow. I forgot my anger for a moment. He had the bluest eyes I'd ever seen. Even now, with a furrowed brow, and an air of concern, he was, quite simply gorgeous.

Stop it! I told myself. This weird guy, looks aside, kidnapped you. Blinded you, basically sewed your mouth shut! I ought to be peeing my pants in fear, and I'm admiring his eyes?

I shook my head to force it to stop thinking about anything other than getting home. To Mom and Dad. To Heath.

No matter how good-looking Brennan was, I wasn't where I was supposed to be. I belonged home, with my family. And if Heath was meant to be part of that, no sense in ogling the criminal.

He stared at me, waiting for something.

"What?" I asked.

"I asked you where you thought you were."

"I have no idea. Blind, remember?"

He didn't say anything, then whirled around, the coat flaring out. It did make a swishing skirt noise.

"I don't have time for this! No more biting!" He sounded exasperated.

"What the hell? You don't have time for the person you kidnapped? Oh, I am so sorry to disturb your schedule! Hey! Where are you going?"

He'd walked out the door, and slammed it behind him. I made myself get up, feeling steadier. Went straight to the door, and tried to open it.

Locked. I should have bitten him again.

CHAPTER FOUR

Brennan

He stood, hands on his hips, listening to her bang on the door, and call him names that he felt pretty certain were not complimentary. Well, to be expected. No one liked to be brought somewhere without permission.

Why had he brought her? It was good question. He hadn't wanted to, but Drake insisted. He knew Drake was right—that she had to be made to forget, and that he didn't have enough energy to return them and modify her memory. But he hadn't wanted to bring her. She made him uncomfortable. Seeing her in front of him, tears falling down the side of her face—it had stirred something in him he hadn't felt before. Until she bit him. He sighed. Her reaction was understandable. It didn't mean he liked it.

All the more reason to get her seen by Taranath, and get her away. He didn't need anyone making him feel anything like this girl stirred in him. Not ever. Too risky for everyone.

He started towards Taranath's rooms, hoping to hurry him along. The girl was a distraction he didn't need, for a great many reasons.

As he rounded the corner from his chamber, he nearly ran into Drake.

"Brennan, did you give the mage permission to travel?"

"What?" Brennan found himself distracted by the image of her face in his mind, and he had to pull his attention away from her to pay attention to Drake.

"Did you give the mage permission to travel? The goblins who care for him say that he left on a journey some days ago. They seemed to think it at your behest. Or at least with your blessing." Drake scowled. "They were properly...concerned when I indicated that you had need of him immediately."

Brennan sighed. His goblins were good creatures, if somewhat mischievous to the point of being a major pain at times. With the stunning exception of the goblins who'd attacked them earlier today, Brennan had nothing but positive relations with his subjects. This day kept getting worse.

"Did they have an idea of where he was or when he planned to return?"

"You know them. When they get scared, there's not much talking to them. It's not my habit to beat up on old women."

His words flashed the face of the mage's head chambermaid. She was an old goblin, who'd been in the castle for as long as the mage had.

"Then let us go and speak to her. You frighten them," he grinned at Drake suddenly. "I'm their good king, not like you and your disrespectful self."

"Have at it," Drake gave a mocking bow, indicating that Brennan should leave first. "The longer she's here, the harder it will be to alter her memory properly."

They both turned to look back towards the lounge. Listening, Brennan could hear her pounding on the door.

"That really is a lot noisier than I expected. Why'd you let her wake up?" Drake asked.

"I didn't let her do anything. She came out of the spell on her own."

"What? That should have lasted longer! Brennan, something isn't right here!"

Brennan gave Drake an incredulous look. "Yes, you're right. We dragged back a human girl to our realm and we need to get her home and concentrate on the real problem."

Drake shook his head. "No, that she broke the spell so quickly. That should have lasted for hours."

For the first time, Brennan felt some of the worry that had been driving Drake. "Are you sure? We were in a hurry."

"I don't make mistakes, lordship."

"Even I do, Drake. We all do. I have to ask. I don't want to believe that this is anything more than a coincidence."

"It can be a coincidence when we find Taranath and he tells us that I'm being an old man and worrying too much."

"Very well," Brennan sighed. "Let us go and talk to his servants. See if we can find him."

"Sooner than later would be better."

They turned and walked together, not speaking.

There was no need to.

Iris

I stopped shouting, and leaned against the door. My hands hurt from beating on it. Obviously, Brennan had locked me in here and left. No one else seemed to notice, either. I turned around, still leaning on the door, and took the time to look around the room.

It looked like a castle. Or my impression of what a castle should look like. Stone walls, and a huge fireplace that dominated the room. In addition to the couch where I'd been, there were a couple of chairs.

It looked comfortable. Not like what I'd expect from a kidnapper. I walked over to the tall window and looked out. That wasn't as easy as expected. The glass had that look of being old, and had waves in it.

What I could see was that the sun shone over a garden. He'd said *the human realm*—what did that mean? This looked like a really nice house, but what the hell was that realm business?

It made my head hurt to try and figure it out. I ran my hands around the window to see if I could feel a latch or anything that would let me out.

Nothing. Damn it.

If I were home, I could...

Oh my god! I reached into my back pocket. It hadn't fallen out. I pulled my cell phone out, and swiped the screen to wake it up.

Opened up the phone and dialed 911.

I huddled in the corner of the window, not wanting to be caught. The phone didn't make any noise, and then the busy signal went off.

What the hell? How could 911 be busy? I ended the call, and dialed it again.

Once again, busy signal.

I checked the signal. It had no bars. That meant no cell tower within range.

That scared me. I didn't want to think about it, so I shoved my cell phone back into my pocket. I huffed back to the couch and tossed myself onto it, feeling stray tears leak from my eyes. I had to get back. What would my parents think? Mom was so sick. If I didn't come back...I didn't finish the thought. I'd spent my whole life on a boat with my parents. We'd come back to land, so to speak, because I'd graduated high school and wanted to attend college. Right around that time was also when my mom had begun to feel sick. Moving off the boat had been fortuitous as she'd been diagnosed with brain cancer later that summer.

Dealing with all the things that had to be done had been our focus to the exclusion of everything else. Finally, Mom threw up her hands and insisted we take the boat out for a week. She'd rescheduled all her appointments. While neither my dad nor I would admit it, we were thrilled that she'd made the decision. The boat was our lodestone, the thing we all came back to. We hadn't been out on her since the diagnosis.

I stood on the bow of the boat, the wind blowing my hair back. The sun warmed my face, and for the first time since we'd found out Mom had cancer, I felt normal. "Honey? Come take the helm. I want to get dinner started," Dad called to me.

I walked along the deck. A Hylas 49, Sorcha was beautiful to me. My parents had met when they were both in Ireland as exchange students, so my dad named her Sorcha, the Irish equivalent of my mother's English name, Claire. The name fit the boat. Sleek and graceful, she moved with a purpose. Just like my mom.

Or just like my mom used to. Now, she sat in the cockpit, wrapped up even on this warm day, so thin that the breeze felt cold to her. A cheerful, pink scarf wrapped around her head, she looked up as I stepped into the cockpit.

"Got it," I said to my dad, who nodded and went below to the galley. I checked the compass, and put my hand on the wheel.

"You were right," I said. "Being out here, this is a good thing."

Mom sighed, looking out towards the horizon. I noticed she hitched her blanket up higher around herself. Being out like this brought into even more stark relief how ill she was.

"Do you feel better?" I asked.

"Yes and no," she said. "I get tired more easily, but my heart's at ease here." She kept her focus on the horizon.

I looked forward. I felt the urge to break down and sob. I'd been holding onto the idea since she'd been diagnosed that somehow this would all get better and go away.

I was wrong. Mom wasn't getting better. I blinked as the tears blinded me.

"Iris, it's okay to cry," came Mom's soft voice.

I dashed at my eyes. "Cry over what? We're here, together." If I didn't say the words aloud, they wouldn't be true.

"Over the way things have gone. I cry all the time."

That made me look at her. "When?"

I knew dad worked from home to be with her. Part time IT stuff, because he didn't really need to work. I didn't know all the details, but my parents came from well-off families. All my dad would say when pressed was that he and his family managed money well, and it was lucky for us they did. Usually, when he said that, he and mom would exchange glances, but they never went into much detail. They weren't close to their families, and it had never bothered me. The three of us always seemed to be enough for one another.

That dynamic had changed.

"I make your father go out each day. Take a walk, go for a bike ride, even go down and mess around with Sorcha," she said. "Anywhere but holed up with me, watching me die." The bitterness in her voice surprised me. She generally maintained a cheerful attitude.

"Mom, you're not dying," I said fiercely. I could feel my gut gurgle at the words, twist into a knot at the thought.

"I am, and we have to accept that. No one but me is doing that," she said, equally fierce. "I'm mad as hell, Iris! Furious that I won't get to see who you become, or be there when you have kids. Livid that I am leaving my best friend, the best man in the entire world. It's not fair!" She wiped at the tears coursing down her face.

"Mom, you're better out here," I said. I could hear the begging in my voice.

"Sweet pea, I'm dying. We need to face it. I want you two to live after I'm gone. You take that scholarship you haven't actually told Dad and me about, and you go make something of yourself. Tell your dad to do the same thing. He's inclined to mope around. And tell him to date again! He's not the sort that should be alone."

"MOM!" I knew my mouth had dropped open. "Why are you telling me all this? You're not dead yet!" The enormity of what I'd just said made me let go of the wheel and clap my hands over my mouth.

For an instant, we were both frozen. I knew I'd never forget that moment. The rigging hummed as the wind filled the sails and propelled us forward. The sun was a golden that you only see when you're on the water. It made a halo around Mom's head, and the struggle between horror and laughter hung suspended between us.

Laughter won. We laughed so hard neither could speak. Kept laughing, which drew my dad up from the galley, wooden spoon in hand.

"I...need...a...tee...shirt with...that...on it," she gasped.

"With what?" Dad asked her, his face screwed up in a mixture of love and alarm.

"Not dead yet," she said, looking at him. "I think it would be great for the funeral."

Dad's mouth fell open.

I understood. He didn't know whether this was supposed to be funny. Mom weakly waved a hand at him. "It's time we put it out in the open, Paul. Let's face it, like we always have."

With those few words, we were the family we'd always been.

My eyes teared at the memory. Were they worried? Did they know I was missing? I hoped not. Not just for the selfish reasons surrounding Heath, whom I'd forgotten for the moment, but because I didn't want to worry my parents any more than they already were.

My thoughts broke off as the door swung open. I stood up, ready to fight for what I wanted so I could get home.

Unfortunately, it wasn't Brennan.

A short little—creature—came in, burdened with a large tray.

I shrank back into the couch. I remembered Brennan saying he'd taken me from the human realm. Where the hell were we? And what was this thing?

"Here, miss, Majesty sent this up for you."

Oh my god, it spoke! I rubbed my eyes. Maybe I had been drugged! I rubbed my eyes again, and blinked hard. The creature still stood there.

"Um, what...what are you?"

The creature—I couldn't tell whether it was a he or she—gaped at me.

"What, miss? What do ya mean?"

"What are you?" I got out, my voice a little stronger this time.

"What am I? Well, I'm a goblin, miss! A castle goblin, serving the king, and glad to be doin' it!"

"A…what?" I whispered

The creature put the tray down on a table on the other side of the room. Then it walked back to me, hands on hips, to look at me.

"Miss, is you all right?"

"I don't…I don't know."

The creature looked concerned, and didn't speak, only stared at me. I took advantage of the moment to study it. Since at the moment it didn't look inclined to eat me or anything.

Its head had a football shape to it, with large pointy ears. A small mane of hair rested between the ears, and from this angle, I could see it pulled up in a bun at the base of its head. Because of that, I was going with female. She had on garments in gray and white and she wore a skirt. I felt better about guessing she was a she. Earrings dangled from her ears, although up close, I wasn't sure I wanted to know exactly what they were made of—they had a bone-like appearance. She was a mix of colors. Gray, green, and brown, although no one color stood out. Her eyes were large, and very dark. Right now, they were studying me as intently as I studied her.

"I brought you food, but I think you might need th' mage more than anything else, miss."

I found myself nodding. "I think they're going to look for him. So, uh, not trying to be rude, but what did you mean you're a goblin?"

"I am a goblin, and you're in the Goblin Realm. His Majesty is the king of the Goblin Realm, and a good king at that. Not like that old one," She grimaced. "Knowed 'im since he were little, him and Master Drake. They're not goblin, ya see, they're fae. But they take good care of the Goblin Realm. What's your name? I haven't seen a full-growed human before." She stepped closer to me.

"I'm Iris. What's your name?"

She laughed. "My name? Don't think a human could rightly say it. Ya are human, aren't ya?" Bright eyes looked at me with interest.

"I am. What should I call you?"

The goblin laughed. "Never thought to think what a human would call me. We don't see many around here! Call me Glynan. It's as close as you'll get."

"Thank you, Glynan. What's for dinner?" I walked over to the tray, feeling ravenous. Where had that come from? I thought you weren't supposed to be hungry when you were fearing for your life.

"This isn't dinner. It's a…" she hesitated, "It's more of a small meal, a refreshment. Bread, fresh from the oven, and honey, and a nice sweet cider, made from the castle orchards."

"It sounds delicious. Smells delicious, too." I got a whiff, and it made my mouth water.

"Majesty says to please eat as much as you like, no need to wait on 'im."

I got up carefully and walked to the small table. I took a piece of the bread, already cut, and drizzled the honey on it. "Would you like to join me?"

She looked shocked. "No, miss. But…" she glanced around, "I'd like to talk with you, if I may. Majesty didn't say as we couldn't talk."

I wondered when she'd seen him. Then I shrugged. Like I cared. I took a bite of the bread. It was delicious. Grabbing the goblet that sat on the tray, I went back to my couch. "I'd like the company," I said to her, smiling, once my mouth was no longer full.

She came back over, looking me up and down. "Never seen a grown human. You're not as big as I thought."

"Why haven't you? Aren't there humans here?" For some reason, the thought of no other humans made me very nervous.

"Oh, we get the baby humans. So cute, they are. Master Drake was human, once."

"What does that mean?" I couldn't stop myself from asking. "He was human once?"

Without realizing it, Glynan sat on the stool that Brennan sat on earlier. "Sometimes, we get human babies, sent here to the Goblin Kingdom. Wished away by their parents! Who would wish away a baby! Anyway, here they are. The Fae Realm, though, 'tis a hard place. Most of the babies don't make it beyond a year."

"What makes it so hard? And wait, you're fairies? Or Brennan is a fairy?" I wanted to laugh, but I didn't want to offend her.

Glynan shook her head, making her ears swing and the earrings clatter. "I don't know, miss, only that humans don't live long here. I've never seen a grown human. But sometimes, and I don't know why, the human baby will make it, and if they keep growing, they become more fae than anything else. Fae and fairies is two different things. Fairies are fast little things, given to stealing your earbobs when you're not looking. Fae is something else, like Majesty and Lord Drake."

I tried to remember if I'd really looked at Drake. Nope. Heard him, hadn't really seen him. But Brennan didn't look all that different from me. It must be something I couldn't see. "Drake doesn't look any different than Brennan."

Glynan nodded. "He's been here a long time. No reason why he'd look like anything other than fae."

"Glynan, what do you mean, fae? You keep saying that, and I don't have any idea what a fae is."

Glynan opened her mouth to answer. The door banged open, and Glynan jumped up, looking around. Her expression screamed *guilty!*

Brennan stood at the door, hands on hips, and he looked...ferocious. It was apparent he wasn't happy. I hoped Glynan wouldn't be in trouble for sitting and talking with me.

"*Glanthemaranynas!*"

She jumped when he spoke—I thought it might be her real name.

"What are you doing?"

"I was keeping your guest company, Majesty! Just talking a bit!"

"That will be all." His scowl didn't change as she scurried around him and out the door.

He took a few steps in, hands still on hips. "Did she at least bring you something to eat?"

Wow! Why was he so mean to Glynan? His words and demeanor reminded me that this guy had kidnapped me, and wasn't to be trusted. I would have to be on my guard. It also meant I didn't need to be all that worried about manners.

"She did."

His face relaxed. "Good. I am sorry to report, we have no idea of where the mage might be. It seems we will have to wait."

"Why can't you send me back?"

He stopped on his way to the tray of food. "What do you mean?"

"You're so great and powerful. Send me home. Let's be done with this. You get on with whatever you do," I flapped a hand, trying for dismissive to cover my anger at him, "And I'll get back to my life."

He sighed, his face taking on the expression one uses when talking to a little kid. "As I mentioned before, I cannot focus my magic on two points. I will need to modify your memory, and manage the portal. Both take a great deal of magic. I need the mage to assist so that you are returned safely."

"Modify my memory now, put me to sleep or something, and then send me back."

"You are so eager to go?"

"As eager as you are to be rid of me." He hadn't said anything, but I knew he wanted me gone. That's fine. I wanted to be gone, too. This whole place defied reality, and I knew when I got home, I would sit in the bathtub and have a complete nervous breakdown, but I couldn't do that now. I needed to stay focused.

The oddest thing happened then. It was almost like watching someone draw curtains over a window the way his face closed down.

"There are risks involved."

I shrugged. "No more than the risks of staying here."

"What do you mean?"

"I mean, the longer I'm gone, the harder things will be to explain. You're screwing up my life. I want to go back, as soon as possible, mage or no mage. Go ahead and wipe my memory, and then send me back when you're rested and ready." I couldn't stop the sarcasm on that last bit, and I had the satisfaction of watching his face harden. Other than kidnapping, and me biting him, he'd been perfectly polite. I no longer felt the need to be the same.

"Very well. I try to be a pleasant host, even if the visit is to no one's liking. Let me fetch Drake, and we'll start with putting you to sleep." He turned and strode from the room, the heels on his boots hitting the flagstones hard. He paused for a moment to look at me over his shoulder as he opened the door.

I didn't change my expression or ease my glare.

He slammed the door behind him as he left.

Only then did I allow myself a small smile.

CHAPTER FIVE

Brennan

He all but stomped from the room like a snotty adolescent. What was it about this girl that got under his skin? *Maybe locking her in a room and ignoring her as she screamed and cried?*

The goblin. What had his goblin servant said to her? They'd been sitting together having a chat when he came in. Glanthemaranynas knew better. He needed to see what they'd discussed, what had caused Iris's demeanor to change so.

That would need to wait because he needed to find Drake. In reality, it didn't matter what had been said or what Iris thought. She'd leave soon. While Drake was not as powerful as Brennan with the use of magic, he knew and understood it. Neither of the things he needed to do were all that difficult, but having to do them closely would sap his strength, and having Drake nearby would be helpful.

He strode quickly through the corridor, arriving at Drake's rooms. Knocking once, he opened the door and went in.

"What is it?" Drake, who had been lying in bed, leapt to his feet.

"The girl. She wants to go back."

Drake shrugged. "We all want her to go back."

"She suggested that I alter her memories, and then put her to sleep, and when I'm ready, send her back."

Now Drake looked concerned. "That's a lot of energy to expend in a short time. Particularly as we've had to travel via portals twice in one day."

Brennan nodded. "I know. She has no idea what she asks, but she's rude, and I don't want her here any longer than she must be. As well, she's already been chatting with the kitchen staff."

"Hard to keep a secret."

"Precisely. I want no one to discover this, so even though it's a risk, I agreed to the girl's request."

"You can use me, you know."

Brennan smiled. "I know. I hope I don't need to, but that's why I want you there."

"You don't have to ask."

"I always will." Using the energy of others drained not only the giver, but the person taking. It created a bond between the two as well, which was why Brennan generally refused to employ it. However, he and Drake had an unshakeable bond, and he didn't mind it becoming stronger.

"Well, let's go and get this started. The sooner she's home, the better."

"You think the kitchen staff is going to talk."

Drake nodded as they headed back to Brennan's rooms. "I do. You've finally settled things with Ailla. There's already talk about why it's taken this long. You don't need questions about a human adding to that."

"I don't know why it's such a topic of discussion," Brennan began.

"Because you've been decidedly single for so long. Father has been in despair, even though he'd never admit it."

They reached the door to Brennan's rooms. He was glad to change the subject from his recent betrothal. "Go easy on her, Drake. She's annoying, but I don't want her any more upset than she is. It only makes things harder."

"Yes, your lordship," Drake mocked.

The door swung open to reveal Iris pacing.

"Where have you been? I want to go home!"

"You forgot to mention shrew," Drake muttered.

Brennan shot him a look, and Drake closed his mouth.

"As you wish, my lady. I'll need you to sit down and attempt to calm your mind." Brennan strove for calm and patient. What he wanted was to throttle her. She was so impertinent! And bossy. He did not get bossed about by others, and certainly not some chit!

"Easy for you to say. You're not the one who was kidnapped."

"We were thrown into your world," Drake interjected. "Amazingly, we had no temper tantrums."

Brennan glared at him, and Drake rolled his eyes and moved to the other side of the room near the window. Apparently Drake found her irritating as well. He felt another pang that she was leaving. Why? He wanted nothing more than to be rid of her and get on with the question of who had attacked him.

Didn't he?

He shoved his thoughts about Iris to the side and focused on wiping away her memory. He'd need to have her sleep until he found his missing mage. That in and of itself—an open-ended sleeping spell—gave him cause for concern, but there was nothing to be done. He also didn't need her banging on doors and shouting down the castle. So her request made his life easier in some respects. She'd stay asleep until he could find his mage, and then get her home.

"Close your eyes, Iris. Let your mind go blank, and try to relax. Do not speak," he added as he saw her open her mouth. "I need your cooperation, please."

She blew out a breath and glared. He forced himself to maintain a neutral expression, and finally saw her face relax.

"Oh, all right. Can't get any worse."

"Not with your constant chatter." Drake spoke quietly. Brennan didn't think Iris could hear him. He hoped not. Neither of them were being very helpful or cooperative.

Iris closed her eyes, and Brennan began to speak the words of the sleeping spell. He could see her sink deeper into the couch as unconsciousness took over. He added the words to the memory spell. When she leaned over onto the pillow, he stood.

"I think that's done it. Let's settle her in and go and find the damned mage." He stepped closer to her, taking her gently by the shoulders and laying her on the pillow. Her hair spread out across the pillow in a manner most fetching.

Most fetching? Brennan shook his head. What was wrong with him?

"Drake, ring for staff."

For once, Drake complied without commentary. Brennan stood silently, watching Iris sleep. Her lashes were darker than her hair, lying across the top of her cheeks like miniature feathers. Her cheeks were slightly flushed, and her lips parted ever so slightly...he found himself wanting to run his finger across them...

The door opened and Nezneys, a goblin who had been with him for as long he could remember, came in. Nezneys looked as though she'd rather be anywhere else. It always amazed him how quickly his entire castle knew that he wasn't in a wonderful frame of mind.

"Majesty?"

"Watch the human. She is in a sleep, and I want to make sure she stays well until the mage arrives."

Nezneys nodded. "I won't leave her, Majesty."

He nodded, and walked from the room, Drake at his heels.

"How do you propose to find him?"

Brennan sighed. "I'll have to ask Mother."

"Oh, no, you don't want her involved in this!"

His mother, the Fae Queen Nerida, had what could only be called an imposing manner. If one was being kind.

"No, I really don't, but she is the most skilled scryer I know. We'll need her in order to find the damnable man! Why did he choose now to be gone?" Brennan ran his hands across the top of his head.

"It's bad timing to be sure. Are you *sure* you want to call in Mother?" In spite of the fact Drake had fostered in their home and had been adopted by Brennan's parents, he maintained a healthy respect for the queen.

Brennan sighed again. "I really see no other way. She'll be discreet, as well. I had planned to ask for her assistance anyway, in regards to our scarred friend."

Drake grinned. "You mean Scarry McScarface?" He laughed, then his face sobered. "You're right about calling her. Best get it over with. Let's use the great hall. She's less apt to lecture if she thinks there might be an audience."

In spite of his worry, Brennan laughed. "How well you know her! Don't worry, I won't make you speak. That name, by the way, doesn't do him justice."

"Yes, but it's funny every time I say it. Don't build him up, Bren. He's an interloper, and we will put him down."

Brennan didn't answer. Something about Scarface felt off. More than it should. He felt like he knew him, yet he knew he didn't. Brennan didn't like mysteries.

They walked on towards the hall. Once there, Brennan pulled out the mirror he used to contact his parents. His mother kept a small mirror on her at all times in order to be available to her offspring.

"Mother," he spoke to the mirror.

In a moment, her face appeared. "Brennan! This is a surprise." Her tone suggested the surprise didn't please her.

"Mother, I have need of you. Are you available to travel to my castle?"

His direct approach merited a lifting of her brows. "I have nothing pressing this afternoon. Will that be soon enough?"

"The sooner the better, Mother. I thank you for your prompt response."

"Such formality! With your own mother. I find myself somewhat concerned, Brennan. Where is Drake?"

Drake stepped into view of the mirror. "Here, Mother."

She peered closely through the mirror at Drake. "I'm not going to get a thing out of you, either," she said crossly. "Never mind. Ought I to travel immediately?"

Drake nodded. "It would be best."

Nerida looked at the two of them for a moment, not replying. She gave the smallest of sighs. Brennan knew a lecture lay in his future. Hundreds of years old and his mother still lectured.

"Very well. I shall inform your father and be there directly." She disappeared from the mirror.

"You're in for a stern talking-to, at the very least," Drake grinned at him.

"You're going to be right there with me," Brennan snapped.

"Shall we have an ale then, while we wait?"

They burst out laughing. They'd sat through many of Nerida's lectures as boys. "No, because then she'll add *drunkard* to our list of crimes. I don't want to give her further weapons."

Faster than Brennan thought possible, Nerida appeared through the portal in the great hall. He jumped to his feet to greet her.

"Mother, you look stunning as—"

She cut him off. "Enough. What is going on that I needed to be here immediately?"

"We have need of your scrying."

The brows rose again. "Oh?"

"Let us return to my rooms. I've no wish to discuss this here." The goblins gossiped endlessly. He'd already seen some of them pop their heads into the hall to see Nerida. They all loved her, in spite of her aloof manner. Nerida, for her part, showed them more kindness than Brennan expected. After all, usually the problem child of the fae royal family was sent to the Goblin Realm. They didn't usually choose it. He had been the problem child, and had duly been named heir to the realm. Even after...he shook off thoughts of the past. Nerida followed him out of the hall. She didn't speak as they made their way to his rooms. He stopped at his door.

"Mother, there is..."

"Oh, stop, Brennan. You're in some sort of distress. That much is obvious. Whatever it is, I'll help you." She pushed her way around him and walked through the door.

And stopped.

Nezneys hurried from the room not making eye contact with any of them. She'd been around long enough to know how little Nerida enjoyed surprises. Brennan wished he could hurry from the room, too.

He walked forward to where Nerida stood still. She whipped her head around. "How did a human female come to be here, asleep in your room?"

"If you move, I will be happy to explain it all to you. It's mostly Drake's fault, so you may save your scolding for him."

Drake made a noise of protest as he came in and closed the door. Nerida held up her hand. "Both of you come in, sit down, and tell me exactly what has happened."

They sat in chairs across from where Iris lay, still sleeping. She looked lovely, Brennan noted. Her lips still parted, as though she were a sleeping princess, waiting to be kissed...

He looked up to see both Nerida and Drake staring at him.

"I'm waiting," Nerida said.

Together, he and Drake told her about being ambushed, and how they ended up bringing Iris back. Nerida didn't speak once during the recitation, although her lips pursed several times. After they'd finished, she looked out the window, lost in her own thoughts. Finally, she turned back to face them.

"I am surprised you brought her back."

"Drake insisted, and in spite of the problems created since, I agree with him. I needed to be able to get us back here. I would not have been able to do that as well as manage her memory." Brennan felt worry snake through him. His mother's calm acceptance did not fall into the behavior he'd come to expect from her. Where was the lecture?

"We had no idea the mage was not in the castle." Drake put in.

"So if you would, please, Mother, scry him, I would appreciate it. There is another matter, as well."

"I am indeed fortunate," Nerida said. "So many surprises in such a short time."

"I would like you to see if you can scry the fae sorcerer we saw. He should be distinctive. I've never seen another fae with that scar." Brennan chose to ignore her sarcasm.

Nerida tapped her lips with a finger. "It's odd that he would keep it. There must be a reason. I'll have to ask your father if he recalls any such fae who was so scarred. I'll look for him, though. After I find your mage. I think that is the most pressing need at this point. Do you agree?" She looked from him to Drake.

Brennan nodded. "The sooner the girl is away, the better."

Nerida didn't answer. She looked intently at him, and Brennan felt exposed in her gaze. It had always been so. Her ability to see beneath the surface made her exceptionally skilled at scrying.

"For this, I'd like a basin of spring water."

Drake stood, and went for serving staff. *Traitor,* Brennan thought. He just doesn't want to be questioned by Mother.

Nerida walked closer to Iris, peering down at her. "There is something different about your human, Brennan."

"She's not mine, not in any fashion, Mother," he couldn't keep the annoyance from his tone.

She continued as though he'd not spoken. "There is something not human about her. She's...she's what the humans would call gifted. Interesting. It's too bad she must be sent back. I should like to talk with her."

"Why?"

"Because I enjoy learning, Brennan. Even about humans. Do you forget that Drake came to us from the humans? While he is human no longer, were it not for that realm, we would not have him."

In spite of his general concern, Brennan smiled. He liked to hear that Nerida thought highly of Drake, even after all this time. "I do not forget. He makes it impossible," he raised his voice to be sure that Drake heard him in the doorway. "But this human is here at a most inopportune time, and—"

"And for one so young, she has a biting tongue." Drake finished, coming to stand beside Brennan. "She yelled at Brennan. While beating on the door when he locked her in here."

Nerida smiled. "Did she indeed? It's a pity she must be returned so quickly. Well, perhaps the mage can come up with something."

"No, Mother. Let's just send her back where she belongs. We have enough to deal with." Brennan felt a pang again. Yes, it would be better when the girl was gone.

Nezneys came back in carrying a black basin carefully. Brennan knew it held water from the well in the courtyard, spring water from beneath the castle. Nezneys set it on a table in front of the closest window, apparently remembering that Nerida preferred to be close to sunlight.

"Thank you, Nezneys. Please see that we are not disturbed." He gave a ghost of a smile to her, knowing that she worried.

"Majesties," she muttered, and with a slight bob, left the room.

"Quiet," Nerida said, looking into the basin, sitting down at the chair in front of the table. She placed her fingers at her temples and closed her eyes.

It seemed an age before she opened her eyes. "He is in the Dwarf Realm."

"Are you sure?"

Brennan got a quelling glare from his mother.

"I'll get the mirror for the Dwarf Court," Drake practically raced out in front of him. Brennan glared at his friend's fleeing back.

"Restrain yourself and I'll see about this fae sorcerer," Nerida said, closing her eyes again. Suddenly, she opened her eyes and clutched at her forehead. "He's hiding, whoever he is. Describe him for me, everything you remember, Brennan."

Painstakingly, Brennan went through the encounter, stopping only when Nerida held up her hand and closed her eyes again, leaning towards the basin. She paled. Opened her eyes and leaned closer, so close that her nose nearly touched the water.

Suddenly, she gasped and leaned back so quickly she hit her head on the back of the chair. When she opened her eyes, tears stood in them. "Whoever he is, he is powerful. He felt me, Brennan."

Brennan didn't know what to say.

"How could he feel you?" He couldn't believe it.

"I don't know, but I felt him turn, and he looked at me as though I stood in front of him. Then I felt as though someone had pushed me on the head." She sounded shocked. "The only good things is that I was able to see his face. It will help your father and I discover..." She stopped, closing her eyes and breathing deeply, "His identity, and who his family is." She took a few more breaths. "It can't be," she said. Softly, as though she spoke to herself.

"Are you all right, Mother?" She had not regained her color. And what did her words mean?

"I will be fine, Brennan. Just taken aback. I can't remember the last time someone felt me scry and had the ability to respond. He presents an interesting challenge." She sounded like herself.

"An interesting challenge? Mother, he did his best to kill me."

Nerida turned eyes to him that were dark and serious. "No, I don't believe he did his best. Had he, you would have been dead. He's that powerful, Brennan. Please do not take any action until I can speak with your father on this matter. Will you give me your word?" She stood, brushing herself off. He felt the intensity coming off her.

Brennan stood with her. "Are you leaving?"

"I must. I need to let your father know about this." The intensity again. It puzzled him.

"But what about..." He gestured at the sleeping Iris.

"Your mage will return. He'll adjust her memory and send her home." Nerida stopped to look down at Iris. She let her hand fall gently to Iris's cheek. "Be well, little one," she said softly. She looked back to him. "Then you can turn your full attention to this other mage." She walked to the door.

Brennan made to follow her.

"No, stay here." She held up a hand to stop him. "Drake will return, and then you can contact the Dwarf Realm. And Brennan," she stopped, halfway out the door.

"Yes?"

"It would be nice if you contacted Ailla. I know she enjoys hearing from you."

He sighed. "Yes, Mother."

"Thank you." With a brief smile, she left, her skirts whispering behind her.

Brennan sat back down after the door closed. Ailla. He didn't want to think about her. She was lovely, somewhat younger than he, and a perfect match. He knew she actually had the approval of Drake, which didn't happen often. Why did he find himself so reluctant?

He glanced at Iris. Why did she look so lovely? Not what a distracted fae needed. Fae were drawn to beauty, to the loveliness of all things. Even humans. And Iris was lovely.

He gladly put all thoughts of Iris aside as Drake entered, carrying the mirror that connected to the Dwarf Realm.

"Set it up here," Brennan pointed. "Make sure that Iris is not visible."

"We can go into your study."

"No, this will be fine." He ignored Drake's eye rolling.

Swiftly, he contacted the other court. The steward confirmed that his mage was indeed there, and went to fetch him.

Brennan impatiently tapped his fingers as he waited. Wisely, Drake kept silent.

The mage's face appeared. "Your Majesty? Is aught amiss?"

"Yes, it is, Taranath. I have need of you. You need to return immediately."

The mage looked troubled. "I traveled to read some documents in the Dwarf King's library. I am not quite finished, Your Majesty, but I can hurry and be back within a few days."

"No. I need you to return now. Make my excuses to Thadrieck. You may return after you have assisted me in a court matter."

"Of course, Your Majesty. At once." Taranath inclined his head. Brennan could feel his curiosity through the mirror. There hadn't been pressing court matters in some time.

"You have my permission to use the portal into my chambers." He didn't want the entire castle alerted. If he could get Taranath in and then Iris away, the mage could return to the Dwarf Realm with no one the wiser. Too many people already knew of the human.

He handed the mirror to Drake, who went to return it to the mirror cabinet in the great hall. All the courts kept mirrors to communicate quickly. Mirrors were the only thing that couldn't be corrupted by spying spells. It allowed for speed and secrecy, when needed.

He heard a shuffling from his study. Taranath came through the door. "I am here, Your Majesty. What is amiss?"

Brennan stood. "This is what is amiss," he stepped aside to allow the mage to see Iris. "Drake and I were attacked and sent from this realm. We landed in the Human Realm, and this girl witnessed our arrival. I wasn't able to erase her memory and get us back, so we brought her here for your assistance. As you were not here, I have set the spell of forgetfulness on her and sent her to sleep. Now if you would, I would like to send her back immediately."

Taranath walked to Iris, leaning down. He muttered to himself. Brennan waited, albeit rather impatiently. He was extremely gifted, and Brennan had learned to keep quiet and let him work.

The mage ran his hand above Iris. He stood up straight and whirled around to face Brennan as Drake came back into the room.

"She's not sleeping!"

"What? Of course she is!" Brennan stepped closer to look at Iris. "I put her to sleep myself."

"She is not sleeping, Majesty. Not the sleep of the dream world. She is sleeping the sleep of death. We must send her back. She is dying."

"What are you talking about? This is not complex magic. I know how to cast a sleeping spell!"

"I do not think it your spell, Majesty, but something within the girl. We must wake her up."

"That will undo whatever Brennan has already done." Drake broke in.

Taranath gave him a stern look. "Good. For whatever reason, she's dying from the magic practiced upon her. I know you have no wish to have this on your head," he looked at Brennan.

No one spoke. Brennan saw that both the mage and Drake waited for his answer. "Very well. I don't want her to die merely because she accidentally came upon us."

"The spell might yet still work. We shall see when she awakens," Taranath said before turning back to bend over Iris's sleeping form.

She doesn't look to be in distress, thought Brennan. The pink is still on her cheeks. What did the mage see that he couldn't?

Taranath ran his hands above Iris again, and Brennan could see a faint lilac glow.

Iris sat up suddenly.

CHAPTER SIX

Iris

"What are you waiting for?" I glared at Brennan. Oh, great. Drake and some other guy were there, all peering at me like I'd grown another head.

"What am I...?" Brennan trailed off.

"Yes! Why are you just standing there? Get on with it! Take care of my memory and send me back."

"Miss, what do you remember?" The new guy asked gently, leaning in towards me. He looked at me as though I were a bug in a jar.

I didn't like being a spectacle, or a curiosity. "I remember everything! From the moment I went into the bathroom, to your freak boys dragging me here, and him," I pointed at Brennan, "Promising to send me back! Every moment you wait makes my life harder! This isn't my fault! It's yours! So fix it!" I could tell my voice raised while I spoke. I didn't care.

"The bathroom? The room where you bathe?" Drake asked.

"No, the room where you...uh..." How the heck did I translate what a bathroom was?

Drake laughed suddenly. "Oh, you mean the necessary. We landed in a necessary, Brennan!"

The other two men looked taken aback. Brennan crossed his arms and glared at me. "I don't see the need to dwell on it. Nor will getting angry help you, Iris."

"Well, since you're not listening to me, it's apparent that I need to tack and change course."

No one responded immediately. Perhaps they didn't understand the sailing lingo. I didn't care. I wanted— needed—to get back.

"Your spell didn't work," Bug Man said to Brennan. He peered at me again, reinforcing the idea of a scientist peering at a new and interesting specimen. "I cannot tell why, but it sent her into a sleep that would have ended...Well." He stopped. "It's lucky that I got here. You'll need to tell me what you said, Your Majesty, as best as you can remember. It should have worked." He tapped his chin, lost in thought.

Great. He *was* a scientist. No wonder he was looking at me like a specimen. And just how would the spell have ended? His changing the subject abruptly made me nervous.

Drake stepped in. "How has this become so complex? Wipe her memory, Taranath, if you please, and let's get her back to the Human Realm. We have greater concerns that need attending to!"

Bug Man—the mage?—held up a hand. "It's not that simple, Lord Drake. She's human. The realm of the fae is not kind to humans. They don't have the resistance to the environment."

"What are you talking about?" Drake interrupted.

"Have you forgotten that many human children who arrive here don't live past a year? This environment is hard on the human form. You are one of the few who survived and adapted. This young woman's body has resisted magic that ought to work on her and in doing so seems to have accelerated the process of decay. If we act in haste, we may kill her."

"What are you suggesting we do?" Brennan still sounded calm.

Good thing, because listening to this was doing anything but calming me. I felt a scream bubbling up and I clamped my lips shut and squeezed my hands together. I could feel the sweat on my palms.

"Miss, I know you are anxious to return home, but may I request some more of your time? Just to see why the spell didn't work. I wouldn't want to make the same mistake."

I heard Brennan make an impatient noise and had to hide a smile. Apparently he didn't like being judged critically. Oh well.

I could also see why this mage character fit right into my Bug Man descriptive. He wanted to study me before sending me home. I'm a sucker for people who love what they do, so I sighed. "Yeah, sure, I guess. Not long, though. The longer I'm gone, the more things fall apart for me." Now I glared at Brennan.

The mage looked at Brennan, surprise all over his features. "But why can you not—"

"We will do our best to get you home in as timely a manner as possible," Brennan spoke over the mage, who looked mystified. "Taranath, I do not want Iris wandering around the castle. You'll need to make your observations here, in my chambers. We will, of course, surrender the lounge to you in order to facilitate your work." He and Drake exchanged what could only be described as stink eye.

"I'll need a few things, Your Majesty. Would you please call for Riensea? She'll know what to bring for me."

Brennan nodded, and swept from the room, along with Drake. I'd thought only women in long skirts could do that, but somehow he managed. I'd never met a more graceful man. I couldn't help but watch him as he left.

I turned my attention back to the mage, and found that he watched me, almost as intently as I feared I'd been watching Brennan.

"We'll need to know your history, my dear," he said comfortably.

"What's your name?" I needed to have something other than Bug Man to call him.

"Most people call me Mage."

I shook my head.

"Very well. You may call me Ta—" and he said something that I couldn't understand. "It's my given name."

I tried it out. "Ta-ra-nath?" Whatever he'd said, it didn't roll easily off my tongue. It sounded like what Brennan and Drake had said.

Taranath smiled at my efforts. "See why Mage is easier? But Taranath will do."

His expression was so rueful, I had to laugh. "You can call me Iris."

He inclined his head. "It's delightful to meet you."

"Personally or as something to study?"

That made him smile widely. "Both, of course. I don't get to see many people from outside of this realm. I prefer not to travel."

"Where were you when Brennan went looking for you? I thought he might burst a blood vessel," I snickered at the memory.

Taranath looked out over my head towards the window. "I had some research to do. Nothing more than poor timing. Let's not waste any more of that, shall we?" He sat down in one of the chairs in front of where I sat. I hadn't done much other than lay around on this couch. Oddly, I didn't want to do anything else.

Taranath began asking me about my parents and stopped when I told him about my mom. Tears welled up, and he waited for me to compose myself.

"Sorry. It's hard to think about losing her."

He sighed. "It's so easy for you in the Human Realm to pass on. I am sorry, Iris. What about your father?"

Before I could answer, the door swung open, and another goblin came in, carrying a bag. Behind her, as I guessed by the clothing it was a her, came a fae woman so beautiful she nearly made my eyes hurt.

Taranath stood and bowed. "Your Majesty," he said respectfully.

She nodded. Your Majesty? Was this woman Brennan's...wife? Why did the thought of him having a wife suck so bad? He meant nothing, so why?

"Taranath, Brennan tells me that you've found something different with the girl."

Taranath looked at her calmly. "I have. The magic Brennan used didn't work. She woke up unchanged. Other than the fact that the spell was killing her."

The woman sat down next to him, staring intently at me. It made me really uncomfortable. She had a direct stare like nothing I'd ever seen. "Nish, you may leave the Mage's bag here. That's all." She never took her gaze from me.

"I am Nerida, the Fae Queen. Brennan and Drake are my sons, and you are?" Her brows went up in a question.

"I am Iris. You're Brennan's...mother?"

"Is that an odd thought?"

Oh, great. I'd just offended the fairy queen. "You don't really look like a mother."

To my relief, Nerida smiled. "Fae age differently from humans. I know you mean it as a compliment."

The goblin Nish set the bag down, bobbed, and with a quick, furtive glance at the queen, hurried from the room. Taranath reached for it and drew out something that looked like a wand. Oh, great. Wand waving, too. Before, I hadn't been sure about having my memory wiped. Now, I wanted to forget all this. It was too much to take in.

He actually waved the wand up and down from my head to my feet. Nothing beeped, or did anything. I waited.

He turned to the queen. "My lady Nerida," his voice came out far too calm. "She is still fading. But...not all of her is fading."

That made Nerida jump, just a little. She composed herself quickly. I got the impression I wasn't supposed to see or notice it.

"What does that mean?" Nerida had a very respectful tone towards Taranath.

"I don't know. I wonder, however," he looked at me again, his gaze considering. "Iris, how far back do you know your lineage?"

"My what?"

"Your lineage. Your grandparents. How far back do you know?"

"I know their names. Neither of my parents are close to their families."

"Why not?" Nerida asked.

"I don't know," I shrugged before wondering if it was rude. "My parents have never been close. They always said that we were better off without them."

Nerida and Taranath exchanged a glance. "What are their names?"

I gave the names of both sets of my grandparents, I didn't really know any names beyond them. I'd been wondering, since my mom got sick, how we'd tell them. My dad's parents, I'd never known if they disliked my mom, or found her lacking, or what. But my mom's parents? Wouldn't they want to know if their daughter was dying? Neither of my parents wanted to discuss it. It fell into the list of *one more thing screwed up by cancer* things.

"You're sure you don't know any more names?" Nerida pressed me.

"I'm sorry. I don't."

"Very well." She stood up, and I had the feeling I'd disappointed her. It didn't feel good. Then I thought, *Why should I care?*

"I'll look into it," she directed this at Taranath. She left the room, majesty trailing behind her with her skirts. I envied that presence.

Taranath waited until the door closed behind her to speak. "Now I want to try and open a portal for you. If you reject the sleeping spell, there must be a reason. I need to make sure you will be able to pass through the portal before even attempting the memory spell."

"Why wouldn't I be able to pass through?" I could feel my heartbeat speed up. I had to get back. I had to.

He shrugged. "I don't know. There is much about you that presents a mystery. If you could stay here and allow me to study you, I might have an answer. I think, however, that it's nicer with you alive, so I shall be unable to do so." He smiled to take any sting away from his words.

I laughed. "I am sorry to be such a bad guest! The nerve of me, trying to die!"

He joined me. "I do love the human sense of humor. You can take something horrid, laugh at it, and make your way through it without magic or spells or anything else. We fae are much more somber."

"So I noticed." I thought of Brennan, and Drake. I'd seen them laugh, but it seemed like as much of a surprise to them as it was to me.

"Would you lean back and relax, and let me see if I can open a portal for you?"

"I don't seem to be able to do anything else," I said reluctantly.

The Bug Man scientist came back instantaneously. "What do you mean, you can't seem to do anything else?"

"I was thinking that here I was in another world, apparently, and all I've done is lay around on a couch. Then I thought I really didn't want to do anything else. The thought of moving around makes me tired."

He nodded. "It's the effect of Fae. It's very hard on humans. Something in fae biology has adapted to what is a more hostile environment than that of the Human Realm."

For the first time, I thought about that. "Am I really not on Earth anymore?"

He tapped his lips with a finger. "Well, you are on Earth, but not the Earth you know. It's very complex, how the realms all exist. How much do you want to know?"

I shook my head, waving my hands in front of me to stop any further explanation. "I don't want to know all that much. Only, am I really in a different world? You keep talking about fae, and the Fae Realm. What does that mean?"

"You live in the Human Realm, Iris. The realm humans inhabit. You are currently in the Fae Realm, ruled and inhabited by fae. But we're not the only creatures here. We have goblins, as you've seen, and dwarves, trolls, and dragons. Each race has a place that is theirs, although the races may live wherever they choose. The entire thing is ruled by Brennan and Drake's father and mother, the Fae King and Queen."

My head spun from all the information. I felt sick.

"Can I get you something?" Taranath looked worried.

I waved a hand again. When I could, I looked at him. "I'll be okay. It just hit me that this isn't a dream, is it? And you reciting the facts and history so...so matter-of-factly, it made it real." I knew that I made no sense. But I'd been ignoring that I might actually be in a different place, a different world, altogether. Being concerned with the immediate need to get back home allowed me to ignore anything else. Sitting quietly with Taranath talking let my brain wander.

"I'm sorry," He said simply.

His manner calmed me like no one else had so far. I guessed a mage was something like a doctor in the Fae Realm. He had the comforting bedside manner of a good doctor.

"Why am I dying?"

"Because Fae is hard for humans. I don't know why."

"Is that why so many babies die here?" I couldn't get Glynan's words about little babies not making it to one out of my head.

Another nod. "They are wished here. They were not wanted in their own world, and they end up here."

"I thought that was just some horrible, old story!" I hadn't believed Glynan when she said the babies were sent here.

"When parents wish to be rid of their children, sometimes the goblins hear and will steal the babies away."

"They might not really mean it!" The thought horrified me.

"Then perhaps people should take greater care with their words?" His brows raised.

He had a point. A horrible point. I didn't want to admit it. "So they are stolen by goblins, and then what?"

"They foster with a fae family. If they live, the family will adopt them. It's what happened with Drake. He came here many years ago as an infant and grew up with the royal family. Eventually—" Taranath pursed his lips. He looked like he was considering his next words. "Drake was adopted formally by the king and queen."

"That explains his relationship with Brennan. They're like brothers."

"Do you have brothers?"

"No. It's just me. They remind me of what I think brothers would be like."

Taranath continued the lesson. "When human children live to about five, they begin to take on the characteristics of the fae. It is possible for humans to survive here, but they grow into it. Most have never seen an adult human, an actual human. This world is too harsh for you."

"So you're saying I should be dead?" This got better and better. I started to think that Brennan owed me a hell of a lot more than just an apology. Maybe a wish or something—although that was more of a genie thing.

"I don't know what you should be. I am surprised the spell didn't work. Other than that, I don't know what to expect. You're the first, my dear." He beamed with scientific pride, as though he'd brought me here himself.

"Well, let's see if we can get me back to where I belong, I guess," I didn't feel confident after our depressing talk.

"I think we need to. After all, you're an unknown!"

Did he have to be so cheerful?

"Relax, Iris, and imagine where it is you wish to be."

That was easy. In the bathroom, after Brennan and Drake took their magic carpet ride out of the ladies. I closed my eyes and concentrated hard.

"Here we go."

CHAPTER SEVEN

Brennan

He paced along the corridors, heading back to his rooms. Where was his mother? When they'd left his rooms, leaving Iris in the hands of Taranath, he'd gone in search of his mother, wanting to know more about Scarface—he laughed to himself at Iris naming the fae— and to see if she'd spoken to his father. He knew, in spite of her earlier words, she hadn't left. He could always tell. Their family all could. Even Drake, once he formally became a member of the family.

"Where is she?" He ground out to Drake, who'd tromped along with him all over the blasted castle.

"I don't know," Drake spoke calmly. "Why are you so out of sorts? I know the girl is annoying, but she'll be gone soon."

"Oh, I don't know, Drake. How about because she's still here, despite promises to the contrary? Or that we still have no idea of who this Scarface is? Or that he hurt my mother?"

"You didn't tell me that."

"She scryed him while you were fetching the mirror to the Dwarf Realm, and said he saw her. Basically pushed her away."

Drake rubbed his chin. "That makes things a lot worse."

"Your grasp of the obvious is outstanding."

"She didn't recognize him?"

"Not that she mentioned."

They rounded a corner and ran right into Nerida.

"Watch where you are going, clumsy boy!" She scolded.

"Why are you still here, Mother? I thought you had to get back to Father."

"I messaged him and gave him all the details. Once I'd spoken to Iris, I knew I needed to be here."

"Why were you speaking to Iris?" Brennan snapped. In spite of his irritation, he saw that Nerida didn't have on her usual mask of calm. Interesting.

He also didn't miss the glance that Nerida and Drake shared. "It came out of some of the questions Taranath had for her. Based on that, I went to the castle histories. There is something you need to know, Brennan."

"Well? No need to draw this out. What is it?"

"I think I know the reason that Iris is fading the way she is." Nerida looked pleased with herself.

Brennan rubbed the bridge of his nose, stalling for time.

"What is it, Mother?" He felt like for every step forward, he took several steps back. All he wanted was to get back and speak with Taranath, and get Iris home. Nothing had gone right since they'd come upon her. Nothing. If he was being logical, he'd concede that nothing had gone right since he and Drake had been ambushed. It was easier just to blame Iris. Made it more palatable.

"Iris *is* fading, but hasn't died. She's being kept alive."

"What are you talking about?"

"Iris is part fae."

He glared. "Mother, you're going mad. Iris is not part fae. She's human, albeit troublesome, but human. And she's going home."

"She may not be able to," Nerida said.

"Why is that?"

"I think the human side of her is dying, just like they do when they come here as babies, but because she is part fae—I believe her grandmother was fae—that is keeping her alive."

"What is it you want me to do about it?"

Nerida gasped. "You're not going to tell her? She has a right to know, Brennan!" Her face showed her shock. Even in the semi-dark corridor, he could see the disbelief on her face.

"What difference will it make? Her world is not ours. She doesn't have a life here."

"She could." Drake had been silent up to now. "I think you need to tell her."

"Why am I to be the one to tell her?" Brennan couldn't stop the irritation.

"I can tell her," Nerida said. "I knew her grandmother."

"What happened that she ended up with a human granddaughter?" Drake spoke before Brennan could. "I've never heard anything about it."

"We don't speak of it. You both know that it's not done for us to involve ourselves with humans. Too many complications." When Drake nodded, she continued. "When her grandmother, Imara, was younger, she accidentally opened a portal, by falling through it, actually. It's why your father and I made an effort to find all the spots that were weak, where the portals were easily available," she directed that at Brennan.

He gave a tight nod. He couldn't tell how he felt, how a flare of hope had spiked in him at his mother's words. He didn't want to hope, hope for…what? He didn't want to go there. So he crossed his arms and said nothing, willing Nerida to continue, while the hope flickered around the edges of him. He did his best to ignore it. He hoped that Mother and Drake couldn't feel his emotions.

Nerida continued. "But before we did that, Imara fell through, and she ended up in the Human Realm. She was there for some time. While there, she met a human man and fell in love with him. She came back to Fae, of course, but she was greatly changed." Nerida stopped, her gaze distant.

Brennan could tell that she wasn't with them just then, that she relived things from the past.

Nerida shook her head. "I asked and asked her, what happened to you there? Prior to falling through, she'd been happy, merry. Many fae asked for her hand, and she'd not accepted anyone yet. With her odd behavior, her parents were pressing her to choose a suitor. They were worried. They were right to be." Nerida sighed. "She came to me, right before she left forever. She cried," Both Brennan and Drake drew back in surprise. Fae did not cry often.

Nerida nodded at their expressions. "I was taken aback, as you might imagine. She told me of her time in the Human Realm, how she'd met a human man and she'd fallen in love with him. She came home when she could, but once home, she didn't want to be here anymore. She told me she no longer felt this to be her home. She wanted to go back. Back to the Human Realm and her human mate. She wanted me to sneak her across one of the portals."

Nerida sighed. "She asked for my help. I was shocked and told her I couldn't. I begged her to go to her parents. I told her that they'd rather see her happy than miserable, even if it was in the Human Realm." Now she looked away.

Brennan could see the sadness, and…guilt? On his mother's face.

"I was wrong. Oh, I was so wrong. She took my advice. She did go to her parents, and her father was so angry. It shook the court, the level of his anger. He went to the king, to your grandfather, demanding that he send her far from here and bind her from portals. Before that could happen, Imara disappeared. We all knew where she'd gone, of course."

She met both their gazes. "I've never been able to shake the thought that I gave the worst advice possible to Imara. Had I made another suggestion, she might not have come to the point she did. Because she followed my advice, she was exiled. Her father died pretending Imara never existed. And now, her granddaughter is here. We have to tell her, Brennan."

"To what end? Do you think she'll actually want to stay here? Where will she live? How will she be cared for? There are no families that will take her in."

"I will," Nerida's tone brooked no discussion. "I failed my friend, her grandmother. I will not do the same to her granddaughter. If you will not tell her, Brennan, I will. She may decide to go back. If she does, I will support that. It's her choice. But she must be able to make the choice with all the information that she has a right to know. She needs to know how she might be changed when she returns. It's not easy being of two worlds." She turned, walking towards the door to Brennan's chamber.

"What, you're going to do it right now?" He leapt forward, trying to get between Nerida and his door. "We don't have to do it right now!"

Nerida shoved him away. "Yes, we do. Who knows how much time we have left? How much time she has left? It is my responsibility. Let me pass."

"Mother," he said, unable to deny her.

She didn't answer, but opened the door and swept in.

Drake followed her, and Brennan slowly walked in behind the pair of them.

Why did he continue to feel such unease about the girl? The mage would determine if there were any magic within her. If so, Iris herself was not aware of it. He'd questioned her carefully, paying attention to her reactions and answers, and didn't feel that Iris had anything to do with Scarface, or why he and Drake had ended up where they had. Brennan could tell, without any discussion, from the way Taranath spoke to Iris that he felt it all just a series of coincidences and nothing to concern himself over. Brennan had learned to trust his mage over the years.

So why did Iris elicit such strong emotions from him? He felt a pressing need to get her out of the Fae Realm altogether, while at the same time, he felt an overwhelming desire to keep her here, by his side, forever. He found he was jealous of anyone who spent time with her. Odd, as he seemed to snap at her every time they were alone together.

"It's her choice. I will not take it from her," Nerida tossed over her shoulder.

"How is it you support this?" Brennan turned his frustration onto Drake.

"My concern stems from questions regarding whether or not she is a spy, or working against you," Drake said levelly, not meeting Brennan's eyes. "We both know Taranath doesn't believe so, given the way he is speaking with her. You know that as well as I. Therefore, I have no opinion either way. I am, however," He looked up at Brennan now, "In support of people being told the truth at all times. You know that."

Brennan made a noise that sounded like a strangled yell. "You and Mother will be the death of me. Who is king here?" He didn't realize Drake read the mage as he did.

He could see the ghost of a smile turning up the corners of Drake's mouth. "Why you are, Your Majesty."

"Yes, and the two of you are very respectful. Move," He walked past Drake to where Nerida stood in between the mage and Iris.

"Mother," he put warning into the one word.

"No, Brennan. She has a right to know. As would any other of our realm."

"What is it?" Iris asked. She looked from Nerida to Brennan.

"I believe we have discovered why you are so ill. Do you remember your grandmother?"

Taranath's brows raised, and he sat back in his chair, awareness dawning in his expression.

Iris hadn't gotten to the same place yet. "No. My parents aren't very close with their families, on either side. They always said that they didn't see eye to eye with their parents."

"What are your grandmother's names?" Nerida asked.

"Uh...well, my dad's mom is named Carolyn, and my mom's mom is Mara."

Nerida gave a triumphant glance to Brennan. "Are either of them still alive, Iris?"

Iris shrugged. "I guess so? I don't know. I wasn't kidding when I said we didn't see them. We don't."

Taranath leaned forward. "Do they know of your mother's illness?"

Nerida cocked her head. "Your mother is sick?"

Iris's entire demeanor changed. Suddenly, she looked like a scared little girl. Watching her, Brennan wanted to take her in his arms and comfort her fear away.

"My mom has brain cancer. It's not operable. That's why I have to get back. If I disappear, it'll kill her faster than the cancer will." She bent her head low, and Brennan could tell that tears weren't far off.

The mage rested his hand on hers. Brennan wanted to knock it away, but he couldn't. It wasn't done, not for the king. A king with a betrothed, and a fae king who had no business holding hands with a human. He stood very still, struggling with his emotions. Drake moved closer to him. Probably alerted by the strong emotion he felt coming from Brennan. He'd always been able to discern Brennan's emotions more than anyone other than Brennan himself.

"Let go of that anger," Drake murmured towards Brennan. "It won't do anything for you. The mage isn't where you need to focus your anger."

Brennan looked at his friend. His brother. "Thank you."

Drake shrugged. "It's what I do. Keep you out of your own way."

Brennan leaned in, wanting to hear what Nerida said to Iris.

"I knew your grandmother, Mara," she said. "At least, I think I did."

"How do you know?"

"I believe she is a fae named Imara, who left here to live in your realm, the Human Realm, with a man she fell in love with."

"Wait, wait, what? You're serious. You think my grandmother is a fae? That would make..." she stopped.

Nerida smiled. "Yes, that would make you part fae. Shall I tell you what I think is happening?"

Iris nodded.

"Has Taranath shared with you how our world affects those from your world?"

Iris nodded again.

"I think the Fae Realm is killing your human side. You are ill, but since you are one-quarter fae, that quarter is keeping you alive."

"What will happen if the rest of me dies?" Iris looked very small as she asked, looking first to Nerida, then the mage.

Iris

I couldn't take it all in. Why hadn't my parents known about this? Why hadn't I ever met my grandmother? Was this why my parents didn't talk to their families? I could tell that Nerida thought she'd uncovered a great secret that solved things, but for me, the questions had just multiplied exponentially.

"I'm having some trouble here. What does my grandmother have to do with anything?"

"Are you not listening? You are not dead because you are not fully human! Or so my mother thinks." Brennan glared at Nerida.

"What do you think?" I didn't understand what he was so pissy about.

"I think that while I question the theory, my mother is not given to flights of fancy. She's terrifyingly practical. So it's worth it to see if she's correct." The words sounded dragged from him.

"I don't understand why you're being such a jerk about all this!" I burst out. "Aren't you glad that I'm not dead? I mean, you know, since it's your fault I'm here? Even if I am part fairy too?"

"We are not fairies," Nerida and Brennan said together, giving me some royal stink eye. Oops. I'd forgotten my conversation with Glynan.

"Actually, it's my fault." Drake leaned in, giving a small wave of his hand. Unlike Brennan, he didn't look bothered at all. He seemed to be trying not to laugh. "I'm very glad you're not dead."

I gave him a *what the hell?* look. This is the guy who had been as rude to me as possible, and now he decides to be nice? And fae call humans odd, not to mention all the other uncomplimentary things I'd heard since I'd been here! I didn't get these people all.

Brennan divided his anger—why anger?—between his mom and Taranath. "Figure out what needs to happen to send her back. I don't see why her heritage stops her from being returned to her own place."

Nerida stood, anger showing. "Because if I am correct, which I know that I am, she has a right to be here as well."

"Being less than half fae?" Brennan stepped closer to Nerida, even angrier. "I don't know why you're hanging onto this so fiercely, but Iris is more human than anything else. She needs to go back to the Human Realm."

He whipped around and stalked from the room. No one spoke, then Drake burst out laughing.

"I haven't seen him this rattled in...I can't even think how long."

Nerida looked at him, her face sad. "You think that's something to laugh over?"

"Oh, I do. I'll go, make sure he doesn't cast himself off the tower walk. It's not a bad thing, Mother. Trust me."

With a smile—a smile!—at me, he left.

Nerida turned back to me. She started to speak, but I held up my hand.

"If my grandmother is fae, and we don't know that yet, that means my mom is half, right?"

Nerida nodded.

"Then can you save her?"

Both Nerida and Taranath glanced at one another.

Taranath spoke first. "What do you mean?"

"Is there some kind of fae medicine, some healing or magic or whatever, that can help her? That can save her?" I could hear the pleading in my voice.

I didn't have to hear the answer. The expressions of the people sitting with me told me what I didn't want to hear.

"I don't know," Nerida said. "We would need to go to the Human Realm and see her. Could you tell?" This was to Taranath.

He shrugged. "I can't answer that from here. But I would be pleased to see if there is something I can do to help."

I felt hopeful about something for the first time since I'd been dragged here. "Then maybe you could help her? Let's go back home, back to my realm! Let's see!"

No one spoke. "What? You can help my mom!"

"There is no guarantee," Nerida said quietly. "I would hate to raise any hope."

"I've already accepted that she's going to die. What I don't accept is that there are people who can help her not helping!" I stood, feeling the anger well up.

"Iris—" I cut Nerida off. I didn't care if I came off as rude.

"No! If you can help her, you have an obligation to do so. If she's part fae, isn't part of your job taking care of your people? She's one of your people, even if she's not fully fae!"

"I don't know that it's my place to interfere with this."

"You certainly felt it was your place to tell me about my grandmother and make my life more complex than it already is. No hesitation there!" I struggled to keep myself from screaming at her.

Taranath started to laugh. "I do beg your pardon, Your Majesty, but she has an excellent point. I am willing to make the trip, and we can see if Imara is still in the Human Realm. Perhaps we can help her—we may not be able to, and I won't have your abuse if not—" this directed to me.

"But let's try. With you at my side, I can focus on what I need to do for the woman, and maybe even Iris, and you can help direct us." Taranath glanced between Nerida and I, wanting something. I didn't have the energy to try and figure it out.

His comment reminded me of something else. It gave me a break from wanting to smack Nerida into doing the right thing, so that could only be good.

"Why do you all need to help one another so much? The magic you use seems so...hard. I thought it was supposed to be easier."

Taranath shook his head. "Magic is not something that can fix all things. It's a helpful tool, something we can use to ease some aspects of life, but it's not there to take all your cares from you and make life simple."

That thought blew my mind a little. I'd always thought magic involved the waving of a wand, and all would be well. Here, in the Fae Realm, it seemed far more complex.

"Will you come? Please. I don't want to lose my mom."

For the first time, Nerida's eyes softened as she looked at me. "I can understand. No one cares for losing a parent." She stepped away from us, looking out the window. No one spoke, even though it nearly killed me to be quiet.

When she turned, I knew I'd won my point. "Very well. Let us all go now. We shall return—"

"Can we please return to where Brennan took me from? It's important I get back to that moment."

"Why?" Taranath asked.

"Because I need to look as though nothing has happened. I will make an excuse to Heath—"

"Who is Heath?" Nerida asked.

"The guy I went to the game with. He went to get me a soda while I went into the bathroom. I don't want draw attention to myself. Not important!" My earlier concern over the potential loss of Heath's affections seemed petty and unimportant compared to this.

"I'll tell him I have to get home. I met him there, so you guys can come back with me."

"Wait." Taranath held up a hand. "Do you not travel in iron and steel carriages?"

I nodded. "So?"

"We do not stay well around iron. We shall have to use a portal."

I started to pace as I always did when I found myself frustrated. I stopped. "The hell with it. Can we just portal to my house? I'll tell Heath that I had to get home quickly. I'll...I'll text him." I'd forgotten that I did have a phone. Since the failed attempt to call 911 the thought of using it here hadn't occurred to me.

"Will you be able to pinpoint a way to Iris's home?" Nerida asked Taranath.

He nodded. "If you lend me your support. I will guide us. Once there, I'll have enough strength left to see if Iris's mother is indeed fae."

"We'll need to talk to Imara." Nerida looked sad and concerned. That was interesting. Why would she be sad to see an old friend? I thought that would be a happier thought. I pushed her worry aside. I had to focus on my mom and getting her help, making her better. Nerida could deal with her own problems.

"Let me leave a message as to where we've gone," Nerida moved away, rubbing at her forehead.

I watched her, fascinated.

"What is she doing?" I whispered to Taranath.

"Some families have the ability to communicate across distance, without words. Nerida is one who can."

She returned, smiling weakly. "I've left word with one of Brennan's goblins. Shall we begin?"

I wanted to ask Nerida how she'd done it, but her expression didn't invite questions. Anyway, there were more important things to deal with.

Taranath smiled at me, I guess to be encouraging. "Iris, I'll need you to sit and take my hands. I want you to focus on your home, see it and allow me to see it with you. Then I can be more accurate in where I open the portal."

I sat down and took both his hands in mine. Nerida went behind Taranath and put her hands on his shoulders. I closed my eyes and focused on seeing our living room.

After a moment, I heard Taranath inhale. "Good, Iris. Show me more."

I forced myself to look around the room, seeing all the details, letting the memory fill my vision.

Without warning, I felt the world around me—the only way I can describe it—shimmer. It was like the ripples that spread when you drop a rock into water. The ripples change the shape of the surface of the water, making it shift and move before becoming still once more.

We weren't at that stage yet. We were trapped in a ripple. I thought we'd walk through something like Brennan had done before. I guess everyone had their own personal portal style, kind of like everyone had their own car?

The ripple stopped, and my breath felt it had been sucked from me. The darkness I'd seen in the ripple gave way to a near-blinding light.

I opened my eyes a slit and saw that I sat on the floor of my own living room.

"Iris?" My dad was standing next to the couch where Mom stretched out. Our arrival interrupted them. Mom looked weaker than normal.

"Iris, what the hell? Who are these people? How did you get here? Weren't you at the game?" My dad fired the questions at me. I could tell he was rattled.

I turned to see Nerida and Taranath sitting in a jumbled heap. Taranath's portal left dignity in the dust.

I got up. "Mom, we need to talk."

CHAPTER EIGHT

Brennan

Brennan paced along the castle walls. He stopped, looking out over the Goblin Kingdom. Where was the scarred sorcerer? What plots were forming among Brennan's own people? What had they been told to encourage them to rise up and contemplate rebellion? These thoughts made him sad. He knew nothing for certain, only that his people would suffer more than anyone else, himself included, before this ended.

"You can come out." He kept his voice bored.

"Thought you'd be out here."

"Clears my head." He didn't move. He could tell Drake walked up behind him.

"I hope so. Telling Iris the truth was the right thing to do."

"Since when have you become her champion?" He whirled to face Drake, his calm broken.

"Since I saw your thoughts."

The simple statement swept Brennan's anger away like a strong wind.

"What do you mean?" He already knew what Drake would say, but wanted to hear him say it.

"You like her. You like her more than I've seen you like anyone else, and that includes Ailla. That gives me hope for you, Brennan. You deserve to be happy, and if this girl could be involved in that, I am willing to support it."

Brennan could only stare at his friend in amazement. Iris had not been at the castle for even a day and Drake made this sort of pronouncement? He must be mad.

"I think you are confusing concerns with—"

"Save the protest, Bren. I know you. I've known you my entire life and much of yours. I know when something has set you down a different path. Lie to yourself if you must, but do not attempt to lie to me."

Drake walked towards the other end of the walkway. Brennan could only watch him go, wondering what Drake saw in him that he couldn't see in himself, feeling a sliver of hope that Drake just might be right.

"I thank you for your concern, Drake, but I am to be married. My fiancée is a fine woman, from a fine family. She'll make me happy enough." He tamped the hope into ashes.

Drake stopped and faced him. "Make you happy enough? How can you say that? You live for a long time, Bren! Is happy enough all that you want in a mate? Is that all you want to give your mate? I'm surprised at you. You're so compassionate to the goblins when everyone else mocks and looks down upon them. Why would you do that to a woman who married you?"

Brennan found himself speechless. He'd not heard such impassioned speech from Drake in some time. When his engagement had been negotiated, Drake had been steadfastly against it, in spite of his approval of Ailla herself. He said that both parties deserved better than a good political match.

Brennen considered his fiancée. She *was* a good woman, the daughter of the king of the Dragon realm. Like all fae from that realm, she moved carefully and deliberately. Her beauty was legendary. He didn't know if she had the Dragon temper because he'd never seen her angry.

"I know you were not particularly in favor of this match..." He felt the need to tread carefully with Drake.

"No, and I'm still not in favor of it. I think your parents pushed you, and you gave in because it was easiest. Iris excites something in you! Reach for that, Bren! Don't let that go. When was the last time you got excited about anything?"

"About one day ago, when you and I were attacked by goblins."

Drake stared, mouth slightly open. Then he muttered something in the Fae tongue that Brennan didn't catch and stomped away. He wrenched open the door leading back to the castle, and disappeared down the stairwell without another word or backwards glance.

Sometimes Brennan wondered if Drake remembered that he was the king. One didn't stomp away from a king, no matter if they had grown up together.

He followed Drake down the stairs, taking care to close and latch the parapet door.

Was Drake correct? Were the unease and his rude, angry behavior because he actually liked Iris? Did Drake actually believe he should throw over the Dragon Princess for a human? Brennan shuddered at the thought of facing two irate fathers.

"It's time for this nonsense to end. She goes back. No more involvement." Whether Drake was right or not, he'd made a promise. Not only to Ailla, but to their respective kingdoms and parents. He wasn't going to toss all that away on a foolish whim.

No matter how much he desperately wanted to believe Drake. Even though he knew that he, Brennan, couldn't ever have such a thing. Even though—Brennan shook his head. No. It wouldn't do to head into such thoughts. He'd learned long, long ago that he had no choice but to keep a tight rein on his emotions to keep everyone around him safe.

***

He walked for a while, not really paying attention to where he went. He heard over and over Drake's words, debating the merit of his friend's observations. Every time he went over all that Drake had said, he felt a rising of hope and a sweep of emotion so strong that he felt he stood on the edge of a high cliff, ready to fall over. He nearly ran into Drake at the door to his rooms.

"What is amiss? No need to stand out here as though these are not my rooms," he grumped.

Drake took two steps in and then stood to the side. "Where have they gone?"

"What? What do you mean, where have they gone? We left them not that long ago!"

"Yes, your lordship, we did. However, they are no longer here."

Brennan opened his mouth to bellow for one of the goblins who took care of him when Glynan came in. Her head bowed, she twisted her hands in front of her.

"I have a message for you, Majesty," she said. Everything about her said clearly that she didn't want to pass the message on to him.

"What is it?" Brennan asked. He tried to throttle down his anger. His goblins were loyal and they worked hard. Other than his own foul temper, he had no need to shout at them.

"Her Majesty, the queen, she bade me tell you that they, her and the mage, have taken the girl home. She will contact you when she can."

"That wasn't the plan at all. Not in any fashion," Drake said. "What happened while we were out?" He looked to Glynan, but she didn't look up.

"Glynan," Brennan asked, feeling rather smug that Drake now shared in the general upset, "What else did my mother say?"

"Didn't say anything, Majesty. Only told me, and not even in person, that they needed to go, and I was to tell you."

She stopped. Brennan could see he wouldn't get anything else out of her. Probably because she knew nothing more. She also felt horrible for bringing him news that she felt sure would upset him.

"Thank you, Glynan. You may go." The little goblin almost ran from the room.

"She sent a message to Glynan. She never sends to anyone outside the family." Drake looked more worried than annoyed.

Brennan nodded. He felt the same way. "That suggests they left quickly. Otherwise, why not speak with me or you directly?"

"Because she didn't want us to stop her?" Drake asked with a slight smile. "She is, after all, your mother. The acorn grows directly from the tree."

In spite of his anger over her skulking away, Brennan had to laugh. "Yes, she and I are a lot alike. Doesn't mean I have to like it when I have to deal with it. She's supposed to be my elder, and what does she do but sneak away like a youngling?"

"There's a reason for it. Mother is nothing if not deliberate. Perhaps we should trust this?"

"Yes. That's what worries me. What told her that this would be the correct move?"

CHAPTER NINE

Iris

"Mom, Dad! Stop! Just stop and listen to me, okay?" I couldn't remember the last time I'd raised my voice at my parents. We all worked well together. You have to when you live on a small boat. Well, she wasn't small, but in terms of space for three, she was. We were a good team, and I counted on that to keep them from freaking out.

"What is going on, Iris?" Dad looked angry.

"Mom, we need to talk about your mother."

This made my mom sit up, and exchange one of those married looks with my dad.

"Why?" She asked quietly. I felt Nerida start next to me. When my mom spoke, the intensity of her illness stood out in stark relief. Even the one word took something from her.

"I am Nerida, and I believe your mother was a good friend of mine, one I haven't seen for a long time." Nerida took the bull by the horns and stepped right in.

"Why would you think that?" This from Dad.

"Why do you not see your families?" Taranath interrupted.

"Who are you to be concerned?" I could feel my dad getting mad.

"Dad, will you trust me? Taranath means nothing bad. We really do need to know about this, though. Please. We never have talked about it. But we need to now."

"Why?" Mom asked again.

"Because I don't believe your mother is human, and having encountered your daughter, I think we can help you."

Nerida's blunt statement took me aback, and I knew what she planned to say. Sort of. I also felt a thrill of hope that Nerida had agreed to try and help Mom. She hadn't been willing to say as much when we were still at the castle.

My parents were rocked.

"What?" Dad whispered. "What the hell is this? It's not funny." His eyes filled with tears.

"I am not joking. Why don't you see your families?"

"My mother had a different life planned for me. I chose for myself, and she told me I was on my own." Mom spoke over Dad. I couldn't believe that she'd gotten all of that out.

"And you?" Nerida turned to my dad.

His anger gave way to sheepishness. "My parents knew Claire's. They knew that her mother was against our marriage. They were offended by her attitude towards me, as though I wasn't good enough. They told me that if I married Claire, I was making my own bed to deal with her snotty family."

"Needless to say, we told them all to go to hell." Mom said in a whisper.

Dad laughed, and sat down next to her, cuddling her close. "Yes, we did. And they went away muttering about how stupid we were, and not to come crawling back."

He and Mom smiled at one another. It filled my heart to see the love still strong between them.

Taranath watched them as well. His expression altered only a little, but I could tell that their love affected him, too.

Nerida didn't allow the massive quantities of sentiment to deter her.

"Does your mother know you're ill?"

Dad answered, shaking his head. "They have not been part of our lives, just as they promised. They don't need to be part of it now."

"That is where you are wrong. We must contact your mother. Contact Imara."

"Mara," Mom corrected her.

Nerida smiled at her, and for the first time, I saw her empathy for my mother. "We knew her as Imara. If I address her so, and she recognizes it, I shall know I have found her. How can you contact her?"

"Call her?" I suggested.

"I do not call in the same way you do, I think. Will you call her?" She looked around at the three of us. "One of you must do it. I must speak with her. Immediately."

I could tell that my dad didn't care for her dictatorial manner. It could be annoying, but there was no time to get stuck on that now. We needed to see if there was anything to be done for Mom.

"Can we get to it, please?"

Everyone looked at me in surprise. "Mom, we're here to figure out some stuff about your mother, but we're also here to see if Taranath can help you. We don't have time to waste. So save all the arguing or whatever for later."

Dad looked from me to Taranath, and Taranath stepped forward. "I cannot promise that there is anything I can help with, but I have told Iris I will look and see."

"What can you do that the doctors can't?"

"Was there anything odd about your mother growing up?" Nerida again. The woman bore a strong resemblance to a pit bull with an agenda.

"She loved the water and sky." Mom's voice had a dreamy quality. She'd leaned back against the sofa and was looking at something the rest of us couldn't see. "I didn't understand when I was younger, but she and my dad would fight because she'd go out back naked and lie under the stars when the sprinklers were on."

Nerida laughed softly. "Of course she did. That's because we fae take strength from the natural world."

"Fae? What are you talking about?" Dad asked.

Taranath stepped close to where my mom lay on the couch and knelt down next to her. Whatever Nerida planned to say, she suspended as we all watched Taranath move his hands above Mom. Like some crazy healer, I thought, feeling hysteria swirling through me. If this didn't work, I didn't know what I would do. I hadn't realized how much I pinned on him being able to help her.

"You are very ill, Claire. But you know that. The fact that you are still with us is, in part, due to your fae heritage. It refuses to die." His voice soft, the words heavy. Weird, how hard those words were to hear.

"I wondered what was keeping me going," she answered, her eyes closed. "I thought I should have died some time ago."

I gasped, then covered my mouth. Stepping closer to Dad, I took his hand. I could tell he felt as shocked as me. We hadn't talked about this with Mom ever. Yet here she was, telling someone who was basically a complete stranger things we didn't even talk about!

I covered my mouth with my other hand so I didn't cry out. Horrible as this was to hear, I didn't want to miss any of their conversation.

"Your fae wants to live. Being with us will help you, Claire. We need to bring your mother to you."

"She won't come," Mom whispered. "She is probably still angry that I married Paul. He wasn't the one she chose, and…she doesn't let go of grudges."

"Claire…" My dad found his voice, his hand still gripping mine tightly.

"I am not surprised," Nerida spoke up. "We choose our children's mates. It's unheard of for the children to marry otherwise."

"Rather pushy and barbaric, isn't it?" I couldn't believe how much my mom could keep up with conversation. Normally, this much tired her out, and she'd be napping by now. Taranath was right. The presence of other fae did help.

"Of course not!" Nerida sounded impatient. "A good parent talks with their child, knows them well, and selects a mate based on that. It's not a random choice, done on a whim."

"Yes, Brennan is most content with your choice, isn't he?" Taranath spoke quietly still, not turning around when he asked.

I had to keep myself from speaking up, from saying *NO!* to the thought of Brennan marrying anyone. What did I care if he married some poor, unfortunate girl? Why hadn't he mentioned that fact? You know, when he was carrying me? Nerida's words dragged me away from examining this matter.

"Brennan is not the matter at hand. Claire, how can we get in touch with your mother?"

Mom opened her eyes and looked at Dad. An entire conversation flew between them. His shoulders sagged.

"I'll call." He let go of my hand, and went to get the phone.

In a moment he was back, dialing the numbers. I didn't realize that they kept up with their parents like that. Maybe it had happened when Mom got sick.

"Hello, Mara? This is Paul Mattingly. Claire—"

The phone was snatched from his hand by Nerida. She moved faster than anyone realized. She spoke rapid-fire into the receiver in a language no one could understand. A pause, and then more rapid fire speech.

She smiled, a smug smile of satisfaction, and looked around at the rest of us. Even Taranath had looked up to see her progress.

"Yes, Imara, I am here. With your daughter, who is dying. If you wish her to live, you will need to come here. At once."

I could hear the grandmother I'd never met speaking, but couldn't make out the words.

"I can open a portal for you. Mage," she moved the phone from her ear, "I need you to help me. Imara," This to the phone again, "Concentrate on me. And your daughter." She handed the phone to Dad, who took it silently.

If I wasn't watching this, I wouldn't believe it.

Taranath stood, after patting Mom's shoulder, and took Nerida's hand. They both closed their eyes, and I could hear a hum. This wasn't like when we came through. This whole portal business didn't seem to have any rules or general guidelines for how it was done.

A bright light grew from a spark in the middle of the living room. Dad drew back, taking my arm and pulling me with him back against the sofa, shielding me and Mom. I let him, even though I knew it would be okay.

The light grew and grew. Mom lifted her hand to her eyes, and suddenly, the light had a shadow across it. A tall, lovely woman with fair skin, who did not look like a grandmother should, stepped from the light.

"Mom," said my mother weakly. "You're really here." She closed her eyes.

"Oh, Claire." For all that I'd heard of her, Imara went straight to Mom, pushing past Taranath, and falling to her knees to take one of Mom's hands. She brushed Mom's cheek with her hand. The expression on her face nearly made me cry. It shifted as her gaze turned from my mom to my dad.

"Why did you not call me?"

He stiffened. "You wanted nothing to do with her before, not even when Iris was born. Why would we think now any different?"

I felt so proud of my dad. I knew his heart broke every time he looked at Mom. I knew it had been hard to call the woman who had cast Mom out. I knew he had a fair amount of anger towards my grandmother, but that moment his voice held steady, his head was high, and he didn't cower before her. I had to admit, her gaze fell into the ferocious category.

"My daughter is ill. You should have called." Imara pinned my father with her look.

"You didn't even care about Iris," Mom whispered. All eyes went to her. "Paul's right. Why would we think you would care if I was sick?"

Imara stroked Mom's cheek again. "You are my child. I will always love you."

"Great way you have of showing it," my dad said, with a ton of bitterness in his words. "Hey, at least it's nice you've showed up now. I'll give you that." He stood, after giving my mom's hand a squeeze, and turned his back on everyone in the room by walking to the doorway to the kitchen and leaning against it.

I could practically feel his anger. I didn't blame him, but I appreciated that he made the effort to keep his temper from exploding all over the place. I didn't think that anyone else knew how much restraint he had.

My grandmother—how weird to even think that after not having her around or part of my life before now— looked at him, and I saw a moment of sadness pass across her face. As quickly as I'd seen it, it disappeared. She turned back to Mom.

"I do wish you'd contacted me. I also wish I'd not been so stubborn and pigheaded," she said quietly.

Mom smiled. "That makes two, no four of us. I've missed you so much, Mom." She sighed, and closed her eyes. Then opened them again. "You've missed so much of Iris's life. Look at her. She's beautiful, just like you."

"Just like you," Imara said, not taking her eyes from Mom. Then that intense gaze turned to me. "But she is beautiful. It runs in the family."

My dad stiffened, and I ached for him. My head swiveled back and forth between where he stood and my mom and grandmother. I couldn't tell if my grandmother was being insulting or not. I hoped that he would be able to keep it together.

"Can you help her?" I asked. Touching as it was to see my mom reunited with her mom, this wasn't moving us forward towards the goal, the goal of healing my mom.

Imara looked up. "I don't know. It's been a long time since I used anything of my fae side."

"It's all your fae side," Nerida interrupted impatiently. "You have no other side."

"How little you know of the Human Realm," Imara stood, keeping a hand on Mom's shoulder. The frost had returned to her expression as she looked at Nerida. I suddenly remembered Nerida's look when we had first discussed my grandmother, back in Fae. There was obviously history here.

"Things are not as you might assume. This is not Fae, Nerida," Imara continued. "I can tell the difference, being here with you and this one," she gestured at Taranath," But I haven't practiced magic in years."

"How could you not?" Taranath, silent until now, spoke up. "Didn't you miss it, in some form?"

"It's not easy for everyone," Imara snapped. "Surely you're aware of that. Are you not a mage?"

"I am," Taranath answered calmly.

Imara gave a small, tight nod. "I presumed as much. No need to drag you here otherwise. Are you part of this mission to help Claire?"

He nodded. "I am. Your granddaughter is most persuasive, and I am sworn to help fae in need. There are no limits on how much of a fae one must be. Claire is fae, thus I must try to help."

"What are you going to do?" They spoke as though no one else was in the room with them.

That didn't sit well with Nerida. "We are going to do what we can," she interrupted. "It will take all of us."

"Not Iris," My dad turned to face everyone once more. "Whatever this is, if Claire agrees, I'm not going to stop you from trying to help her. But not with Iris's help. Whatever the hell it is you're doing, she's not going to be part of it. I won't lose her too."

Mom spoke up then. "I agree with you, sweetheart. Iris is not to be part of this."

"Don't I get a say in this?" I interrupted angrily.

"No!" Mom and Dad spoke together.

A moment of silence, and then everyone but me started to laugh. Not a lot, more of a whisper of a laugh than anything else, but the mood, the pressure, the atmosphere lightened.

Suddenly, I felt about five years old with how all the adults in the room were looking at me.

"Let's get on with this," Imara said, a rough tone to her voice.

"We need to gather around Claire," Taranath took charge. "Paul, we'll need your help also. It's important to have someone present who loves her dearly."

Imara glared at him. My dad, however, hesitated.

"Will this hurt me?"

"Are you afraid?" Taranath asked as Imara and Nerida rounded on him, both of them ready to tear into him.

Dad walked back to Mom and held up a hand. I could feel the anger coming off of him. "I'm not afraid for myself!" He said scornfully to the two women. "However, if this grand plan of yours doesn't work, Claire will still...die. I don't want anything to happen that will leave Iris an orphan."

The anger faded immediately from both Imara and Nerida. I took two steps to my dad and took his hand. "I'll be okay, Dad."

He kissed the top of my head and hugged me with his other arm. "I'm not ready to leave you on your own yet, honey."

"It's a fair question," Mom whispered.

"You will be all right. Tired and in need of rest afterwards," Taranath said, "But you will not be harmed. I will take care to ensure we don't take too much from you."

"What are you taking?" Mom asked before Dad or I could.

"Energy," Taranath said. "Magic is draining, no matter how skilled one is with it. If we can help you, I am guessing it will take a great deal of energy to do so. So the four of us will need to pool our resources, as it were." He smiled at me, letting me know it was okay that I wouldn't be part of those providing help.

That pissed me off, but my parents were on the same page, so I knew I wouldn't get anywhere with them.

"Everyone take hands, please." Taranath moved around Imara to stand close to Mom. "Imara, take her other hand. Paul, Nerida, I will need you to complete our circle."

I watched as this unlikely group of people all did as he told them, taking hold of one another's hands. It looked like the craziest grouping of Duck, Duck, Goose ever. I had to sit on a little giggle that threatened to escape. I wasn't laughing. I could feel myself as tense as I'd ever been, and on the verge of losing control in some way. The stress of everything that had happened was catching up to me. Maybe Dad was right to insist that I stay back. Not that I'd admit it. I wondered, crazily, if I could get a picture of this. The thought of what Nerida, or my grandmother, would do if displeased made me stop reaching for my phone.

Taranath took Mom's hand and closed his eyes. He began to chant in a different language. I'm guessing the Fae language. I closed my eyes too, to listen. His voice had a soothing, hypnotic quality.

It felt warmer. I opened my eyes a little bit, and took a step back. Taranath had a glow around him, and the glow moved down his arm and towards my mom.

In spite of knowing he meant to help her, it scared me to see that light moving towards my mom. I could feel my hands itching to separate her from Taranath, from whatever it was that they were doing to her.

I took a step forward.

Brennan

He paced in the lounge, wanting to lash out, to hit something, to knock things over and hear the satisfying crash of things breaking.

Although he knew his mother wasn't a nitwit, this certainly put that supposition to the test. What in the name of all that was sane was she thinking? Had she stopped thinking? What had led her to believe that leaving with Iris and his mage was in any way a good idea?

His frustration spilled over. "Damn that meddling woman!"

Drake chose that moment to put his opinion in. "I'm sure that she felt this was a good idea."

Brennan ran his hands through his hair. "Why? Why involve herself in this? Over one human girl."

"She's more than that," Drake's voice lost its teasing tone. "I won't allow you to ignore that."

"I plan to do just that," Brennan said in what he hoped sounded like an unconcerned voice. "While annoying, as are most things that Mother takes it into her head to get involved in, it will allow you and I to figure out what is going on in our kingdom. I do have a kingdom to run. In case it's slipped your mind."

Drake gave him a wry smile, one that said he wasn't bothered by Brennan's lofty manner. "I am always at your service, Majesty, as you are well aware."

"Good. I'm glad to see you remember what it is we need to focus on. Let's portal to the clearing where we were ambushed and see if there are any of the goblins left." Brennan's face fell, remembering the fallen numbers of his people. "We will also need to find their families, if we can."

Drake nodded. Brennan appreciated that he didn't offer any quips or light-hearted remarks. The sight of all the fallen must have stayed with Drake as well.

"I think that we can manage it, even without a mage," Drake said.

"Let's be a bit more prepared. Wear your armor and take more than just your sword."

Drake nodded again and left the room silently. Brennan went to the back room of his chamber, opening the cupboard where his armor resided. He couldn't remember the last time that he'd had to wear it, outside of ceremonial events.

Like his engagement.

He shoved the thoughts of Ailla aside. He had enough to consider without adding Drake's comments about the match to it.

Why then did those very comments keep running through his head like goblin children at the end of a feast day?

He shook his head and armed himself. He slid his long-bladed sword into the scabbard hanging by his side and crossed two more short swords in a back harness. Better to be over-prepared than caught unawares as they'd been before. He knew how lucky he and Drake were to have not suffered worse than being cast into the Human Realm.

Other than meeting Iris.

No, he thought. No. I will not think about her.

His thoughts were mercifully interrupted by Drake's return.

"I see we think alike," Drake grinned at Brennan's crossed pair of swords.

Brennan returned the grin. He and Drake had been working at swordplay for years. They were formidable.

Prepared, aware, and with six swords between them, they would be a match for even the scarred, traitorous, murdering fae sorcerer.

"Let's go," his grin deepened. He knew he looked more like his subjects when he headed into anything resembling a battle. It was as though being the Goblin King for so many years had altered him. Drake told him that his teeth lengthened and sharpened, like the goblins. His eyes darkened from their normal brilliant blue, and his thoughts became narrower and focused.

"I hope we meet him again."

Pulling a crystal from his side pouch, he tossed it in front of them with a sharp phrase, and a blur of light appeared.

Together, he and Drake stepped into the light.

***

An hour later, Brennan had to admit defeat. He and Drake had been all over the clearing. They could find no side of the scarred mage.

The fallen goblins still lay where they fell. Brennan walked among them, sorrow replacing the warlike feelings he'd had such a short time ago. He knew some of these goblins. They'd been in the castle, or were clan to those who lived near the castle.

Reluctantly, he opened another portal and summoned his steward.

Tall and skeletal, Bronoor didn't truly look like a goblin. Brennan suspected that he had fae blood due to his height and some of his facial features. He'd not dare mention it to Bronoor, however. The goblin was one of the proudest he'd ever met.

Stoic though Bronoor was, his mouth fell open as he stepped through the portal to join his sovereign.

"Your Majesty, what has happened here?"

"Drake and I were attacked yesterday." Was it only yesterday? Iris had set everything on its head. "We were able to fight them off, but unfortunately many perished. I want to bring them home, Bronoor. Find their families. Take care of them."

The scale of death hit him and he stopped speaking, overcome.

"But why would they attack you?" The disbelief stood out in Bronoor's question.

"I wish I knew. We stopped to have something to drink and eat, and they came rushing from the trees. It's well known that I stop here. I like the peace this clearing offers. Offered," he amended. "Once Drake and I were able to overcome them, a tall, scarred fae appeared. He told me I needed to agree to surrender the throne."

Bronoor gave the closest thing to a gasp that Brennan had ever heard from him.

"He did not!"

"He did. I, of course, declined such a demand, and he cast us into the Human Realm."

"This is a powerful magician," Bronoor looked thoughtful, although the horror of the situation hadn't left his features. "How did he convince all these goblins—I know some of them, and they were good and loyal—into daring to attack you?" His voice rose in indignation.

"I am hoping that you will be able to help me discover just that," Brennan said. "I cannot believe that they could be so angry or so unhappy without anyone mentioning it. Is there unrest I am not aware of?"

Drake had come to stand with them. Brennan glanced at the man who was his brother in all the ways that mattered. He could see the same sorrow he himself felt.

"We will discover it. I wouldn't be surprised to find that the accursed Scarface who has disappeared at the heart of it."

"Your Majesty, I will return with help," Bronoor bowed his head and walked away to organize the removal of the bodies.

Brennan nodded to him.

"Well, of course," he said, continuing the conversation with Drake. He looked around the clearing. "But what could he have told them, Drake? What prompted this? We haven't seen this sort of open rebellion since before I came to the throne. I have been going over and over this in my head. I keep seeing them," he looked down, overcome at the memories. "They came with swords raised, and anger and hate written all over them. They were ready to die." He looked back at Drake. "You know that it takes something very powerful to push anyone, fae, goblin, dwarf, dragon—"

"Well, perhaps not dragon," Drake interrupted.

They shared a wry grin. "No, maybe not the dragons. But generally, for a man to be ready to die, he's been told something very powerful, something that goes bone deep."

"I agree. The question is, what did he tell them, and for that matter, how do we find him?"

"We must send emissaries among the villages. Go out beyond the reach of the castle, beyond a day's travel. Those at the outskirts of the kingdom are not as directly affected by the affairs of the castle and might be persuaded to rebel."

"Again, it comes around to why? Even those who are several days' journey over land have always been treated well by you."

Brennan didn't answer. He had seen what a shoddy leader had done. The fae who'd been king before him had cared nothing for the subjects he ruled. A distant cousin, he'd taken the throne as a stepping stone to try and oust Brennan's father from the Fae throne.

It hadn't worked. The former king had lost his life, courtesy of an axe. Brennan had already been declared the heir, but he'd taken the throne earlier than planned because his father didn't want anyone other than close family to act as regent. It had been, at the time, a volatile situation.

"Do you think he could be somehow related to the former king? There had to have been those who supported him, and were angered at his removal and death."

"Then perhaps they shouldn't have backed a poor ruler who was nothing more than a selfish child," Drake didn't hesitate in his response.

"That's all well and good, but you must be more realistic, Drake. You know the politics that swirl round all the courts, and my father's is no exception. There are those who bear the name of our family who would end us in a moment if they could get away with it."

Reluctantly, Drake nodded. "It's possible. Hell," he swore softly. "It's the best reason we have at the moment. Until we find a goblin willing to talk, it will have to do."

"Where are they?" Brennan turned round. It was taking longer than he liked. He would not leave the clearing, however, until all his fallen people had been removed, and returned to the castle for burial.

Regardless of the fact that they had attacked him, he would see them cared for.

His steward approached. "Majesty, we have help."

"Good." Brennan crossed his arms. He could feel his face tighten and an iron band squeeze round his heart as a line of goblins trooped by. "Carefully collect all of them. When you return to the castle, wrap all of them for burial after they have all been identified and their clans notified."

The steward nodded, and moved away, head down.

In spite of the many beings in the clearing, no noise broke the silence. Brennan could hear the small clanking of weapons and armor and the many decorative items goblins loved to wear. Other than that, no sounds came through to distract from the somber task. Not even the birds sang.

At long last, the steward approached again. "That is the last of them, Majesty. We have them all."

"Let us be gone, then." He stalked forward. Watching the fallen being carried away had created an anger that by now had reached nearly a boiling point.

Drake kept pace with him as he walked towards the portal, and he stood aside to allow Bronoor and Drake to pass.

"Brennan, let us go."

"Go, Drake." His tone brooked no discussion. Drake turned and followed the steward.

Brennan cast another look around the clearing. It lay empty. It would never be a waypoint for them again. The times he and Drake spent there together, as one of their favorite spots during travel were a distant memory replaced by the vision of the bodies of his fallen people. He would have a stone placed here to remember them.

Angrily, he whirled and went through the portal, snapping it closed behind him. The immediate response of the portal to his magic made him smile ruefully. It always seemed to be more effective and work better when he had a base of anger behind it. One more reason to keep his temper. The thought of what his anger could do with magic was something he didn't want to contemplate.

It was, he realized, where the problem lay with the human girl, Iris.

She threatened his calm. As when he'd felt anger at Taranath touching her hand, at Drake holding her. He didn't like the potential loss of control. He'd seen what happened, and knew the histories, of fae who chose not to exercise control over their emotions. To say nothing of his own personal history.

As much as he'd replayed Drake's words regarding Iris in his head, he knew it a better thing to marry Ailla and keep himself under a tight reign. Better for him and all those who were around him.

He dismissed thoughts of the human from his mind, even though a part of him wanted to go over all their interaction again. To contemplate the difference between his own six hundred seventy-four years of age and whatever young age she was.

He had no time for that, however. He needed to see his father, to see who the allies of the former Goblin King might be. If any were still living, and if so, would they still be willing to act.

Much better than thoughts of a human girl who flitted through his head.

CHAPTER TEN

Iris

As I moved towards them wanting to stop the light that traveled down Taranath's arm from reaching my mom, my father pushed me back.

That movement rippled through the three fae, and Taranath fell back.

"Iris! What are you doing?" Nerida demanded.

"Don't talk to my granddaughter like that!" Mara was having none of Nerida's anything.

"Both of you stop," Dad said quietly. "Iris, are you okay?"

I looked at Mom. Something had gone out of her. "I'm sorry. I don't know what happened. I watched the glow going down his arm, and I needed to stop it." Tears fell down my cheeks, and I knelt next to Mom. "I'm sorry." I put my head down, ashamed. I didn't want to look at anyone.

"It's all right, Iris." I felt a hand on my head as Mara spoke. It must have been her hand. I felt something pass from her to me. I felt slightly less suicidal than I had mere seconds before, like maybe I hadn't just doomed my mom.

"Why did you feel the need to stop me?"

I looked up to answer Taranath. "I don't know. It was very strong, an urge I couldn't control."

He nodded, looking like the scientist again. "How interesting. Your fae is very strong and very protective."

"What does that mean? And can you still save her?" I looked from my mom to the three fae, who were all grouped around her.

One of them—I couldn't remember which one—had said that fae felt better when among their own kind when they were in other realms. Maybe they all felt the need to be close because all three of them, Nerida, Mara, and Taranath, had huddled close to Mom when I wasn't looking. Mara held her hand, and Nerida had her hands on Mara's shoulders. Much like when Taranath had been focusing on getting here earlier, I realized. They drew strength from one another.

Mom looked better. I know that sounds stupid given the fact that cancer had wasted her to a shadow of herself.

But she had color in her cheeks. Her eyes were more alert, not the bright shine they often had when she was taking morphine.

I felt the tears spring to my eyes and spill over. Until this moment, I hadn't realized how hard I had pinned my hopes on the fae being able to help her.

I dashed at my eyes and looked for Dad. I knew he couldn't be comfortable with this. Not only because his daughter and two weirdly dressed people had fallen into his living room, but because his mother-in-law, who'd turned her back on his wife and her entire family sat there, holding Mom's hand as though they hadn't spent twenty years apart.

I moved to him and took his hand. "You okay?" I asked quietly. I still felt guilty, and I needed to be reassured.

He nodded with short, tight movements. He crossed his arms and exhaled.

"It's not easy seeing her here," he gestured towards Mara. "I think I might be in some kind of shock as well. I haven't grounded you to within an inch of your life." The ghost of humor hovered around his eyes.

I gave him a smile with no ghosts. "We're a little beyond that now, don't you think? Dad, is it me, or does she look better?"

"I think we want her to look better," he didn't hesitate in his response. "I understand that you don't want her to leave us, but I don't think anything will change that."

"Don't say that," I whispered. "Please don't say that." I let go of his hand and covered my mouth with my hand. I had to, or I would have screamed at him, screamed horrible things at him. His acceptance of this, his refusal to take the offering of hope I'd brought, made me want to scream until he hurt as badly as I did. Even though I knew he did.

"Honey," he put his arms around me, even as I stayed facing away from him. "I want to hope more than anyone. I don't want to lose her. But I don't want to entertain some kind of fairy tale."

I looked at him then, eyes wide. "Don't let them hear you say that. They get kind of pissy when you call them fairies."

"What the hell is this?" He whispered.

"Can I tell you later? It's a little complex, and I'd rather not do it right now."

I thanked the fact that we'd lived together for so long in confined quarters where you had to be able to trust your crew. He gave me that trust, no questions asked.

"We can wait until the circus leaves, then." He didn't bother to lower her voice on that one.

Mara turned around and glared.

"We are not the circus, and I am not leaving my daughter."

Dad pushed himself off the table he'd been leaning on. "Really? Because you have such a great record of being there in the tough times?" His voice didn't raise, but the anger came across clearly.

"Paul, it's all right. Mother, do not agitate my husband. He's been the best man in the world to me, just as I knew he'd be. You were wrong about him, and us. You need to admit it so we can move on."

Everyone turned to stare at Mom. Her voice sounded stronger than it had in months, and she looked between Dad and Mara.

Neither spoke. I guessed that they were as surprised as I was.

Mara sighed, a sigh that spoke of being greatly put upon. Maybe it was better I hadn't known her growing up. She seemed very formal, more like Nerida than my fun-loving and huggy mom. She didn't seem like she would have been a comfortable, squishy grandmother. No cookies baked by her—they'd be served on a silver tray with a teapot and eaten with only the very best manners.

The image made me want to giggle, and I covered my mouth again to stop it.

"I was wrong, Paul Mattingly. I believe my daughter when she states you have been a good man, and your home shows the signs of a happy and successful family. Much better than the boat."

What? "That we still have and were out on recently," I spoke up. She wasn't going to get away with a half-assed apology like that. "That boat was our home and still is. We're only here because Mom needed treatment. I would have cheerfully lived on the boat while going to school. This—" I gestured around scornfully, stepping closer to Mara, "is not ours, and honestly, it's a big waste of space, in my opinion. It's not material crap that makes a family happy and successful." I rolled my eyes to emphasize my scorn, and crossed my arms, glaring.

Mara didn't say anything. I heard a little gasp and though vaguely it must've come from Nerida. Maybe fae kids didn't tell their parents when they were being asshats. Too bad.

Then Mara looked at Mom, and they both started to laugh.

"She is all you, isn't she?" Mara asked quietly. I glared more, and then lost my anger when I saw what looked like the glint of tears in her eyes.

She looked at me again. Yep. Tears. "Your mother looked just like that when she told me she was going to marry your father."

"And what a smart move that was." I wasn't giving an inch.

Dad came up behind me and put his arm around me, squeezing a shoulder. He planted a kiss on the side of my head.

"She doesn't take crap from anyone, Mara."

Mara turned that gaze of hers to Dad, and a smile almost turned up the corners of her mouth. "It seems she is a great deal like both of her parents."

Dad gave her a nod, and I felt his fingers tighten briefly on my shoulder before letting his arm drop.

"What is it you think you can do for Claire?"

Thankfully my dad decided to gloss over the fact that I had screwed up the first try.

Nerida, who had a decided look of relief on her face— didn't she ever have clashes with either one of those boys of hers? Finally spoke.

"How are you feeling, Claire?"

"Better," Mom said. "Like I've had a big dose of morphine, but without the cloudiness of the morphine." She smiled at me, and I felt my shoulders relax.

"That is the effect of being among us," Taranath said calmly. "You'll feel it as long as you are with us."

"Wouldn't it be better to take Mom to your realm?" I asked.

He shook his head before anyone else could reply. "No. Even though Claire is half fae, with her illness, she is weak, and the effect of Fae on her human side would kill her."

I felt the blood rush from my face and fall somewhere into my shoes.

"How are you going to make her better?" I whispered. "That's what you're supposed to do."

Nerida let go of Mara's shoulders, and took the two steps towards me. "There is no guarantee that we can help, Iris. You knew that."

Her calm, matter-of-fact tone made me want to slap it right off her face.

"Then why the hell did you come here? To find your old friend? You used my mom and my hope to get what you wanted? Thanks for nothing! Selfish cow!" I screamed the last word at her and ran from the room.

I could hear the burst of talk erupt after I left, but I kept going.

I ran out the front door and around the side of the house to the carport. My bike leaned against the side of the house, and with blurred vision, I yanked it upright and threw myself on it.

It wasn't far to the marina. That had been one thing we'd all agreed on when we decided to move ashore. We'd live somewhere close to the marina where we docked Sorcha.

That bitch, I thought angrily. Say whatever to your face, but when the truth came out, it was about what they wanted.

I pedaled harder, wanting to erase the sight of my mom's face, and all the hope I'd been carrying. No wonder my mom wanted nothing to do with them. Even without knowing about the fae side of things. Even Mara, who didn't seem all that warm or cuddly, abandoned them. The fae were not a kind race. No wonder someone wanted to kill Brennan.

Maybe when I finally went home, they'd all be gone, and leave me, Dad, and Mom to ourselves.

To pick up the broken hope and go on as best we could.

I could forgive a lot of things, but the raised hope just so Nerida could reach her goal—I didn't think I could forgive that. Part of me knew I spoke in anger, and really wasn't being fair, but I didn't care. I had no hope left. My mom would still leave me.

I hoped like hell they'd be gone when I finally went home.

Brennan

He tapped his foot impatiently as he waited for his father to appear. He used the family mirror, so Jharak would know to take the mirror to a private setting. While the day shone brightly, the arrival of the bodies of the fallen goblins cast a gloom over his castle and made him impatient. He needed to get to the root of this, and as quickly as possible. He had no proof of this, but he'd learned to trust his instinct over the years.

Glynan came in, clearing her throat.

He held up a hand after glancing briefly at her. "I cannot be disturbed at this time. I am waiting for the Fae King."

"But Majesty," she squeaked. "The Lady Ailla is here!"

That broke his concentration.

"What do you mean, she's here?"

"She came through the throne room portal asking to see you immediately."

Brennan ran his hand through his hair, wanting to yank it out. Her timing could not be worse. He didn't have the time or desire to go over wedding details. He couldn't even pawn it off on his mother, as she'd run off with the mage and Iris—his mind shied away from further thoughts of her—the moment his back turned.

He groaned. "There is some sort of conspiracy, isn't there?"

"Why would you think that?"

Wonderful, he thought. Just perfect that his father appeared in the mirror at that moment.

"Father, give me a moment, please." He didn't allow Jharak to reply but turned the mirror down and spoke to Glynan.

"Bring her to the queen's quarters and offer her refreshment. Give her my apologies, and let her know I am in the middle of matters of the kingdom, but will wait upon her as soon as I am able."

Glynan hurried from the room. It occurred to Brennan that she seemed afraid of his bride. To his knowledge, Ailla had never given any of the goblins reason for fear, other than the fearsome reputation the Dragon Realm carried. No one ever wanted to make them angry. They did, after all, have a special relationship with the dragons of the realm.

He picked up the mirror again.

"Thank you for meeting with me, Father."

"Why is Ailla there? And where is your mother?"

Jharak sounded as frustrated as Brennan felt. "And why are you so cold to your intended?"

"Father! Your part in my marriage negotiations is at an end. The bargain has been struck, and the marriage is now in my hands. That is not what I wanted to speak with you about."

"Very well. Where is your mother?"

"Off on one of her missions," Brennan ground out. Would no one cooperate today?

"Oh." Jharak seemed mollified, if grumpy. "Very well. What is it, Brennan?"

He told his father of being ambushed, and of the words of the sorcerer. He mentioned being tossed into the Human Realm, but not of bringing Iris back. She was back in her own place now, and was now nothing more than a slight mishap in the scheme of what was important. What his mother chose to tell Jharak when she returned was up to her and not his concern.

"So," He finished. "In speaking with Drake, it occurred to us that perhaps some of the allies or family of the former Goblin King might have a grudge they wish to exercise. What do you think?"

"Why now?" His father asked.

Brennan shrugged. "I don't know. It's one of the many things I don't know, Father. I am guessing in the dark at this moment. Do you think this is a consideration I need to leave be?"

Jharak stroked his chin, thinking. "No, it's a reasonable guess, Brennan. There is no other foe who would rise against you in this manner."

Brennan laughed, but it wasn't a happy sound. "I doubt that, Father. There are plenty who not only don't care for me, but don't like that we are aligning with the Dragon Realm, and who have no regard for my goblins. They wouldn't see their deaths as of great import." He couldn't keep the bitterness from his voice.

"What are you doing with the fallen ones?"

"I have had them identified and their clans notified. I will speak to those at and near the castle tomorrow, when the heads of the clan come to collect their relations. All honor will be paid."

Jharak nodded. "That is wise, Brennan. I don't have many answers for you, but I will go and confer with the historian to see who is still alive who might carry on such hatred. Go and see your fiancée." He winked out from the glass of the mirror, which meant he'd put the mirror down.

Brennan sighed. He put the family mirror into a pouch at his belt. Somehow, he knew he'd need it sooner rather than later. Better to keep it with him.

He went to the large mirror on his wall, one with no magical ability. Sadly, as he could wish that it would go and see Ailla for him.

He straightened his coat and made sure that he looked like a king.

With another sigh, he left the room for the queen's quarters.

He couldn't decide why he felt so nervous and unwilling to meet with her. He'd done nothing wrong, nothing for which he owed her any apologies. Why did he feel guilty?

The queen's quarters were not far from his own. He took a steadying breath and opened the door.

Ailla stood near the window, framed by the afternoon sun.

She stood nearly as tall as he himself. Her hair, dark like his also, had an auburn tint that glowed in both sun and candlelight. Her lips were full and red, and her face was smooth and serene. When she walked, he could barely see the movement of her feet beneath her gowns.

She didn't turn when he entered. He kept moving towards her.

"Ailla? Is something amiss? I am sorry, I didn't expect you, or I'd have not kept you waiting."

At his speech, she did turn, and he saw that the red of her lips mirrored the red in her gown. She looked like a living flame.

The thought didn't stir him. Not as it ought to.

Ailla held out a hand. "I came because word of your distress reached me."

"Already? I have not yet made public the attack or the numbers of the dead."

Her brows rose slightly. "I do not know of an attack!"

"Then what distress do you speak of?"

"I have been told that you had a human here, and it proved difficult to return her to her realm. Is she still here?"

Brennan frowned and silently cursed the goblins' tendency to gossip. "I did. Drake and I happened upon her directly after we'd been attacked. I needed to ensure that she had nothing to do with the ambush. Once the Court Mage determined she had nothing to do with it, she was returned home." Once again, he felt no need to let anyone know that his own mother had gone with Iris.

Ailla stepped closer, curling her fingers into his. "I am curious to hear how a human female came to be here. Is she still here? I would love to see her, see what one looks like. I haven't even seen a human child in ages," She smiled at him.

Of course. Humans were a curiosity in Fae. It made sense. But something in Ailla's manner didn't feel right to him. Why did she care about this? He still couldn't fathom how she'd heard of Iris being her so quickly.

She led him towards a bench near the window with the gentlest of pressure on their clasped hands.

He put a smile on his face. "Of course. I am glad you wish to sit, as it is a tale of some length."

"Indeed? I am greatly interested." Ailla sat close to him, and leaned in. Now Brennan heard the quiet steel behind her words. What might have been brushed off as general curiosity had moved into something else. Ailla had some other reason for being here. Iris' presence was a mere diversion. Was Ailla on some mission from her father?

Brennan didn't like the varying emotions that flooded him as he considered his betrothed. His feeling of something being not quite right increased. This all felt planned. Even her concern for him.

He started at the beginning, keeping his voice steady, almost bored. When he told her of his goblins, however, he couldn't keep the emotion from the telling. He stopped speaking, looking away from her.

"Your devotion to the goblins is admirable," she said. He felt it was the first unplanned thing she'd said since he came in.

"No more than you and your family are devoted to the dragons. They are not fae, but they deserve no less."

"Of course not." The calm mask fell back into place. "It speaks well of you, however, Brennan. I am sorry, please continue."

He went on, making light of the situation with Iris, and finished with, "Taranath has seen her home. She did not fare well in her time here, and I wished to have no further deaths on my door."

He didn't tell her that Iris was part fae. There seemed to be a lot of things he wasn't telling those around him.

She patted his hand with the one not holding his. "Very understandable. Who do you think the attacker is?"

For the first time since he'd entered the queen's quarters, Brennan relaxed.

"I don't know. I wish that I had some idea. Have you in your kingdom heard any word of unhappiness with my rule, or heard of some grudge or other reason for anger among the goblins?"

She shook her head. "The realm is looking forward to our wedding and the increasing ties between our two kingdoms."

"I need to find him. I cannot have this instigator running free causing death among my people. I will not have a return to the time before my rule."

He snuck a glance at her as he said it. He wanted to see if she reacted.

Nothing.

Damn these dragon women. They were skilled at hiding their secrets. If she even had any secrets. He didn't want to think too hard about what had him doubting his future mate. Ailla had done nothing to incur this sort of suspicion from him. Only a sense of unease that had not stopped since he'd joined her.

"I will, of course, speak with my father. He may have some ideas as to why this is happening now. Did the attacker seem to be an elder?"

Fae didn't age much, but those who were older had an aura about them that alluded to their age and experience.

Brennan shook his head. "No, but I will admit that I wasn't paying attention to detail during our encounter."

"That is understandable. I don't know that anyone would have."

"You would have," he admitted ruefully. For all his ambivalence about Ailla, he didn't discount that she was a spectacular woman. She would, as his father reminded him, be a strong partner.

She smiled, and again he had the sense that the real, unrehearsed Ailla sat with him momentarily.

"I thank you for the compliment, Brennan. I'd like to think so, but one can never tell. If my people were lying dead before me, I cannot say that my attention to detail would be all that competent."

"I am sorry that this has made you travel," he said. He hoped he didn't sound as false as he felt. In fact his mind hummed with possibilities. Ailla, while concerned for his safety, showed more interest in Iris than anything else. If there were some reason…it would be better to know before they married. She shrugged. He wondered why he hadn't seen the more relaxed Ailla before now.

"I don't mind. We will be wed soon. Your concerns are mine."

Brennan wasn't sure he believed that. Not with the Dragon King as a parent. No need to debate that now.

"I am not sure where my mother is. Otherwise, you could both make progress in the planning."

Ailla stood, an air of briskness about her. "I leave that to my mother as well. I will return home and confer with my father. If he should have any answers about who might have attacked you, I will contact you."

He stood with her. "Let me escort you to the portal, Ailla."

She smiled up at him. "That would be nice, Brennan. I am," she said suddenly, "Sorry that I missed my chance to see a human girl. What was she like?"

Brennan heard the tension in her tone. Why did Iris bother her so? He stumbled over what to say as they walked out of the queen's quarters and towards the throne room.

On the way, Drake appeared from a side hallway.

Saved by my brother, Brennan thought. He didn't think he could speak calmly about Iris, and he certainly didn't want to speak of her to one as perceptive as Ailla.

"Bren, I thin—oh." Drake's voice changed. "My lady Ailla. I am sorry. I didn't realize you were here." He bowed respectfully to her.

Ailla nodded, and Brennan noticed something in her that hadn't been there a moment ago.

"I needed to confer with my intended. Now I must return home."

"Not home for long, though?" Why did Drake seem overly cheerful? And polite? What was that about?

Ailla gave Drake what Brennan could only describe as a sharp look.

"The Dragon Realm will always be my home of my youth. The Goblin Realm will be home for the rest of my life."

"That is good to hear, my lady. Brennan, I would speak with you once the Lady Ailla has departed. My lady," he bowed to Ailla and went the opposite direction.

"Drake seems born to annoy all those around me," Brennan said, hoping to lighten a shift in the mood he didn't understand.

"He is lucky to have you," Ailla replied. Whatever had caused her flare of temper had passed.

"No, I am fortunate to have him. He is true and loyal." *Even when I don't want it*, thinking about their conversation on the castle parapet.

Ailla tucked her arm through his as they walked into the throne room.

He led her to the portal and passed his hand across it to activate it.

As she took her arm from his, he lifted her hand to his lips and kissed it gently.

She clasped his hand in both of hers.

"I am glad that you were able to send the human female home so easily. That she didn't create much trouble."

He looked down at her, puzzled at her words. What did Iris have to do with anything they'd been discussing? Why did Ailla keep bringing her up?

Everything. She has everything to do with everything, his traitorous mind whispered. *Stop it,* he told himself. Admitting it, even just to himself felt...wrong while he stood here with Ailla. Worse, what if she could see his thoughts? Every fae had different skills. If she could tell what his thoughts were... "She was..." He stopped. He didn't know what he'd been about to say, but it wouldn't have been good in the context of standing and talking with his betrothed. He cleared his throat.

"How could I have done otherwise? Drake was not correct in his fears, but he was right to be cautious." He hoped that his voice didn't sound strangled. He couldn't stop the snarl of his thoughts at what he'd just admitted to himself.

"Then I am glad you have one another," her voice dropped to a near-whisper. "Take care of..."

"Yes?" He smiled at her, wanting to assuage whatever it was that concerned her. Reassure himself that he'd given nothing away.

"Yourself." She let go of his hands, settled her gown, gave him one last sharp look, and stepped through the portal without a backwards glance.

Brennan stood for a few moments after she left. What had all that been about? Nothing she did made any sense. He'd seen more emotion from her in the short time she'd been here today than he had for as long as he'd known her. He couldn't contain his fear that he'd exposed his thoughts and what that would mean for the future. Why did she focus on Iris? What did she know? What did she suspect?

His musing broke into scattered thoughts as Drake came into the throne room.

"So what did she want?"

"She came here because someone, no doubt some of my talkative staff, spread the word that we had a human here, and that the human took some work to return to her realm." He walked towards the large window opposite the portal, not wanting Drake to see his face. He couldn't hide from Drake. Not when his thoughts were in such turmoil.

Drake cocked his head. "Why would she be concerned about Iris?"

Brennan glared at him briefly before facing the window again. "I don't know. You haven't been talking to her as you have to me, have you?"

"Of course not! I save my insolence and truth for your ears alone, your lordship., " Drake mocked.

"Well, that's good. I'd hate to subject anyone else to your tendency to rattle on."

"That doesn't mean I don't rattle the truth, Bren." The teasing note had disappeared.

"I appreciate your concern for my—"

The portal behind them flashed with sudden light, indicating that someone allowed to use it had opened it.

He stood back and then jumped forward to catch Nerida as she tumbled through.

"Damn the Human Realm!" She steadied herself against Brennan as she regained her balance. "Nothing can be easy with it."

"Mother, how goes things?" For once, Brennan appreciated his mother's tendency to focus on her own concerns. Anything to shift his thoughts from his own.

She swatted his arm. "Not well, and I don't need any of your talk."

"I merely asked what I thought was a general question, as I was not sure what to ask," Brennan protested.

Nerida stood and brushed off her skirts. "I need your help, Brennan. I didn't wish to ask you, but I feel I have no other choice. I need your skill. The skill of the Goblin King."

"Mother, are you serious?" Drake looked from her to Brennan.

Did she need help with Iris? What could she need his help for? What in the Human Realm had stumped her? He found his initial irritation diminish a bit at the thought of what might have happened. "What is it you need help with? Did you not return Iris to her home?" He ignored the specific request that Nerida had made.

To his surprise, Nerida leaned against him again, and he could feel sadness rolling off her.

"I did. We did. Taranath and I found her home and saw her mother. The mother is as sick as Iris said she is. Then we contacted Imara, and Imara used a portal to come at my request."

"And?" While he couldn't deny his feelings, no one else needed to know. The more they continued to talk of Iris, the longer it would take to lock her away in his memories.

"Oh, Brennan!"

Brennan drew back from the pain in Nerida's words.

"Mother? What is it?" Drake led her to one of the benches in the throne room and made her sit.

"I made a complete muddle of it all! Of the entire thing! I told Iris that I wasn't sure we could heal her mother. Iris wanted us to bring the woman back here, to use the fae magic to heal her, and Taranath told her no. I told her that we'd promised nothing. Then Iris yelled at me, screamed at me, and called me names, and told me I was an awful person for using her mother to get what I wanted. We could have healed her, I believe. But…" She stopped, lost in thought.

"Mother, is what Iris said true?" Drake asked gently.

"Well, yes, but not entirely. I was more than happy to see if we could help one of our own, even if she is not fully fae. It wasn't that I intended to break a promise! Iris got in the way!"

"Where is the mage?" Brennan interjected.

"He is still there, with Imara and Claire—Iris's mother—and her father. Our being there did help, everyone could see that. Unfortunately, Iris had a reaction, which was odd and ought to be looked into," She frowned, obviously thinking about it again. Then the sadness returned to her face. "Because of Iris' interference, we were unable to heal Claire. Taranath is trying to ascertain if he can do anything more."

"You found the grandmother? It was the fae woman you thought it was?"

"Yes, yes, it is Imara. Interestingly, she behaved just as her parents did when her daughter chose on her own. That's neither here nor there. I need you to return with me, Brennan. I would not ask it if you were not my son, but I need the aid of the Goblin King." She put weight on the last two words.

"Mother, why do you care so much about this?" Brennan hadn't seen his mother get disturbed like this in a long time. To ask him to use the full force of his magic as the king of his realm! She'd never made such a request of him.

"Because of the way that Iris looked at me when she shouted at me. Full of hurt, and anger, and…" Nerida's voice trailed into silence.

"And?" Drake prompted.

"She is right. I promised to see if we could help her mother, and I did actually promise, but my main concern was to find her grandmother. I didn't mind helping the woman if we could, but Iris saw straight through me, and she called me…"

Brennan felt his ire rising. No one had the right to call his mother anything. Other than himself. She was a dreadful meddler.

"What?" Drake again.

"A selfish cow," Nerida whispered.

Drake and Brennan looked at one another over her bowed head, and both of them burst out laughing.

CHAPTER ELEVEN

Brennan

"Mother, really? How old are you exactly that you allow a human child—an infant, practically—to upset you so?"

Nerida sniffed. "Probably because she is right. I have been selfish."

Brennan met Drake's eyes over his mother's head. Nerida never admitted she was wrong. She merely switched course, and carried on as though that had been her plan all along. What was it about Iris that forced everyone around him to behave so differently? Drake, Nerida, even himself. All of them, as though bewitched. No one made Nerida feel guilty. In spite of the confusion Iris brought in him, he found himself admiring her and her abilities. He doubted she even had any awareness of them.

Which he would not consider at this moment. Iris could not be his priority. His kingdom, the promises made by his father—those were his concerns. Put anything else away. Lock it inside.

"What can we do to make this better for you, Mother?" Drake asked kindly. "I am sure it's not comfortable to come up against someone else's pain."

"It's not. It's quite dreadful. I don't lie to myself, though, and Iris is correct. It might have been better had you just left her where you found her, Drake," she said, a spark of her normal self returning. "That is neither here nor there. I did make a promise, as much as I wish I hadn't, and Iris's words reminded me of it. You must bring the full power of the king, Brennan. I cannot fall back on my promise. No matter how irritating I find it to be reminded."

"I am sure many feel that way," Drake grinned, not making eye contact with Brennan. "Nothing to be done now, however, other than move forward."

"So will you please come back with me?" Nerida asked again.

Brennan had to contain his shock. Iris had really affected Nerida. If he could keep his temper in check, he'd have to ask her how she'd done it. Nearly seven hundred years, and he hadn't been able to be as effective as one argument with Iris.

"If you're taking him and drawing on the power of the King, I'm going with you." Drake's tone brooked no discussion. "With everything that's going on, he will have need of extra protection."

"Very well. I need to contact Jharak, to let him know what has happened. I do not wish to leave your kingdom without you for long. Let me have a moment to speak with him and then we shall return," Nerida busied herself with searching for her mirror.

"Very nice to be asked," Brennan glanced up at the ceiling. "Almost like there is no king in the room at all."

"You really need to move past your overly strident concern for dignity at all times," Drake said. "I know you too well. Mother knows you even better."

"It would be nice to be consulted, rather than ordered," Brennan snapped.

"Welcome to how the rest of us live," Drake snapped back. "Mother, take your time. Catch your breath. How long has it been since someone got the better of you?"

"Oh, be quiet, rude child," Nerida flapped a hand at him as she walked towards the other end of the throne room. "Where is the family mirror, Brennan?

Brennan felt grateful to Drake. He'd calmed Mother pretty quickly. That was only to everyone's benefit. "I have one here, Mother. Please take it and stop searching through my room."

Nerida hurried to him and snatched the mirror away from him without a word. Brennan rolled his eyes. Oh, she was in a rare mood.

As for coming with them, Drake made sense, and his reasoning was logical. He didn't care for the being ordered about, but he knew better than to continue protesting. It wouldn't get him anywhere. It would also make him feel awful if he stood by and let Iris's mother die. Not when he could possibly help. No matter how much the idea bothered him.

"Very well. Let us be off once she's done," He gestured with his head where Nerida held up the mirror, speaking rapidly. "Might as well get this over with."

"I know you do, and I appreciate you helping me to assuage my guilt, Brennan," Nerida said as she joined him and Drake. This was uncharacteristic appreciation from her. "I don't care for this feeling, and I know I am putting you out somewhat."

"That will have to do," he smiled at her. "How often does one have the upper hand on Queen Nerida?"

"Not often," Nerida took his hand. "Let Drake and I open the portal. I need you to save your strength for healing."

Together, Drake and Nerida concentrated, and a portal of mixed colors opened in front of them. First Nerida, then Drake stepped through, and Brennan followed behind.

As he took another step, he was blinded by the bright, artificial light of the Human Realm.

Iris

I stared out at the ocean. Why had mom gotten sick? Why did we have to leave the life we'd built? Ever since we'd come ashore, things had gone to hell, and that put it mildly. *Sorcha* rocked gently on the swells that rolled through the marina. I tried to force the last several hours from my mind.

I kept coming back to Nerida lying to me, and my mom still sick.

The ring of my phone dragged me from my thoughts. It was Dad. I had to answer.

"I'm at Sorcha," I said as soon as I answered.

"Come home. We need you."

"What for?" I wasn't running around on the whims or broken promises of anyone else. "Are they still there? No need for me to be if they are."

"Iris." He had his Dad voice on. "Come home now." He hung up.

Well. That meant I didn't get a say. Great.

Reluctantly, I got up and hopped off the boat. Swinging onto my bike, I headed for home. For whatever next level of shit was headed my way.

***

When I opened the front door, I felt the overwhelming attention of many eyes on me. There were too many people, too much for me to focus on. I found Mom and Dad, and then...

"What is he doing here?" I gestured at Brennan.

"I brought him." Nerida answered me.

I glared at Nerida. She'd disappeared like cake at a birthday party after I'd screamed at her. I walked towards the couch and sat next to my mom, trying not to sob like a baby and pull myself together. I hugged her, and she raised a hand to put around me.

I kept my face buried against my mom, loving and hating the feel of her thin arm around me. All the anger I'd felt came rushing back at the sight of Nerida, with Drake and Brennan in tow. I stood and glared at Nerida as she spoke again.

"Brennan is one of the most skilled healers in the Fae Realm. I brought him here at great personal risk and inconvenience because I don't want to break my promise to you to try and help your mother."

Nerida hadn't lost one ounce of her haughty demeanor. So much for humility.

"Really? Or is she just saying that because she's your mother?" I glared at Brennan.

Drake answered. "No, it's true. We'll need you to move away from your mother, Iris."

"What exactly are you going to do to Claire?" My father, quiet until now, spoke.

Brennan and Drake turned almost as one towards him, standing with crossed arms at the end of the couch.

"Sir, I am Brennan, and this is my brother, Drake. We are the sons of Nerida, and she speaks true, I am skilled at healing. I understand Nerida promised your daughter that she'd try to help your wife," Brennan turned his head slightly and smiled at Mom. "With my mage, I will see if we can vanquish the illness that resides within her."

Dad didn't respond immediately. I could tell he was keeping himself together with great effort. Suddenly, his shoulders sagged as he looked past them towards Mom.

I stared at Brennan, amazed at how polite and caring he seemed towards my dad. Wow. He was a smoothie when he wanted to be. Seeing him smile at my mom, like he cared...it made all the positive thoughts I'd had about him before he opened his mouth, kidnapped me, zipped my mouth shut—they all went away.

Wow. When he smiled...

"Claire?" My dad said softly.

She gave the merest of shrugs. "What can it hurt, sweetie? It won't make things any worse."

"Will it hurt her?" Dad turned back to Brennan.

"I don't know. I am unsure if I've come across this sort of illness. I'm sorry," he said to Mom. "I don't have a sure answer for you now.''

Mom shrugged again, closing her eyes and leaning back against the sofa.

"Let's get on with this," I interrupted. Something about Brennan in my home made me uncomfortable, like my skin itched all over. I wanted to know what he thought of my home, I wanted to tell him this wasn't really our home, not to judge. Then I felt anger at myself for even worrying about it.

Brennan was maddening. That's all there was to it. Maddening man.

Who looked really, really amazing right now, with his dark hair and blazing blue eyes. He had black trousers on and a blue shirt and the ever-present cape in a darker shade of blue. He could be one of those guys on a cheesy romance novel cover, he had so much sex appeal going on.

What the hell was wrong with me?

Brennan met my eyes at that moment, and I felt the heat rise through my cheeks. Could he read thoughts? Dear lord, I hoped not.

A smile tilted one corner of his mouth, and he broke eye contact. Thankfully. I could feel myself sweating.

"Taranath, if you will join me?" Brennan moved closer to Mom, and Mara took a few steps back.

"Madam, you are Imara?" Brennan sounded very formal as he addressed her.

She inclined her head regally. Who was royalty here? Or were all the fae this formal?

"I am. It is a pleasure to meet you, Your Majesty."

Brennan nodded briskly. "I would like to speak with you later, but let us tend to Claire first."

Imara nodded. I didn't know whether to be impressed or annoyed with all the elegant formality.

Taranath moved next to Brennan, and the two of them knelt down next to Mom. Taranath placed his hands on

Mom's head. Brennan took her hands and crossed them over her chest, still holding both of them.

I stepped back and tucked myself under Dad's arm. He squeezed my shoulder hard. I could tell he had just as much fear and anxiety about this as I did.

Brennan and Taranath closed their eyes. Like before, I could feel the hum. Feel it, rather than hear it. It thrummed through me, and I leaned in more to Dad, needing to feel him. If I didn't I felt like I'd drift away, sort of like a stray balloon.

As before, Taranath glowed as he touched my mom and focused on her. This time, Brennan was part of that glow. Actually, Brennan glowed more brightly. Perhaps that was only my impression of him.

I could see part of the glow leaving them and moving down their arms towards my mom. I stood up and slightly away from my dad, feeling the need to be close to this, just like before. That scared me, because I had stopped the whole operation once already.

This was different. I took one, then another step until I stood very close to Brennan.

"Iris, what—" my dad said.

I reached out and put my hands over Brennan's on my mom's chest.

Brennan

He hadn't noticed her coming closer until she put her hands over the top of his. Then he felt the jolt that her touch elicited in him, and almost as quickly as it was there, it disappeared into something else. She had healing powers! Whatever Iris had, it amplified what he himself did.

Claire sat up, her eyes open and bright.

She met his eyes, and then moved to her daughter.

"Daughter," she said.

Brennan heard the gasps behind him. It took him a moment to ascertain why.

Claire had spoken in Fae. Not the human tongue.

He risked a glance at Iris. Like he and the mage, she glowed with the healing magic. All of her features seemed accentuated. Her hair crackled and sparkled with the light of a summer's day, and her eyes were the color of the moss on trees. Her lips were parted, and all Brennan could think of in that moment were cherries, or some other fruit that he wanted to take a bite out of.

Where did this magic come from?

He lost his train of thought as Claire eased her hands from beneath his and took one of his and Iris' hands. Taranath still had his hands on her head, but as she sat up, they slid away. The mage staggered back, and Drake moved to catch him.

Brennan felt suddenly that there were too many people in too close a space.

"You can let go now," Iris said. Her voice didn't sound like her.

Nevertheless, he stepped back, and Iris leaned down to take both her mother's hands.

"Mom, let's get up."

"Claire, Iris, no!" Iris's father stepped forward, arms out to—help? Stop?—his wife and daughter.

"It's all right," Claire spoke. While low, her voice held strength, strength that hadn't been there before.

"We need to go outside," Iris said, still speaking in that strange voice.

He and the mage stepped back further to give the women room. Iris helped her mother to stand, and then walked, holding her arm, towards the door that led outside.

Paul had moved around them all and opened the door. "You sure?"

Brennan couldn't tell which of his women Paul asked.

Iris answered for both of them. "We are. Come on, Mom."

He didn't know why, but Brennan was glad to hear that Iris sounded more like herself, inasmuch as he knew what she sounded like.

"What just happened?" Drake murmured in his ear.

"I don't know. Mage?"

Taranath shook his head, his eyes glued on the little family as they escorted Claire outside.

"I'm a fool," Imara said quietly. "That girl is as much fae as I am."

Nerida responded. "You think so?"

"Did we not just see the same thing?" Imara rounded on his mother. "That was not the action of someone more human than fae. Logically, Iris shouldn't be able to do that sort of magic right out of the box, so to speak."

"Right out of the box?" Taranath asked.

Imara waved a dismissive hand. "It's a human saying. Regardless, this is not logical. She has a lot of fae within, and I am foolish and riddled with stupid pride."

"Why did you continue to keep your distance?" Taranath asked.

Brennan loved having him around for this very reason. The mage had such an inoffensive manner that he could ask things without being insulting.

"You're just like your parents," Nerida said.

Imara nodded. "After being so affronted at their actions, I did the same to my own daughter."

"Your mother is still with us," Nerida said softly. "I know she would love to see you."

Imara's eyes brightened with hope. "That is something I would like to discuss, but not right now. I want to tend to my daughter. I've let things go too long with her." She walked out the door.

No one followed her.

"Taranath, what did we just see?" Drake asked as soon as Imara left the small room.

The mage shook his head. "Iris is very powerful. Brennan and I were finding success in eradicating the disease but the healing sped up when she took part."

"Have you ever seen such a thing?" Nerida asked.

"Maybe it was a good thing that I didn't leave her where we found her," Drake added.

"I don't know about that. More problems than anything else," Brennan said.

Taranath looked him with a mild expression. "Don't discount something merely because it presents a greater challenge than one is used to," and he walked outside to join the others.

"What does that mean?" Brennan allowed his frustration that had been present ever since he fell into Iris to come out. He felt even more frustration at the leap of hope and longing that this new side of Iris brought out. Why did these small bursts of hope keep occurring? Why did they feel they were getting larger, not fading? The thought of emotion growing in him made him even more uneasy. Unchecked emotion brought only danger, and hurt.

Drake grinned, laughed a little, and clapped him on the shoulder. He too walked outside, leaving Brennan with his mother. That was never a good thing.

"Brennan, I really think you might want to engage in a bit of self-reflection and be honest with yourself," she said kindly. "It would do you good."

"I am fine, Mother. I need no reflection. Happy though this is, I need to return to my kingdom before some wretch destroys it."

"It won't happen in the next hour. Come, and let's see how Claire is."

Then she walked outside to join the others.

Brennan watched everyone else from inside. Claire had stretched her arms up towards the sun and turned her face upwards. He hadn't seen such naked joy in a long time. Slightly apart from Claire, Iris and her father stood together, arms wrapped around each other, both smiling and crying.

As Brennan watched, Imara approached Paul, and said something he couldn't hear. Paul's face closed and then relaxed, and he leaned down and gave Imara a hug. Brennan could see that Paul did not feel entirely comfortable with Imara, but some of his strong anger seemed to have dissipated.

Brennan could only assume that the happiness of knowing he wouldn't lose his wife brought this on.

So much emotion. Why did anyone think this a good thing? He shook his head.

Still, watching Iris's family and his own before him, he had to admit that the only thing he got from them was happiness, relief, and a great deal of love.

Emotion might be all right for others, but not for him. He'd learned that lesson all too well all those years ago.

With a reluctance he didn't want to think about, he turned his back on the happy scene before him and took a stone from his pouch. Drake had been right. Helping Claire had drained him. He would need help to return.

He cupped the stone in his hands and summoned a portal. Without fanfare, and with a quick glance over his shoulder, he stepped through it. Imara would have to wait until later.

The stone winked closed behind him, and he stood in his cool, dark lounge.

Wondering why he felt so empty.

CHAPTER TWELVE

Iris

I couldn't stop smiling as my dad and I stood together. He even hugged Imara, and we all turned to watch Mom. She was well, everything about her said she felt better, normal...cancer-free.

Finally, I reached for her as she turned her face upward, eyes closed, drinking in the sky. My dad came up behind us and put a hand to her arm.

"Claire? How do you feel?" He stumbled a little over the words.

I got it. The hope felt so big, so overwhelming that you were afraid to really let go and hope that your hope had been justified. And we'd been down this road before.

"I feel fantastic," Mom said, opening her eyes and turning to look at both of us. "I can't remember when I felt this good."

"It's not only due to the healing that the king provided. It's also because you're among your own kind," Taranath said quietly. He stepped forward when my mom stopped communing with the sky. "It's good for fae to be around other fae."

Suddenly, Mom's eyes narrowed. She whipped her head around, searching. Stopped when her gaze met her mom's.

"You knew this? You knew I'd be better, even if you didn't know I was sick, but you knew I'd be better if I was near you? And you never told me? Not once," Mom pushed past Dad and me, brushing off our hands, "Did you ever say anything about why I might benefit from being close to you. Not once, Mom, did you give me any idea that there might be something I needed to know!"

Mom looked primal as she got closer to Imara. Imara shrank back, leaning into Nerida. I could see Nerida lean into Imara, offering that aforementioned strength. "Would you have listened? I had just told you we didn't agree with your marriage. Would you have listened to anything I said?"

Imara obviously didn't take grief from anyone, not even her own kid who she'd basically disowned. I felt both impressed and sorry for her. What a way to live. I had a sudden flash of insight. Imara was probably her own worst enemy.

"You couldn't have told me this earlier? Maybe when I was still in high school or something? You know, like a normal mom?"

"I have never been a normal mom," Imara drew herself up.

"No shit," Dad muttered.

I turned my head so no one would see or hear me trying not to laugh. Dad looked down too, both of us caught up in how funny this drama was. In a sad, sob-story, black comedy kind of way.

"She's been asking for this for years. It's okay if your mom has a go at her," He hugged me, mistaking my actions for distress.

"Oh, I'm sure she has," I said.

"It's always better to be honest," Taranath interjected mildly, watching the fray with his hands clasped in front of him. "There've been a lot of less-than-honest actions here."

"What are you, the Buddha?" This from Dad.

"Dad, I think Taranath has to stay low-key. Look who he works for."

Taranath raised an eyebrow at me and smiled as I laughed.

Even though I understood my mom's anger, and Nerida deserved everything I'd said to her earlier, and Mara had some serious issues, I didn't care. I couldn't care. This had to be the best day ever for me. My mom was healed. Oh, no doctor had confirmed it, and deep inside I could feel that evil little voice we all have asking, *What if she's not?* I shut it up. I even felt as though I had the luxury of examining my part in things later. Nothing mattered other than she had become well. She'd stay well, too. I just knew it. The evil little voice could buzz off.

We'd have to go and let the doctors poke and prod her, of course. She'd be the miracle of the moment, and then we'd go back to life as normal.

That thought caught me. What did normal mean, now? I couldn't go back to what I was...god, only four or five hours ago? I'd never be that girl again. Heath, college, everything that had been important at the start of today seemed faded, like looking at an old home movie or something.

Drake appeared from the shadow of the house where he'd been lurking.

"Brennan has returned already. If you have no further need of me, Mage, I shall return also."

"He left?" I couldn't control my disappointment.

"This is not his only concern," Drake answered, but it wasn't said rudely. If anything, he gave me what looked like a compassionate glance.

What the hell did that mean?

"Tell him..." I stopped.

"Yes?" Drake prompted.

Even Taranath looked interested.

"Thank you," I managed. "I can't thank him enough for what he's done."

"Will you allow that he's done you a service, a favor?" Taranath looked off in the distance as he spoke.

"Yes, but he owed me for dragging me back with him in the first place."

"That was me, remember? So if I owed you, I've returned the favor by assisting your mother." Drake seemed far too intense for this conversation.

"Well…okay. I guess. Then yes, Brennan has done me a favor."

Taranath nodded. "I would agree. So if he should have need of you, may he call on you?"

"Are you sure you ought to be collecting a favor on Brennan's behalf?" Nerida spoke for the first time since she'd joined us outside.

Taranath snapped out of it and met her gaze, smiling as he did so. "I am collecting nothing on his behalf, Majesty. Merely sorting what has happened. I like things to be neat and tidy."

"What does that mean, she owes him a favor?" Great. Now Mom decided to get in on the conversation.

Nerida tried to answer but Imara, looking grateful to interrupt my mom, answered.

"It means that Brennan has the right to ask for her help at a later date. She does not have to give it, but he has the right to ask. It's a big deal, but it's not binding."

Nerida glared at Mara. I had to look down to stop the laughter again. Nerida was a proper manipulator, but Mara was slamming the door in her face.

"You're not dragging my daughter into whatever mess you have," Mom said. The light of battle still shone in her eyes. I wouldn't want to take her on.

To her credit, Nerida didn't flinch. I guess being a queen for thousands of years gave you lots of practice in not flinching. "It's no mess, but as Taranath said, it sorts things out."

"Sort them without my daughter."

"How old are you, Iris?" Taranath interrupted.

"Twenty," I got in before the claws came out.

"She is old enough, in both the Human and Fae Realms, to acknowledge that she owes Brennan the courtesy of listening to a request for a favor," Taranath stared off in the distance again.

Silence greeted his words. How did he do it? He had a calming aura that just floated around him like perfume, and drifted over everyone else, diffusing the situation.

"Well, Iris? Do you wish to acknowledge that Brennan may, at some time in the future, ask you for a favor if the chance arises?"

I glared at Drake. He sounded a lot like someone trying not to laugh, and I couldn't figure out what would be so funny. I didn't like the feeling that there was more going on than I knew.

At the same time, the thought that I might get to see Brennan again excited me. Even though I had no business being excited. At all. I needed to keep my thoughts in check. Heath. Potential boyfriend. Actually from *this* world, remember? I ignored the fact that my hope from earlier left me feeling flat and deflated.

I realized that everyone had stopped their bickering to look at me, waiting for me to say something. Oh, great. I loved being the center of attention.

"Yeah, sure. I do owe him. He helped Mom." I smiled at her.

"Now that it's settled, I must go." Drake looked to Nerida. "Mother, would you accompany me?"

Nerida hesitated. "Imara, will you please come back with me?"

My grandmother crossed her arms. "Why are you so intent on my returning?"

Nerida flushed. "I feel responsible for how things occurred when you left. I've never felt right. I feel as though I might make amends if you come back."

Imara glared. "You were not correct in your assumptions years ago. I have no reason to believe that you are correct now. I don't wish to have my hopes dashed again. Thank you, Nerida, but I will decline your offer."

Nerida looked like she wanted to say more. Drake took two steps towards Nerida and pulled her back towards the house.

"Mage? I think you should return as well. We have work to do."

Taranath ignored Drake to speak to me. "Iris, I would like to stay with your family for some time longer. I will make sure your mother continues to do well."

"I think that a sound idea." Imara chimed in.

Drake huffed. The guy really needed to ease up, but it didn't seem to be part of his DNA. "I will convey your wishes to the king. You may converse with him when you finally choose to return. Mother, let us go."

He left, his anger trailing behind him. What the hell just happened there? These fae changed emotion like changing underwear.

Why did I care?

My mother was well. She wasn't going to die.

I shrugged and moved closer to my mom, who stood arm in arm with Dad. Imara murmured something I couldn't hear, and at that moment the sun came out from behind a cloud to shine fiercely on the back yard.

My mom and grandmother turned their faces up towards it. In that moment, I saw possibilities that I'd never considered.

Brennan   .

He sat on his throne, annoyed. There was much to do, and all he could manage was to sit and brood.

Where was Drake? His mage? His mother?

Why had Iris captivated them *all?* To the point that he was effectively abandoned. He didn't want to delve into the fact that he experienced jealousy that others were still with her.

His sorry musings were interrupted by the hum of the throne room portal. It had to be at least one of them. Brennan wanted to kick himself for being so glad to see someone in his inner circle.

His mother and Drake stepped through the rose-colored light.

"All is well in the Human Realm?" He allowed sarcasm to slide into his question.

"It appears so. I'm annoyed that you left so abruptly, Brennan. You might have been able to persuade Imara to return with me."

Drake said, "No, Mother, I don't believe he would have. She wanted nothing to do with you. Did you not see that?"

Nerida waved a hand. "Everyone is far more unyielding when they are angry. She is still angry and—"

"Doesn't that indicate something?" Brennan couldn't believe his mother's ability to turn everything into what she wanted it to be.

"Well, of course! She hasn't been able to express her anger, and it's got to come out before she can move on. She'll join me. It may take a bit longer, however, and I would have liked her here now, Brennan," she snapped.

As though this was somehow his fault. How his father didn't rend his hair from his head, Brennan couldn't fathom.

"Where is Taranath?" He moved away from his mother and her machinations.

Drake answered. "He has decided he will stay there for a while longer to make sure the human woman is well, I believe." Now Drake employed sarcasm.

"Has everyone gone mad?" Brennan threw up his hands. "It's as though the accidental meeting of one human girl has turned everything on its head!"

"She is a most extraordinary girl," Nerida said. "Let him know what she has agreed to, Drake. I will leave you now. I must go to your father." Without waiting for a response, she opened the portal again and disappeared.

It didn't happen often but Nerida could still surprise him. Iris agreed to something? Why? "What? What is she talking about?"

Drake's face showed no expression. "Iris agreed that by helping her mother, you have the right to ask her for a favor at a later date."

Now he found himself momentarily speechless. "She what?"

Drake nodded. "She agreed that you may ask."

Brennan found himself upset for Iris. "Did any of you bother to explain to her the significance of such an agreement? A promise made in Fae, between fae…" Such a promise was binding. The rational part of him knew that Iris should not be further tied to him.

"Well, she was not actually in Fae, Brennan. She gave her agreement while in the Human Realm. I told her that she was under no obligation to agree—at least, I think I did," Drake scratched his chin, thinking. "But that she did need to listen to you. That's what she agreed to."

"You do realize what you've done?" Brennan could feel his temper rising once more. His anger hadn't been this unsettled in ages. It needed to stop. His own realizations were problematic enough, now Drake had handed him a key to a door that he didn't know if he wanted to open. He didn't feel good about knowing the door could be opened.

"Yes. I've ensured that you are not taken advantage of."

"As the king, don't you think I might have the upper hand in terms of advantage?" Brennan had to raise an eyebrow at Drake. "Honestly, Drake, I'm not the babe-in-the-woods in this encounter. Iris is."

"Well, at least you've stopped calling her *the human*," Drake said cheerfully, as though he hadn't just involved Iris further in the realm of fae with his stupid agreement.

"I know she's the human!" Brennan snapped, unable to think of anything else, but unwilling to allow Drake to get the last word.

"It's good you know things," Drake still sounded cheerful. "That's usually one of the requirements of being king."

Brennan had to resist the urge to strangle him.

"I'm sure the mage will return shortly. He's being a good steward of fae. Why don't we contact Father and see what he's come up with regarding any allies of the former king?"

"How good of you to remember what we're dealing with," Brennan couldn't stop the sarcasm.

It was also good that Drake was his brother in all the ways that counted. He ignored Brennan and his bad mood, and made the call to Father.

For once, Brennan didn't mind Drake taking the lead in gathering information. He couldn't settle his mind to the task at hand.

Bronoor entered as Drake spoke to their father. "Majesty, we have identified most of the fallen goblins. Those of whom we are unsure, we have been able to at least discern their clans. The heads of the clans are here to take home their kin." He bowed his head.

"Father," Brennan turned to the mirror, speaking over Drake's shoulder. "Please excuse me. I must meet with the heads of the clans here. Drake, you can use my quarters to continue this conversation."

Drake nodded, and the mirror with the image of the Fae King winked out. Bronoor bowed as Drake passed. Once Drake had left, Bronoor rose.

"Shall I bring them in?"

"Yes," Brennan hated this part of being the king. Even more so because it had been so long since he'd had to take on this aspect.

Bronoor moved from the room, and too soon returned, opening the doors to the throne room and standing aside to allow the clan leaders to file in.

Brennan hadn't returned to his throne, but received them standing. He wanted them to be clear that he was with them in this.

"Majesty," said Horgath, the oldest of all of the heads of the clans, and obviously the one chosen to speak for them. "What has happened to our kin?"

Brennan sighed. It appeared they didn't truly know, or were being extremely disingenuous. That wasn't likely. Goblins were fairly honest. There were liars among all the races, but goblins preferred to be upfront and damn the consequences. He'd never had any reason to doubt Horgath or the others. He wouldn't start now. If they gave him reason later, that would change things. But for now, they all mourned.

"My lords," he began, walking to them. "I am sorry to have to share sad news with you. Will you sit and have a drink with me?" He gestured at the council table that sat off to one side of the throne room, behind a light curtain. He didn't use it often, but it allowed for larger groups to meet in the formality of the throne room. Brennan thought the formality was called for now.

Muttering among the clan heads, but they all trooped towards the table. Brennan waved a hand at Bronoor, who exited the room and before everyone had seated themselves, kitchen goblins were scurrying in carrying trays of drink and food.

Brennan sniffed delicately. Good. Bronoor had sent in the light ale, rather than the heavy mead or the stronger spirit. This wasn't the time to have too much spirit—that led to fighting and weapons, and he didn't need more of that.

Once everyone had a drink in front of them, Brennan walked to the head of the table and sat. He wanted to make sure he kept himself on equal footing with them.

Not the king, but a fellow leader mourning the loss of their people. He didn't know who was behind this, and better to tread carefully until he had a grasp on who or what was involved.

"Yesterday," was it just yesterday? He felt he'd aged one hundred years since then. "Lord Drake and I were traveling, and we stopped in one of our regular resting places to eat and water the horses." He glanced around the table. Slight nods. The clearing was as well-known, as he'd thought.

"Before we'd even broken out the packs, we were ambushed. A large number—"

"Who dares to attack you?" The goblin next to Horgath—Fievolt, Brennan remembered—asked.

"It was close to fifty. A few trolls, who looked to be from the mountain tribes, but most of the attackers were goblins. From my kingdom. From your clans."

He waited to see their reaction.

Silence greeted his words. He could see a few glancing at one another, wanting to know if anyone knew of this. Brennan himself couldn't see any sign that anyone had knowledge of it, but that meant nothing. Anyone could dissemble with practice.

"Drake and I had no choice. We had to take up arms and defend ourselves."

"Did any survive?" Horgath growled.

Brennan shook his head. "No, none. That is not all, my lords."

Now he detected some rising tension. "A troll attempted to drag Lord Drake off and kill him. Drake managed to escape, and as he rejoined me, a man—a fae— appeared and walked among the dead." He knew they would be affected by his words.

"He approached Drake and I and demanded my unconditional surrender as the Goblin King."

Loud shouts and talking burst out. Every clan head had something to say, except Horgath.

Horgath crossed his arms and stared at Brennan. When the rest of the clan heads noticed that their spokesman waited, they stopped talking.

"What did you tell him, Majesty?"

"I told him that I would not surrender, would not abandon my people. He laughed and told me that this kingdom was not my people, and I challenged that assertion. He asked me to surrender again, and when I refused, he cast me from Fae and into the Human Realm."

More talk, but Horgath held up his hand.

"What do you wish us to do, Majesty?"

Brennan leaned forward. "I cannot tell why my people are upset enough to take up arms against me. I have ever encouraged anyone with a concern to come to me, regardless of how large or small the concern may be. I have heard nothing of unrest, or unhappiness. Yet some of those slain were goblins of my city, or who'd been here in the castle. I need your help, my lords."

"Who was the man, Majesty?"

"Lord Horgath, he was not known to me and did not tell me his name. He had a long scar down one side of his face. He also is a sorcerer of some skill. He took Drake and I completely by surprise, and managed to send us from the clearing. He was not young, but not an elder. I need to know what the whispers are that allowed him to drag our people to their slaughter." His voice deepened, as he saw again in his mind's eye the field of his fallen goblins. "I will not allow my kingdom to descend into the chaos that ruled before I came to the throne. I will not allow a malcontent to sacrifice my people for his own ends! But I need your help, my lords." He leaned in, making sure to meet the eyes of every leader around the table.

Every one of them met his eyes. Even Horgath, in spite of his questioning. It wasn't any of them, then. At least, he hoped not.

Horgath stood. "Have we leave to return our kin to their clan?"

Brennan stood as well. "Yes. Bronoor has also prepared what you will need to bury them with honors."

Horgath's face darkened, a feat for a goblin who had a dark tone to begin with. Brennan could hear the slight clanking of the ornamentation on Horgath's clothing.

"They were traitors, Majesty."

Brennan held up a hand. "I am unwilling to decide that at this point, Lord Horgath. The strength of the fae I encountered leads me to think that he might have manipulated our people. Until I know differently, I want them buried with all the honors they would have had they died in another manner."

Horgath put his hands on his hips and took several steps away from the table. Brennan didn't say anything. He recognized the signs of a leader trying to decide the best path.

Finally, Horgath turned back to him. "We will do as you ask. But we will make note of them all and if a different tale emerges, we will make amends. May we take them home?"

"Of course. I think you have made a wise choice," Brennan said. "I agree with it. Should you need anything, I want you to come to me. Me, alone."

Horgath nodded and looked around at the other clan heads. "We will. This ain't like them, Majesty. And we'll see if there's been a fae of your description hanging about."

He gave a quick bow and turned to leave the throne room. The other clan heads followed him.

"My lords!" They all stopped as one.

"I am sorry."

"As am I, Majesty," Horgath replied. Within a moment, he had left the room.

Brennan let out a breath and sat down on his throne. That had gone better than expected. Almost too well...he stopped himself. There may indeed be a traitor within that group of goblins, but there could be a traitor anywhere. He had no idea where the traitor was, and until he knew more, he would still any thoughts of who it might be. To continue to ponder without proof was a path to madness, delving into paranoia and poor choices.

Exactly what Scarface wanted, he thought, sitting up. Dissention and discord, a breaking of trust and bonds that had stood for hundreds of years.

The more he thought about it, the more he felt certain this was someone carrying out a grudge. It would be one thing to attempt to topple Brennan from his throne, perhaps shake the power of his family, but this had the feel of something more personal.

Drake returned. "Your father has found some leads." "What?"

"They are in the Dragon and Dwarf Realms. The old king had a wife. She fled and later married a man from the Dragon court. Her sons are still there, but her daughter married into the Dwarf Realm."

"These are not the heirs of the old king, surely?" The thought staggered Brennan. His father wouldn't have barred the lawful heirs from the throne in his favor? He'd always understood that there were no heirs. He'd forgotten than when he'd been named heir, the Goblin King was married, and there was still hope for children.

Drake frowned. "The sons are from the Dragon man she married. The daughter is the old king's, born after he was put to death. His wife told no one she was expecting."

"What did Father know of the wife?"

"Nothing. He knows nothing of them."

"Ailla and her father must know." A cold hand squeezed the center of Brennan. "She is part of their court. They have known all along, Drake."

"Her father, perhaps. Ailla, I do not think so, Bren."

"We have to operate as though they both know and have kept that fact from us." Brennan could feel the cold hand turning to ice.

CHAPTER THIRTEEN

Iris

My mother. Her mother. Both of them facing the sky, and even though it sounded crazy, I swear I could see them grow, somehow. Almost like the slow motion of watching a flower unfurl in the sun. You didn't really see it move, but suddenly, it lay open, and beautiful.

"Mom…" I breathed. She turned, and she once more was my mom. Not the fae woman stranger.

"You look amazing." My dad had come over, and I could tell he saw what I did. Mom still looked like Mom, only…different. Sharper.

Dad looked over her shoulder to Mara. "This is something you ought to have told Claire long ago, Mara."

My grandmother startled and spun to face him. "I should have. I am sorry that I waited until nearly the last minute. I won't let that mistake happen again."

"What happens now?" I asked. As much as I enjoyed seeing Mom healthy and healed, I felt a growing fear that just as I had been forever changed, Mom would be too. I didn't know whether the fae influence would turn out to be good or bad. Not yet. Even though the fae thing had saved her.

"You go on to live and make the most of your lives," Taranath spoke. He'd been so quiet that I'd forgotten he stood there.

"Although, I think you might consider coming back with me, Iris."

"What? No!" Three voices nearly shouted at him.

He didn't even blink. I really, really wanted some of the no-flinch all these fae seemed to have bred in them.

"Iris is of age, in both our realms. Her fae side allowed her to live where her human side would have perished while she was in Fae," he looked to my parents and Mara. "There is something different about her, and how she reacts to her two sides. It would be interesting to have time to observe how she responds to being in Fae for more than a day."

"Oh, now I see!" I laughed at him. I could afford to laugh now. "You really want a chance to study me, don't you?"

Taranath smiled the biggest smile I'd seen from him since I'd met him. "I cannot lie, Iris. Yes, I do. So I leave the door open to you." He reached into a pouch along his waist and pulled a smaller pouch from it. Held it out towards me.

I hesitated to take it.

"It will allow you to open a portal and bring you to me. All you need do is open it and speak my name. I don't want you wandering all over Fae should you decide to join us again. But if you wish it, I want you to be able to come at your convenience."

"Are you leaving?"

"My king has need of me. As interesting as this has been, as gratifying," He smiled over my head towards Mom, "I need to be home. Helping the king."

Brennan. I knew he was in some sort of battle. In my focus on myself, and my mom, and...everything, I'd not thought of him. Or his trouble. I felt my heart give a strange leap at the thought of him in some kind of struggle, or worse, hurt.

"I hope he's okay. Please thank him again, from all of us," I stepped closer to Taranath, wanting to say more, not wanting to open up that part of my brain that had so much more to say.

"I will tell him of your promise to allow the request of a favor. Should he be in need, he will ask. Fae see no weakness in seeking help. They are only careful from whom they seek it."

With a last, intense look at me, he stood back, nodding at my parents and grandmother. "I am glad you are well, Claire. Imara, you are welcome home at any time."

Without warning, a flash sparked in front of him, and then as suddenly as it appeared, he disappeared.

I looked at my parents. My mom looked intrigued. Dad held his hands up to shade his eyes. "They're all pretty dramatic. Is that really necessary?"

"Everyone opens portals differently. Even Iris," said Mara. "In order to get here from Fae, Iris had to direct the portal. I'm assuming she is the only one who knew the location of your home?"

"That would explain why we all fell on the floor in a pile," I said, scowling at the memory.

Mara didn't look bothered. "Who came through with you?"

"Nerida and Taranath."

"Nerida fell into a heap on the floor? I would have paid money to see that!" Mara hooted with laughter. It changed her entire face, her demeanor, everything—to see her laugh so freely.

"That might have explained her mood," I allowed.

Still chuckling, Mara put her arm through Mom's. To the surprise of all of us, she did the same with Dad.

"Let's go in, have a lunch that has nothing to do with Fae, and catch me up on what my stupid pride has allowed me to miss."

She gave me a glance that had only warmth as she passed by me, arm and arm with my parents. My dad seemed to hesitate as she dragged him along.

I watched them walk back into the house.

Part of me had never been so full of joy. I would lose my mom someday, but it wouldn't be today. Or even tomorrow. I'd been given a lot more tomorrows with her.

So why did I feel so sad? So forlorn?

Brennan. The name came to mind unbidden, so swiftly, it must have been waiting to spring forward.

How? Why? I'd met the guy like...yesterday! This couldn't continue. I would not see him again, and I needed to put him out of my head.

Suddenly, blond guys like Heath didn't seem all that attractive anymore. I sighed and followed my now larger family into the house.

Brennan

He and Drake crouched low, eying the modest abode in front of them. They were perched on a hill above the house, and Brennan felt sure they'd be spotted any minute. That was if the imaginary gong that seemed to announce him everywhere that Drake joked about didn't go off.

But their luck held. No activity other than a lazy curl of smoke came from the little house.

"Are we certain this is the right place? It won't do for us to burst in on an innocent member of another realm," Brennan muttered to Drake.

"I am sure," Drake didn't take his eyes off the house. The old king's daughter, Dhasyrha, lives there with her husband. He is a fae with dwarf ties. There are no children from the match."

"Where did you discover all this?"

"Father. I've no idea where he got the information from, but he told me this while you were talking to the clan lords."

Brennan nodded. The fact that the information came from Father eased some of his concern. Not all of it, but some.

"Did Father happen to know anything of Scarface?"

Drake laughed softly. "You're still calling him that? She named him well, didn't she? Brings him down to size."

Brennan only nodded, eyes still on the cottage. Once Drake had imparted that the old king's widow still lived, and her daughter lived in the Dwarf Realm, they had traveled there immediately. Brennan didn't care for the basic lack of planning that this move highlighted, but he agreed that taking action towards the daughter was better than approaching the Dragon King. Or perhaps he just didn't want to face Ailla and her father. He couldn't stop the feeling of betrayal. The widow had been there all along. The court would have known of the marriage of the daughter. All these things were known, and no one in that court had bothered to let Jharak or Brennan know.

The failure to share that knowledge made him very suspicious.

"According to Father, the Dwarf lord she married was not the daughter's first choice. There was a fae whom the old king promised her to before she was even born." He looked at Brennan. "I would be willing to offer a strong bet that is our," Drake swallowed a laugh, "Scarry McScarface." He didn't say anything for a moment, and then burst into silent laughter.

Brennan slid his gaze from the cottage to glare at Drake. "We are trying to be discreet."

"I'm sorry," Drake managed, once he stopped laughing. "Brennan, even you have to admit it's funny."

Brennan shrugged, He could see Iris, feeling the effects of Drake's calming spell, giggling to herself as she said the name. Drake was right. It did bring him down to size. He allowed a smile, and then got back to the matter at hand."

"Why is it you didn't tell me of this before we left?"

Drake shrugged. "I thought it better to get you here. This is where we need to be. The daughter, Dhasyrha, is the key. Father seemed to think the widow wanted nothing to do with what happened, and that could be why we weren't told of her, or how her life moved on."

"Or she was kept hidden as a bargaining tool." Brennan couldn't completely disguise his bitterness.

"I hate to encourage your line of thinking, but it's a possibility. The question is, why hasn't Eilor brought it up before now? He didn't, even when you were dragging your feet with the betrothal and Father had to dance around stalling things a bit. That sort of information is usually something that ought to be shared between leaders."

"I don't know. I don't like the direction of these thoughts, but I can't dismiss them. They sit, whispering in my ear, creating conspiracies out of everything." He glared at the small cottage, willing something to happen.

Drake leaned in, peering at him. "That's not a good place for your thoughts to reside, Bren. You have to put them aside. You don't want to say something you will have to work around later."

"I know, I know! I want to head to Eilor and demand the truth, but I can't see where that would help anything other than my anger at this point. It wouldn't allow us to gather our own answers as I think we need to."

"Look!" Drake nudged his arm with an elbow. "The door!"

The door to the cottage opened. A woman's head peeked around the edge of the door. Clearly, she exercised care before coming outside. Of course, maybe this was just life in the Dwarf Realm. Brennan didn't think he'd get that lucky. This woman, who ducked back inside quickly, had something to hide. But what? What is she, if it is Dhasyrha, hiding? Or who? Or from whom? The questions frustrated him.

Now the door opened wider. The woman who'd peeked out came outside, scanning the area outside and around the cottage. She even cast her gaze up into the hills where Drake and Brennan lay hidden. Brennan resisted the urge to duck down further.

She turned to speak over her shoulder, and a man came out, taking the woman's hand as he came to stand next to her. He had on a long cloak with the hood up. In spite of not being able to see the man's face, Brennan knew, knew in his bones, that he saw the fae who'd started all of this and caused the death of his people. He felt all of his muscles tighten, anger bunching them, and his lips curled over his teeth. The fae sorcerer would pay for what he'd done.

The woman turned to the hooded man, and they embraced. He leaned down and kissed her, partially obscuring her face within the depth of the hood. She broke the kiss and buried her face in his shoulder. Brennan could tell she gripped him, held him close. He felt a momentary burst of empathy, and then reminded himself that the man, if not the woman, had led his goblins to be slaughtered for their own gain. That removed all empathy.

"Ready?" He whispered to Drake. They'd hurried from the castle but lying in wait had given them a little time to discuss what would happen should the cottage be occupied. Brennan realized that he hadn't really thought they'd find anyone here. Or maybe, he hadn't wanted to.

"Ready." Drake's voice sounded tight.

Brennan reached into the pouch at his waist and drew out one of the stones they had brought with them. It would allow their magic to expand its reach, and hopefully help to repel any magic from those they captured.

"Now!" He whispered.

He and Drake stood up and held the stones high over their heads. Together they shouted the spell, and a spark appeared over the couple below.

At the sound of their shouted incantation, the hooded man drew back from the woman. As she turned to see what had caused him to move, Brennan could tell the man saw the danger before she did. The man yanked her hand, pulling her back towards the cottage.

The spark exploded, casting a net of light over the woman. She crouched down with a cry as the net fell over her. Then she dropped to the ground, and with what

Brennan could only describe as a wail, her hand still gripped by the man. The man kept hold of her hand for a moment longer, and then kissed it. He let go of her, ignoring her cries, and, threw back his hood, and Brennan stiffened at the hate he could feel pouring from the man, even at this distance.

Keeping his hand in the air, he and Drake began to make their way down the hill. Brennan took another stone from his pouch and held it in front of him, casting a protecting spell ahead of them.

"Bren, I got her! Get Scarry!" Drake shouted. "Go! Get him before he vanishes!"

Another indiscernible cry from the trapped woman. Brennan broke into a run, not wanting to lose the mage.

He didn't take his eyes off the man, who had his hands out in front of him, and Brennan could feel…something. Some sort of large gathering of magic—what was the man doing?

"Stop! You murderer! Stop it! Leave him alone!" The woman screamed.

Brennan altered course slightly so that he could avoid the woman and get to the mage. He was close—so close! One hundred feet, seventy-five, then fifty…he would make it. He readied his stones and opened his mouth to cast the binding spell when the scarred man flung his hands wide.

It felt as though time stopped. He couldn't see anything other than a blinding light that obscured everything else.

Then a blow to his chest…a dagger? How had Scarface gotten that close?

Then…then…the light began to darken around the edges of his vision.

His chest no longer felt as though a dagger lodged there. No longer felt anything. Good. A glancing blow, at best.

The light in front of him grew smaller and smaller. Drake must have struck out at the mage, stopping whatever it was he planned to do.

Brennan was glad that he had Drake with him. He could rest. He felt tired, so tired that he could barely hold his eyes open...a rest would be good.

In spite of his earlier resolve, he hadn't purged thoughts of Iris. She persisted as his last thought—what was she wearing? She didn't look human at all. She looked over her shoulder at him, smiling. The thought made his heart lift with a hope he thought he'd squashed before he closed his eyes and all went dark.

CHAPTER FOURTEEN

Iris

I sat at the kitchen table, watching and listening to my parents and Mara. The level of joy floating around the room could have choked a horse. Mom had come straight in and made lunch for all of us with a happiness I hadn't seen in forever. Everyone, even Dad and Mara, beamed at one another. I didn't mean to complain, but I couldn't shake the feeling of loss that persisted.

Loss of what? I had nothing to lose.

Don't you? A small voice whispered within.

I felt the hair on the back of my neck rise and without warning, my vision blinked and I felt as though I'd run into a wall of fear, pain and anger and…something else I couldn't identify.

"No!" I cried out, stumbling to stand up and move away from the table. Momentarily blind again. This had to be something to do with Fae. The pain overwhelmed everything else.

"Iris?" I could hear my family call my name but I couldn't focus on them.

"Brennan!" I cried out. "Oh no, he's hurt! He's hurt!" I didn't know how I knew it this came from Brennan. I just did. My hands scrabbled at my chest, trying to stop the pain. I couldn't breathe. My mouth opened but no sound came out.

"What are you talking about, Iris?" Dad asked.

I staggered towards the chair at the table, grasping it now that I could see again so that I didn't fall on my face.

"I don't know. All of a sudden, I saw him, and he was lying on his back, and there was blood, and his eyes were closed..." Just when I didn't think it could get worse, I burst into tears.

I covered my face with my hands, not wanting to see anyone else. I didn't have anything for anyone other than the vision I'd seen.

Finally, I got my sobbing under control, and looked up. Mom, Dad, and Mara were all watching me as though I were a stick of dynamite, about to explode at the worst possible moment. Fair enough. My outburst probably didn't make sense.

But...I looked at my grandmother again.

"What?" I asked her. Her expression held more than mere trepidation.

"What happened when you met Brennan for the first time?" She asked. Her gaze fell to the table, and she fiddled with her fork, not meeting my eyes.

I hesitated in my answer. Not because I didn't remember, but because I did. In Technicolor.

"I went to the game..."

"With Heath," my mother interrupted. "What happened to him, Iris?"

I shrugged. "It's not important, Mom." Although I felt guilty that I hadn't texted him or anything. And I'd been so worried initially. It didn't matter. Not now. I promised myself I'd text him *something*. Soon.

"Go on, Iris," said Mara. She lifted her head, and I sat back a little under her piercing gaze. Why did every fae I'd encountered always seem to be looking at you like they knew something you didn't?

"I was in the restroom at the stadium and there was a flash of light and Brennan and Drake were just there. In the ladies' room. Then I tried to run away, and one of them zapped me or something, and I woke up with them carting me along back to Fae." There was a lot more than that, but I didn't want to get into it.

Mara eyed me intently. "What happened—I mean, what did you notice, or how did you feel, when you first encountered Brennan?"

I got the impression she knew a lot more than she was telling, and knew that I hadn't really told her anything.

I shrugged. "I don't know. What do you want to know?"

Mara stood up, coming closer, and peered at me. "It's not what I want to know. Do you want to know why you saw what you did? It's not me that's having visions." She stepped back and shrugged.

Holy hell. My grandmother had to be more maddening than almost anyone else I'd ever met. My mouth opened to say...what? Then I noticed my mom smirking.

"This isn't funny, Mom!"

She compressed her lips, trying to erase the visible humor. "I know it's not, but it's funny to hear Mom go at someone else like she did to me all throughout my childhood. You may as well tell her what she wants to know."

I sighed. "Does it matter? Something is wrong with him, and he needs help." I couldn't focus on anything else beyond the rising sense of dread I felt. Even though I'd gotten my crying under control, the emotion behind it threatened to overwhelm me.

"It does matter. There's a reason you're feeling what's happening to him." She said, like that answered a question or something.

"This is actually happening to him? He's actually hurt?" I looked down and saw the bag that Taranath had given me. I could go to him and—

My grandmother's hand stayed me from anything I might do in that moment.

"You cannot go to him, Iris. Not like this."

What the hell? Could she read minds? I stared at her, wordless.

"Tell me what happened when you met him." Her voice softened, but the steel of command lay beneath her calm words.

"I stared at him," I whispered. "I don't think I've ever seen anyone more beautiful. He looked at me, and I felt like everything stopped."

The words came out on their own volition. I didn't want to say any of this in front of my parents, but I couldn't resist Mara.

"Mom! Stop it!" My mom pulled her away from me.

"What is she doing?" Dad didn't look happy.

I shook my head a little. What had that been?

Mom glared at Mara who amazingly looked rather guilty.

"She's really good at getting people to say what's really in their heads. I never understood how she did it, although I do now. You don't get to use magic on my daughter!"

Now Dad glared too. "What the hell, Mara? You're back for ten minutes and already meddling? I think you need to leave." He stopped when Mom put her hand on his arm.

Now my grandmother straightened her shoulders, and did a little glaring of her own. "You can fuss at me all you want. There's a reason Iris can see what is happening to the Goblin King. Ignore it and toss me out if you want, it doesn't change the fact that I would bet he's hurt, and it happened recently. Don't you want to know why she sees this?" Amazingly a note of impatience had crept into her tone. My grandmother had some serious nerve.

My dad rolled his eyes. "All right, since you're dying to tell us. Why is it exactly that Iris is affected by that guy calling himself a goblin?"

"He is the Goblin King, whether you buy it or not, Paul. In Fae, most people can't see what happens to others. Not even parents have that ability with their children."

"What are you saying?" Mom asked in a small voice. Like she knew.

"Iris has a tie to Brennan. There is nothing else that makes sense. I don't know why, or how, after meeting only such a short time ago, but she could not have such a vision otherwise."

"I am right here. You can talk to me, rather than about me," I said. I still felt awful. It didn't get better, only worse. My chest felt as though something huge sat on it. I leaned on my hand, unable to keep my head up on its own any longer.

"Honey, are you okay?" Mom leaned into me.

The day didn't seem as bright or cheerful anymore. A shadow lay across the day, and I couldn't shake it.

"Iris, you are tied to him. What else happened while you were in Fae?" Mara knelt down next to me, her hand on my knee.

"Nothing. I don't know, I don't think anything major happened, other than we didn't get along because he wasn't very nice to me."

"What do you mean? I can't believe he was rude," My grandmother said.

"Not directly, no. But he couldn't wait to get rid of me."

Mara leaned back on her heels and a small smile appeared. "Did he say that, Iris? That he couldn't wait to get rid of you?"

I shook my head. "But all he wanted was to find Taranath, and send me home." *I'd wanted to go home*, I told myself. I'd wanted to, yet I'd been angry that he wanted to send me home.

"What else?"

"Mara, can't you see she's not well?" My dad came to stand next to where I hung on to the table. "Ease up."

"She's not well because of something going on with Brennan!" Mara snapped, standing up, hands on hips, to glare at Dad. "Unless we figure out what their tie is and why it's affecting Iris as it is, she'll be unwell until…" Her voice stopped as she looked at me, lounging in a heap against the table, "Until she goes to him." Her lips pursed at the thought. "Little though I like it."

"No. She's not going anywhere." My mom put her arm around me. "I don't want her to go back there again. You heard what Ta—Ta—" She tried to get out Taranath's name, and then gave up. "That magic guy said! The place nearly killed her! And you said she couldn't go! You've changed your mind already?"

I looked at Mara from where my head lay on my arms. She had a look of resignation that showed no signs of being moved by my parents' statements. She gazed steadily at me, and I knew. I knew I would have to go back to Fae, because otherwise, whatever the hell this was, it wouldn't get any better.

"What do I need to do?" I asked her. My head still felt too heavy to lift.

"Use the bag that Taranath," She didn't stumble over his name as Mom had, "Gave you and go to him. Tell him you must see Brennan. Tell him what happened here."

"Can you come with me?" The thought of navigating Fae on my own scared the crap out of me. I'd only seen one room and nearly died because of it. What else lurked that would be dangerous—possibly life-ending dangerous—if I were somewhere that Brennan had been hurt?

Why did I care? I'd screamed that he'd been hurt, but really, why did I care? I looked at what I felt, what I thought and realized I did care. A lot. More than I'd ever cared about anyone else.

"Why do I feel like this?" I said quietly, not really talking to anyone else.

Mara heard me. "Because there are times when fae meet, and their souls know one another. They are right for one another. Remember your initial impression of Brennan? Before he hurt your feelings? Time stopped."

This felt wrong, this clinical analysis. What happened to things happening like they had started to with Heath? The butterflies, the nerves, the anticipation? I didn't want to examine my thoughts or whatever about Brennan. I didn't want to accept that what Mara said had any merit at all.

We weren't from the same place. We weren't even from the same world. He couldn't stand me, and I couldn't stand...I stopped. I wanted to think about how much I couldn't stand him, but it wasn't true. At all.

"I couldn't stop looking at him," I said quietly. "I should have been scared to death, and a moment later, I was. But right then, I couldn't move, couldn't stop looking at him. All that I kept thinking was..." I looked away, trying to remember what I had been thinking. "Was, *You're here.*" Something in my tone made both my parents look at me.

They exchanged one of those married looks I loved to see.

"Looks aren't everything, honey," Mom said, equally quiet.

"I know that, Mom," I couldn't keep the impatience from my voice. "Obviously. His manners leave something to be desired, and..."

"He came here to help your mom." Mara crossed her arms. "You don't know that world, Iris, but I do. He didn't have to do that. Brennan, from what I remember, is a good ruler. A kind man. He's done well with the Goblin Realm. Much better than the last one," she snorted, her eyes going distant for a moment. She focused on me again. "I have never heard of a ruler putting themselves out like that. Of course," she looked down, again lost in her own thoughts, "He would be more kind than most."

"I'm not sure his actions towards me in particular have been kind, Mara." Yes, he'd helped Mom. Only because his mother dragged him here, and Mom was a fae in need of help. That had nothing to do with me, or how he felt about me. What did Mara mean, of course he would be more kind than most? I started to ask her but she spoke first.

Mara shook her head. "I don't think that is what you should be basing your opinion of him on."

Dad glared. "What are you trying to do, Mara? It almost sounds like you're pushing Iris at that guy." His brow furrowed as he waited for her to answer.

I remembered that Nerida had said Mara was from an important family. It showed in the deliberate manner in which she turned her attention to Dad. In that moment, I knew my mom had been as brave as a lion to stand up to her mom. Mara epitomized intimidating.

"I am not pushing my granddaughter anywhere, Paul. I'd prefer she not have a connection to Fae. I am also, as you may know, a realist. The reality is we all saw what happened to Iris. There is no getting around it. Better to face it and deal with it." She looked at me again. "I think you need to accept that there is a tie between you and Brennan. Not," She held up a finger, forestalling the protests from both of my parents, "That you have to accept it."

"What does that mean?" I got in before anyone else could.

"It means you have a tie, but you don't have to do anything about it."

"So what does that mean?" I tried really hard to control my mounting frustration. Part of it—a part I didn't want to admit—was due to the fact that all this chitchat didn't explain what happened to Brennan, and I had no answers to how badly he'd been hurt.

The rest fell into the *I'm mad that I care* category.

"The tie can be broken, but you will need to return to Fae. Taranath could probably do this for you."

I didn't say anything to that. Did I want the tie broken? If I did break it, what then? My mom no longer had cancer. Well, I didn't think she did. It would take a number of doctor visits to confirm it. We could move back on the boat. I liked college, sort of, but I liked the boat far more. College didn't hold the same draw for me it had only yesterday. My parents would be happy to be out again.

My life would be better.

Right?

Right?

"I don't know if I want her to go back to…to wherever it is you're talking about." Mom crossed her arms and hugged herself.

I knew that gesture. It meant she tried to contain her nerves.

"I…I'm not sure I want to either, Mom. I think I need to, though."

"No, Iris," Dad said. "Enough."

"I think Taranath knew I'd come back," I said slowly, pushing myself up from the chair. "Why else would he give me the means to do it? I mean, if this was it, if he knew there'd be no reason for me to come back."

"You can't know that," Mom protested.

"I don't know anything. I'm guessing," I admitted.

"Are you sure it's not just wishful thinking?" Dad put his hand on my shoulder and squeezed. "He's a good-looking guy."

"It's more than that, isn't it, Iris?" Mara still had that intense expression on her face.

I nodded, slowly. Sighed deeply. I didn't know what I felt, what I wanted. I also knew that Mara had a point of some kind, and I needed to face it.

"It's kind of like the storm that covers the entire horizon," I still spoke slowly, looking at my parents so that they would understand. "You see it all day, and there's nowhere to go that doesn't have a storm in the distance. So you prepare, and do the best you can. Sometimes it really sucks, but usually, you come through."

"Yeah, and sometimes you're beat to hell," Dad growled.

I shrugged. "True, but when did we ever run from a storm? We either went through it, or found a way to deal with it. This is me dealing with it. I hope I don't have to go through it but if I do…I'll be ready for it. Maybe not prepared," I laughed a little, thinking about how just unprepared I was. "But I'll see it. It's the best I can do, Dad."

"I don't like it." Mom still hugged herself.

I ached for the pain I knew this caused my parents. Behind that lay an ache to find out what happened to Brennan. A part of me screamed to hurry this up, because he was hurt, and I needed to get my ass there pronto!

I couldn't hurry this, even though it felt like something terrible had happened, and got worse and worse the longer I stayed here. I needed to make my parents okay with this, as much as they could be.

"I think this is the right decision, Iris," Mara came closer and took my hand. "I wish it were otherwise, but as I said, I'm a realist. Until you deal with this, it will plague you. You'll need to ask Taranath to break the tie."

"You're coming with me, right?"

She shook her head. "No. My time there is done."

"But Nerida—"

Mara laughed. "Nerida doesn't hear what she doesn't want to. I knew that I would not go home when I left to come to your grandfather. I made my choice. I understand your fear," Her voice softened. "It's frightening. Taranath would not give you something that would lead you to harm. I think you'll be safe."

"That's not very reassuring, Mom," my mom said. "Would you have sent me out with an 'I'll think you'll be safe'?"

Her mother turned and looked up at her. "Now you see why I protested your marriage. I worried."

Mom opened her mouth, then closed it.

"Not fair, Mara," Dad put his arm around Mom as he spoke.

"Generally I'm not," Mara replied and amazingly, she smiled at Dad. "Fae do what is needed. Fair and unfair—that's more of a human thing. Family and honor are the things that matter."

"As long as they go with the program?" Dad shot back.

Mara's smile widened. "I didn't do much better than my own parents. I have thought that over the years. But you have done well for yourselves."

"No thanks to you."

"Correct, but that is not the issue at hand, Paul." She turned back to me. "I think you need to go, and sooner rather than later, Iris. I think you saw Brennan as something bad happened to him. What could be going on? We don't have warfare in Fae." Her brow furrowed.

I could see the thought distressed her, even though she said she no longer belonged there.

"I'm afraid," I whispered.

"Of course you are. That doesn't mean you shouldn't take action."

I met her eyes. Took a deep breath. "You're right. Whatever happens, I have to face it." I walked away from her, from my parents. When I spun around, they were all looking at me. The fear and worry and love were all over my parents. Mara...well, I didn't know her enough to read her. Maybe I just didn't want to.

I pulled out the bag from Taranath. "What did he say? Open it..."

"Speak his name." Trust Mara to remember.

The little pouch looked so innocent. I opened up the cord that held it tied, mouthed *I love you* to my parents, and then, "Taranath."

The world spun.

CHAPTER FIFTEEN

Brennan

Light…dark…warm…pain…*hurts*…

Drake.

Iris.

Brennan opened his eyes and closed them immediately. *Cowardcowardcoward* some part of his brain screamed. The sound made his head hurt.

He hadn't felt pain to this degree since he'd been a child. Everything hurt. Opening his eyes hurt.

"Don't move."

Drake. Good. He must be safe. Drake sounded like Drake.

"We're almost to Taranath."

It took too much effort to figure out all that occurred around him. What had he been thinking of before…something happened?

Iris.

He'd seen her in…fae clothing. Why? He'd left her safely in the arms of her family. Away from Fae. Away from him. He killed those he loved. Better that she go.

Those he loved…

What happened?

"Taranath, we've need of you!"

Brennan let his eyes close fully. It seemed a shame that Drake sounded so concerned. Much better to relax and go to sleep. He could hear voices talking over him, but it took too much effort to focus, or pay attention.

Iris

Did any portal ever behave the same? The last time I'd gone through one, it had been like walking through water, the ripples moving me along. This time I fell, ass over teakettle. Maybe there were ripples but I couldn't get my bearings. As I contemplated, as much as anyone could while spinning in all directions, how long it would take for me to throw up, everything stopped, and I fell once more.

Straight down onto a hard floor.

"OW!" I yelled. I clutched my head with both hands. I'd be lucky to escape this crap without a concussion. Or brain damage.

"Iris?" I heard surprise in Taranath's voice.

Well at least I'd made it to the right place.

"I had to come," I said, rolling onto my knees. I had to take a moment, let my head hang down. Throwing up was still on the table.

I pushed my hands against the floor and carefully stood. I had to keep my eyes closed. When I opened them, I saw Taranath and Drake gaping at me.

"I know, I know, not graceful. I'm doing the best I can."

"What are you doing here?" Drake cut right to it.

"I had to." I felt tears and the worry I'd suppressed before opening the pouch rise to the surface. "I felt...I don't know what I felt. But Brennan—" Drake's gaze shifted when I said the name to something in front of him.

"Oh my god!" I clapped my hand over my mouth. The thing in front of him stirred. Brennan!

I rushed, as much as I was able, to the table where Brennan lay.

"What happened to him?"

"Why are you here, Iris?" Taranath asked, a lot more nicely than Drake had.

He moved next to me, moving his hands over Brennan gently. When his hand brushed the center of Brennan's chest, Brennan stirred and made a noise that might have been a protest. It broke my heart.

"I felt this," I whispered, unable to take my eyes off Brennan's face. That face, so expressive, always in motion—lay still. Quiet. It didn't feel right. It scared the shit out of me.

Drake had moved around to where I stood without my realizing it until he grabbed my arm that reached for Brennan. "What are you doing here? What do you mean, you felt this?"

"Drake," Taranath said mildly.

Drake's anger showed in every line of his face, in the strength of the grip on my arm.

"Drake, this doesn't help Brennan. Let go of Iris."

Another moment that could be an eternity, and then Drake dropped my arm.

"Now, Iris, what brought you here?"

Shaken, I made myself turn slightly to Taranath. I didn't want to turn my back on Drake. He no longer had the joking, best friend vibe. He had the '*hurt my friend and I'll kill you*' vibe. It scared me to think what he might do if I couldn't see him.

"I was sitting in our garden, and I felt like something had hit me right in the chest, and then I saw Brennan, and he looked...he looked..." My eyes were drawn to his too-quiet form in front of me, "Like he fell down. But with a surprised look. And then my chest hurt, and I knew something had happened. Then," I stopped to wipe the tears I didn't realize had slipped out, "I couldn't see or feel anything more. It happened really fast."

I clutched at Taranath's arm. "Will he be okay?"

"How did you know to come here?" Drake pushed in between Brennan and me.

I didn't understand his anger.

"Because I didn't know where else to go. Taranath—"

I took several steps back in fear, the words choked in my throat. Drake had pulled a knife! A knife! What the hell?

"How did you know how to find him?" Drake yelled. "No one knew where we were going! How did you know to find us here?" He grabbed the front of my shirt. The knife hovered before my eyes.

"Get off of me!" I found my voice and screamed as loudly as I could, grabbing at his hand that still held onto my shirt. I felt his fingers curl tighter next to my chest, and as fast as I could, I changed my grip and pulled his hand towards my face. My movement caught him by surprise and I felt his fingers move away from me. I pulled his hand harder, using both hands, getting it close to me—and then in what quickly was becoming a signature move, I bit him.

Hard.

"Crazy human!" He yelled and let go of me like any sensible person would.

Drake stepped back, bumping into the table. The hand holding the knife dropped, and I lunged for it. I might be able to get the knife and—

I overshot the mark and fell into Drake. We tumbled against the table.

Just as quickly, we were both pushed back, flying in opposite directions from the table. I landed on my back, hitting my head, *again*. I smirked through tears of pain to see Drake also rubbing his head on the other side of the room.

"STOP!"

Taranath hadn't raised his voice since I'd met him. It felt like a thundercloud dropping on my head.

"This is not helping Brennan," he said, dividing his anger between the two of us. "Shall I leave you where you lie, or can you be trusted to behave as civilized people who are concerned for the king?"

No one spoke. I took a deep breath, trying to steady my racing heart. "Yes. If the knife can go away, please." I shot a glare at Drake.

"Of course, Taranath. My apologies for getting in the way of your work. I will not question Iris further until you've tended to Brennan." Drake's voice didn't even sound winded.

How did he calm himself down so fast? I felt a flash of envy at that kind of control. I didn't have it. I wanted to bite him again, maybe tear his head off. Asshole. I couldn't believe he pulled a knife on me.

"Put away all weapons." Taranath's tone brooked no discussion. "And no biting."

He watched us both for a moment, then "You are both free. Get up." He whirled around to Brennan.

How the table hadn't fallen during all that, I didn't know. Taranath must have some pretty amazing moves to have done what he did.

It's always the quiet ones, isn't it?

I walked carefully to the table, taking care to keep Taranath in between Drake and me. I know he promised, but I'm not taking chances. Insane man.

"Iris came here because I gave her the means to come to me if she needed to," Taranath said, not looking up from his examination of Brennan. "She could not go anywhere else. Nor did I want her to. I felt if she must come to Fae, it would be safest to come to me. I do admit, Iris, to wondering at your timing. Did you come because of what you experienced? How did you know Brennan had been hurt?"

His hands busied themselves opening up Brennan's shirt. They moved in a way that seemed independent of the man himself. I watched his hands, unable to turn away.

Brennan had no color. He was so very pale.

"Um...yeah. Yes. I knew something had happened. Mara told me I had to come back here, to see you, to..." I didn't want to tell him what she had said. I didn't want to share that, not now, not with Brennan lying here, and Drake still glaring at me.

No way.

Taranath nodded. Whether he knew what Mara had said, or whether I'd told him enough, I don't know. I felt relief that I wouldn't have to go into it now.

I'd have to, though. At some point.

"So, Drake, Iris reacted to Brennan being hurt. I think you may safely sheath your knife."

Silence, and then I heard the hiss and snick of the knife being put back.

"It would seem that you have some connection to Brennan. Most interesting. I would like to talk with you more about it, but I need to heal him. Iris, I will need the assistance of the both of you. Drake, please move to the other side."

I couldn't take my eyes from Brennan, who seemed to have gone paler while we talked.

"He isn't getting better," I said in a small voice.

"No, he's not." Taranath spoke before Drake could. "But we shall change that. Come here, Iris."

I took a step closer to him.

"Your hand, please."

I held out my right hand.

"No, the other one."

Okay. Weird.

I did as he asked.

"Drake, your right hand, please."

Drake gave him his right hand.

Taranath took both our hands, placing Drake's on top of mine. Both of us jumped. I could feel it in his hand.

Then he placed our stacked hands on Brennan's chest. This felt awful. Not only because Drake and I were still ready to kill one another but because I could feel Brennan's wound. His blood pumping from his body.

"Don't move. Either of you." Taranath spoke mildly, but I heard the command. He walked to Brennan's head, and placed his hands on the sides of Brennan's head.

"When I begin, I want you to think of Brennan healing," he said.

Where was the wand?

The image of Taranath running a wand over me popped into my head right then. Why wasn't he using the wand? Magic didn't seem to have any hard and fast rules here.

He closed his eyes, and began to speak in a language I couldn't understand. I felt Drake's hand tighten over mine. I risked a peek at him, and saw that his eyes were closed. His jaw had the hard look jaws have when the person is clenching their teeth.

I looked down at Brennan, so still and pale.

Oh god, you can't die. You have to get better.

He didn't move.

Like before, with my mom, Taranath had a glow on his arms. It encompassed Brennan's face, and I could see it moving down to where our hands sat on his chest.

It still scared the shit out of me, and I wanted to do something to the glow, but I knew I couldn't move.

Please get better.

Taranath chanted loudly, and the glow brightened. Any brighter, and I'd have to cover my eyes.

Please.

I felt a heartbeat beneath my hand.

For me.

Brennan
—please—
For me.

The words penetrated the dark. Who asked this of him?

For me.

Who?

His eyes opened, and everything that happened burst over him like a shower of lightening.

"Drake!" He sat up. He hadn't left Drake in the Dwarf Realm, had he?

He realized he wasn't alone. Hands were upon him. Drake and...Iris.

"You must rest, Brennan." A voice behind him.

He tried to see who had come up behind him, and when he moved, a jolt of pain ran from his head to the tips of his fingers.

"Your Majesty, please. You are safe. Drake is safe. But you will not heal as you should if you do not allow the body time to rest."

Gentle hands on his shoulders pressed him back.

"What...what is she doing here?"

A spasm of hurt crossed over Iris's face. He saw it, and it made him want to turn away. He didn't want to hurt her.

"Not...safe for her," he caught Drake's hand. "Get her home."

"No." Iris spoke. "Not until you're well."

Brennan ignored her.

"Get her safe." He wouldn't look at her. Couldn't trust himself to hold his resolve if he looked at her again.

"No!" Iris came in close to him. "You can hate me if you want. But I can't go back, not until you're better. Because if you don't get better, I'll keep falling over in my own realm. So shut up and get better." She moved away from him. He could still feel her, as though she sat next to him.

Brennan heard her anger and the jagged edge of pain. He closed his eyes and sighed. Better that she be in pain and go home safe. It wasn't safe here. Not with Scarface. Not after he'd attacked him with magic that Brennan didn't even know, hadn't heard of or seen, nothing. It hit him like nothing he'd ever experienced before, and it kept coming. He'd lost the ability to fight it.

The last thing he'd seen...Iris. Dressed as a fae woman, smiling at him over her shoulder.

"Majesty," Taranath, hovering over him. "I will send for my goblins. They will tend to you."

He nodded, eyes still closed.

"Iris, come with me. You need to rest for a time."

He heard them leave.

"Come and help me up." He knew Drake hadn't left.

He felt hands gently tug him into an upright sitting position.

"Where is he?" He whispered.

He could see the anger and regret on Drake as though he shouted it.

"I don't know. He hit you with that spell, and then I couldn't see much. I was lucky that I saw you as you fell. I carried you away from the cottage and opened a portal. I am ashamed, Brennan. I didn't look back or strike another blow against our enemy. My concern was for you, and to get you to safety."

"Did you recognize the mage?"

Drake shook his head. "No. Why?"

Brennan shrugged. "When I got close to him, I looked hard at him, and something rang familiar. Just as it did before. I cannot put my mind to what piece of his face did it. I've seen him before, though. I am sure of it."

"How? We know everyone."

Brennan glared. "Yes. Like we knew of the old king's widow and her children. Indeed. We know everyone."

Drake's shoulders sagged. "True. I spoke rashly. We don't know much of anything about this, do we?"

"I didn't recognize the magic, either. Did you?"

"No. I've not seen you felled in such a manner."

Brennan glared harder. "Thank you for the words of confidence, Drake. It improves the situation greatly."

A grin swept aside the tension that sat on Drake like a cloak. "You must be feeling better if you are able to give me such sarcasm."

"I'm so weak that a healthy breeze would be the end of me. My mind, however, is relatively unscathed."

"Good. Let's talk about something else for a moment, as our situation in regards to the sorcerer is going nowhere. What is Iris doing here?"

"How would I know, Drake? I was not aware of much of what happened."

"She showed up via a portal right after I brought you to Taranath."

"That's..." Brennan started.

"Suspicious." Drake finished.

"You cannot still suspect her?"

"I would have had an answer to that question had Taranath not stopped me."

"From what?"

"From whatever it took to get the answers I sought."

This didn't bode well. He knew that tone. "What did you do, Drake?"

"I...attempted a bit of persuasion," Drake hedged.

"You pulled a weapon on her?" Brennan didn't know whether to laugh or be angry with his brother.

"I did. Taranath seemed to share your incredulity. He made me stop. Had he not, we'd have no questions regarding the girl."

"Don't you think that perhaps a weapon might have been a..."

"Appropriate?" Drake supplied.

"*A bit much* is more what I had in mind."

"No. You are my brother and my king. She's been in the wrong place too many times, Bren. We need to get the truth from her."

"You mean you didn't when you had her at the point of your weapon?"

Drake snorted. "She actually said she'd come because she knew you were hurt. How would she know, Bren, unless she had reason to know that you'd be attacked? No one but you and I knew where we went today. And Iris was here directly after I got you back here. Just as she happened to be there when we passed through the portal into the Human Realm. I don't believe in so many coincidences."

Brennan pushed himself off the table. "We must go and find them. I don't think that she is involved, but you are right. We cannot afford even the smallest chance that she might be."

Drake caught his arm as he steadied himself.

"Thank you, brother. Thank you for getting me home. I have no doubt that I would have perished if not for your quick actions."

Drake rolled his eyes. "Stop. You'd do the same. That's what it means to be brothers."

Not always, Brennan thought.

"It seems I owe you twice," he said, keeping his thoughts on brothers to himself.

"What do you mean?"

"I heard you, right before I opened my eyes. You asked me to live. For you. It forced me to open my eyes. I remember it clearly. Thank you, brother."

Drake lifted a brow. "That wasn't me."

CHAPTER SIXTEEN

Iris

Me and couches were getting real comfy here in the
Fae Realm. At least I'd gotten to try out a different one,
being in Taranath's rooms rather than Mr. Damned King
of the Ingrates. After I'd used the pouch to come here and
helped to heal him! First words—*take that human home!*

I swiped the traitorous tears that fell without
permission. Taranath had installed me in here and sent for
goblins to help Brennan and to get me a hot drink.

"Something restorative," he'd said.

Nice gesture, but I didn't think that would help. I still
needed to talk to him about the tie Mara was sure existed.
And break it. As soon as humanly—I laughed without
humor—possible.

My spiraling thoughts were broken as Taranath bustled
back in. He held a cup in his hand, and I could see steam
rising from it.

"This will ease you a bit. Not as much as you might
like, but I find it easier to work through problems when
my mind doesn't fly like a flock of scattered birds."

I nodded, taking the cup as he held it out to me.
"That's exactly how I feel."

"I think you might also give some allowance to Drake.
He'd only brought Brennan right before you appeared, and
I believe he still felt the urgency of the battle from which
they came."

"Please! Don't make excuses for him! I'm no threat to
anyone, particularly the great king's guard dog!" I could

smell the drink, and it smelled warm, and soothing. I took a sip, then another.

"Have you ever been in a situation where you were frightened? Did you not act first and then think rationally later? Not anything trivial, but a time where you or others were in danger?"

I opened my mouth, then shut it. I had been. We'd been on the boat, and a squall had come up while we were under sail. It had been so fast that we hadn't gotten the sails down, and the boat was skidding across the waves like a toy jerked on a string as gusts of wind hit the sails. We'd had to time our efforts so we could drop the sails when the wind gusts passed. Not that the steady wind had been any picnic. Mom, Dad, and I worked as a team. At one point, Mom, kneeling next to me, stood up just as a gust hit the boom and sent it towards her.

In sailing, the one place you do not want to be is where the boom is. It's the horizontal arm that the bottom edge of the largest sail is attached to. If it hit you on a small boat, it would knock you overboard. On *Sorcha*, it would catapult you overboard and kill you.

I saw the boom coming. It moved in real time and in slow motion for me. I ran at Mom and slammed into her, knocking her into the cockpit.

We'd both been bruised after that, and she had a limp for nearly a week where she'd hit her knee when I'd fallen on her.

But she lived.

Damn the man. "Yes," I admitted.

"Then you know what it is to take action and speak later. While he may not be very happy, Drake's concern is the king. And he acted accordingly."

"Doesn't mean I have to like him. Or forgive," I added with emphasis, taking another sip of my drink. Whatever it was, it was delicious. There were flowers and honey in it. I could taste it. Anything else, I didn't have a clue. I didn't care, even as I suspected there was something like fairy Xanax in it.

"No, but you may understand. That is as important as anything else."

I didn't say anything. I didn't want to agree with him. Damn him.

The door burst open. I jumped, spilling a little of the drink down the front of me.

Brennan came through, followed by Drake. Great. Just who I needed to see right this minute.

"You really should allow yourself more time to rest, my lord." Taranath's brows raised to nearly his hairline. "Even with your generally robust constitution."

"I need to speak with Iris. Then I will head straight to my chambers. My word," Brennan offered the ghost of a smile to Taranath. Which dropped as he moved his focus to me.

Awesome.

"I apologize for Drake's hasty actions earlier, Iris," Brennan said.

It sounded sincere. I sighed and looked at the wall.

"As does Drake."

Drake made a non-committal guy noise. Then he grunted. Apparently Brennan had given him a little encouragement.

"I am sorry I had you at the end of my knife, Iris. I can only plead concern for my king." Drake moved as I looked at him. He'd sidestepped an elbow from Brennan. I'd been right about the encouragement.

"We still do not know why you appeared when you did. Can you please tell us what happened?" Brennan took over. I guess he realized Drake was a lost cause in the Iris Fan Club at this point.

"I was sitting at home, and then I had…I don't know what you'd call it. Insight? That you'd been hurt. I…" I hesitated. I didn't want to share that I'd felt it.

"We need to know all that occurred," Taranath said in his soft voice.

It calmed me, even with the ingrate and his insane buddy.

"I felt like someone slammed me in the chest. I couldn't breathe, and I saw stars. Like when you've been hit hard. When I could speak, I said your name," I made eye contact with Brennan. "I told Mara you were hurt." I stopped.

Three sets of eyes looked at me expectantly. "What? That's it! Really. My grandmother and I talked, and she told me if I was seeing you get hurt, I needed to talk to Taranath. That's why I came to him. He gave me a bag of some kind of tricks to bring me to him. That's it. I didn't know you'd be there."

I couldn't tell if they believed me. It did sound rather fishy, but I had no other information to give. I'd spoken the truth. They could take it or leave it.

Drake started to speak but Brennan held up a hand to stop him. Brennan himself walked carefully towards me. That was new.

"You felt something hit you in the chest? That is where I was hit, correct?" He glanced at Drake for confirmation.

A short, tight nod from Drake. He looked pissed he had to admit even that.

Brennan turned those remarkable eyes to Taranath. I felt my shoulders sag a little with relief at no longer being the focus. Even if for only a moment.

"Why?" Brennan asked.

Even I could feel the weight of that one word.

Taranath took his time responding. "I am unsure of the cause of this, Majesty. It is something I need to think on. In the meantime, let me escort you to your chamber. You're up faster than I thought you'd be. That way, I can reassure myself that you are healing as you need to." As he spoke, he walked past Brennan and Drake towards the door.

"Iris, I'll leave you here. I'd advise finishing your drink. I'll return shortly."

Taranath opened the door, and stood back, waiting for Brennan to precede him.

Brennan looked from him, to me, and to Drake. It made me wince to see the healing wound on his chest. No blood, though. At least not now. How had they cleaned that up so fast? I could see blood on his shirt. Something passed between the two of them. He gave me a brief bow and turned on his heel without saying anything else.

The door shut behind them, and I found myself alone.

Brennan

"Why did you hurry us out of there?" The door had barely closed before Drake questioned Taranath.

"I didn't want to speak of this before her."

Brennan admired how Taranath allowed nothing to ruffle him. Drake in high emotion, as he was now, had a forceful manner that intimidated many. That, as well as many other reasons, had decided him on Taranath as the Court Mage.

"Speak of what?" Brennan asked.

"There is a tie between you and Iris, Your Majesty."

"What does that mean?"

Taranath sighed. "I suspected it before, but I hoped my suppositions were incorrect. However, her return confirmed things. You and Iris have a tie."

"How is that possible? She's human!" Brennan grasped at the first thing that came to mind in order to not blurt out what he wanted.

Taranath shrugged. "She's not entirely human. You saw what happened with her mother. That is not human in the least. That's her fae side. And now, knowing that you were hurt. The tie means that you two are bound together in a manner. You do not have to remain so, if you do not wish it." Taranath looked straight ahead as they walked.

Brennan stared at him. He couldn't find the words. Did that explain his vision just before he fell? Iris dressed as fae?

Thankfully, Drake jumped in. "What does this mean, being tied?"

"It means that something in them feels so strongly for one another that their souls have become bound."

How could Taranath make these pronouncements as though he discussed the weather? It rocked Brennan to the core.

"She's supposed to be here." His voice came out in almost a whisper.

Taranath heard him. He stopped, put his hand on Brennan's arm. "Forgive my presumption, Your Majesty, but yes, I think she is. Whether we like it or not. I think, perhaps, you aren't as upset about this as one might suspect."

"Wait!" Drake threw up his hands. "We haven't established she's not here to harm him, not here at the behest of that cursed fae!"

Taranath faced him. "She is not part of a scheme to harm the king. This is a coincidence, Drake. I know it's hard to see, but I see no evil or harm in Iris. I've looked." His tone spoke to the depth of his surety.

"You'd stake your life—the *king's* life—on such belief?" Drake asked.

Brennan held up a hand. "I believe him, Drake. When has he been wrong before in the advice he's given?"

"I don't like it."

"Did you not say something similar not one day ago?" Brennan couldn't help but interject a teasing note into his question.

"That's before she showed up one too many times when you were at risk!" Drake didn't back down.

"Will you trust me?" Brennan quietly asked his brother. His heart felt like a bird breaking free from a cage. The challenges presented by this were enormous, but the mere fact that someone other than himself said she should be here made him feel good. Happy, almost.

He ignored the concern over having too much feeling. He would handle it. He glanced down as a pair of goblins scurried past, giving head bobs when they saw him look down.

Who said goblins didn't have a high level of sensitivity? He'd never understood such an idea. His experience showed him otherwise. As the two who'd just gone by showed.

"I don't have a choice, do I?" Drake made a sound of disgust.

Or maybe because Drake made no move to hide his emotions. "How can you change your thoughts on her when you argued so strongly in a different direction?" Brennan wondered aloud.

"After I saw you lying unconscious, and she turned up just as I got you to safety. Again, right after we saw Scarface who bespelled us both times! Does this completely escape you?" Frustration made Drake's voice rise.

"No. I understand your concern. I think, though, that this is one of the few times where I will say it has been an unfortunate set of coincidences," Taranath replied.

"Drake, I am glad you are by my side," Brennan said walking forward again, forcing the other two men to follow him. "Please be watchful. I hear the truth in what Taranath says. I also hear it in your words. So keep watch. Do not harm her. At all. If you feel something is off, come to me immediately." He turned to look at Drake, to make sure he understood.

Drake glared for a moment, then expelled a breath. "If you say so, Bren. I won't harm a hair on her head. Unless she comes at you armed."

"Perhaps you should also promise not to threaten her with any sort of weapon," Taranath interjected mildly.

"Yes, perhaps you should use some restraint," Brennan agreed. The thought of Drake putting a knife to Iris filled him with...not rage, but a protective feeling. He couldn't be angry with Drake. Of all those around him, Drake had proved time and again himself to be Brennan's true brother.

Unlike Cian.

Why thoughts of his lost brother came to mind now, he didn't know. He hadn't thought of him in so long. Drake was the only brother he had, and the one who...Brennan pushed the unworthy thought away. From the distance as an adult, he knew Cian to be a child, with a child's temper, and what could be explained as a child's cruelty.

Drake had never been cruel. Ever.

Brennan shook his head. He had no time for thoughts of the past. Enough lay before him that needed to be addressed now.

First, Iris. "Taranath, I will need you to explain further this tie between us. What does it mean? What will it change for me? For her? I need to understand it before I do anything else. I don't want to hurt her due to lack of knowledge."

Drake muttered something, but Brennan ignored it.

They'd reached Brennan's chambers.

"May I join you within, Majesty?"

Brennan nodded. They entered into his study, and he went to his favorite chair, throwing himself into it. He felt very tired, as if the weight of all the realms sat on his shoulders.

Maybe they did, in a fashion.

Drake and Taranath sat also.

"Majesty," Taranath began, "I didn't want to speak so openly in the corridor, but will you tell me honestly of your feelings for Iris?"

Brennan drew back. He hadn't expected such a direct question. "I...I don't know what I feel," he answered. "I feel for her, which is more than I expected." How to keep some of what he felt hidden?

"Your Majesty, I mean no disrespect, but you are not being truthful. Tell me the truth."

Only Drake and Taranath—and his mother—could speak to him so. Brennan felt relief that Taranath had saved this for the privacy of his chambers.

"He likes her," Drake rolled his eyes. "Why he can't admit it, I don't know. He couldn't before this mess, and apparently that challenge exists still. As it should," He glared at Brennan.

"Enough," Brennan said. "I felt an attraction to her that I haven't felt…"

"Ever," Drake supplied.

"I can speak for myself, Drake."

"I don't know about that, Your Majesty." Sarcasm dripped from Drake's words.

"I think she cares for you as well." Taranath had an amused expression on his face.

"That's been apparent from the beginning," Drake muttered.

"Has it? Were you aware, Your Majesty?" This to Brennan.

"I hadn't thought about it, Taranath. I," He smiled ruefully, "I found that I had a great deal of focus on my own feelings."

"What of your intended? How does she fit into this revelation?"

Brennan shook his head. He noted that Drake had clamped his lips together. "I don't know. I don't know, Taranath. I never expected to…" He stopped. If he said it aloud, it could never be taken back.

"Feel for a human? Or anyone at all?" Taranath asked quietly.

Shock prevented Brennan from any sort of immediate response. How did Taranath know? How *could* he know?

"So what is to be done?" Drake, ever practical, changed the topic slightly.

"She will stay here, with me." Brennan found his voice.

"That will get back to Ailla faster than you can order breakfast," Drake said.

Brennan shrugged, emboldened by the fact that he had a reason to allow Iris to be here. "Will she be all right?" He asked Taranath. "When she was here before you said her human side fell ill."

"That will probably continue. But," he held up a finger, "Given what I have seen of Iris, I think her fae side will compensate."

"She could die," Drake said.

Brennan glared at the hopeful note in Drake's statement. "No, she will not. We'll send her back before that happens. I am to be told immediately if you notice anything of the sort," he spoke to both men, giving Drake a hard look.

Drake threw up his hands, rolling his eyes at the ceiling. "All right. I agree to watch over her, not only to ensure she doesn't try to harm you, but so she doesn't come to any harm. Not because you're right," he gave Brennan the hard eye in return, "But because I do think you have feelings for the girl, and it's good for you to figure out what they mean. As long as they don't get you killed."

"Thank you for such support," Brennan said, unable to keep the sarcasm at bay.

"Of course, your gracious lordship."

"Shall I bring Iris to you, Your Majesty?" Taranath rose, ending the conversation.

Brennan nodded. "Until…things…are settled, I don't want her away from me."

"Convenient."

"Be quiet, Drake."

CHAPTER SEVENTEEN

Iris

I finished my drink and leaned back against the cushions. Fairy Xanax, indeed. I felt far more relaxed than I'd been since...since I'd come here the first time. That Taranath, he made a mean drink.

Brennan was safe. Drake still had homicidal tendencies, but Brennan was safe. Up walking and talking, in spite of the horrid wound I'd seen him receive. He was safe.

I wasn't sure what contributed more to my feeling of contentment—that he was safe, or the whatever Taranath had added to the drink.

The door opened and Taranath breezed in. As before, I noted how graceful his entrance was. Not the same sort of grace Brennan possessed, but his own. A more serene sort of thing.

He sat across from me. "How do you feel?"

"Better."

"Why?"

"I'm okay. Drake didn't kill me, and Brennan...Brennan is okay."

Taranath smiled. "All very true. Drake will not attempt to harm you again. As I said, he is most fierce in his concern for Brennan."

I nodded. It didn't seem quite as bad now, with a little distance from the whole affair. "I'm willing to let it go. I admire his devotion, although I wish he didn't point a knife at me."

"You will be safe, even from Drake," Taranath actually laughed a little. "Can you move about on your own? Brennan wants you to stay close to him."

My whole body felt as though someone had turned on a light switch within. "Why?" I tried to keep my question calm.

"Because he acknowledges, as you do, that something has brought you here that needs to be addressed. Given what happened during your time here before, he wants to ensure you don't fall ill."

I would get to be with Brennan! That made the knife business with Drake worth it.

"All right. Let's go. One thing, though, Taranath."

"Yes?" He asked, rising up and offering me a hand.

I took it as I stood up, taking my time, testing my balance. I could walk. Good. Doing better than before. "I want to see more than just all the couches in the place."

Taranath stared at me for a moment, and then burst into laughter. "I think we can accommodate that."

"Lead on, MacDuff."

"Who is MacDuff?" He asked as we walked through the door.

"Oh, it's...never mind. It's from a play, by Shakespeare. I'll explain later."

As we walked along the corridor, I took the time to look around. It helped that Taranath still held my hand, as though I were some great lady he escorted. He also walked slowly. I appreciated this subtle allowance for my overall state.

The stone walls gleamed, and there were heraldic shields placed along them. We came to a part of the corridor where five arched windows in a row looked out from the castle.

"Can we stop for a minute?"

"Of course," Taranath let me walk to one of the windows.

This must be an outer wall, because I could see grounds out in front of me, and there were a few goblins bent over plants. Further out was a line of trees, and in the distance I could see a town or village or something like that.

"You see the center of the Goblin Realm. Brennan's castle sits in the middle. That is the largest town within our realm."

"It's prettier than I expected," I said. "Not what I expect from a goblin kingdom."

"What did you expect?"

I shrugged. "I don't know. But the idea of goblins doesn't really bring up images of clean castles and attractive gardens," I gestured towards the window. "It usually puts one in mind of dark and dirty, and...you know."

"Fascinating. Where do you get such ideas?"

I looked at him to see if he made fun of me, but his face indicated nothing outside of genuine interest. I'd forgotten he was a scientist at heart.

"I don't know. That's how our world tends to see them."

"Well, I am sure there are misconceptions through all the realms." He put a little pressure on my hand to move me forward. "Let us take you to the king...who is neither dark nor dirty." I could hear the mirth in his tone at the idea.

"Oh, god, don't tell him I said that! I've got enough problems!" I pleaded.

That sobered him. "Indeed you do. You have to promise me, Iris that should you feel weak or as you did previously, you will tell Brennan or myself immediately."

"So I don't die?" I asked, trying to be brave.

"Well, there is that, although I have to tell you that I don't think you're going to. I think what happened with your mother has altered you. Brought your fae side to the forefront." His brow furrowed as he looked at me, and I felt like a specimen again.

I could have gone years without bringing *that* up. "I think you might be reaching."

He shook his head. "How do you feel?"

I laughed. "After the fairy Xanax? I feel just fine."

"What is Xanax?"

"A drug that relaxes your body, helps you let go of stress."

"Ah...fairy Xanax?" He laughed with me as comprehension hit. "You have an unending sense of humor, Iris."

"It's a nice thing to have. You all should try and get one."

He chuckled. "I think you might be trying to change the unchangeable."

"That's me, the trailblazer."

"Here," he led me to a door.

I felt shy. I didn't know why, but I hesitated.

"All will be well, Iris. Fear not," Taranath's voice in my ear propelled me forward as he opened the latch.

"Your Majesty, I've brought her."

Two sets of eyes burned into me. For entirely different reasons.

Drake looked like he wanted to say something. Say a lot, actually. He stood, nodded at Brennan. "I'll see what I can find, Bren."

He looked at me intently as he passed.

I stepped into the room.

"Welcome back, Iris. Please join me," Brennan gestured to the chairs that sat around him.

"I will return later," Taranath bowed, and before I knew it, had left the room and closed the door behind him.

I gave the closed door a look of despair. I didn't expect to be so summarily abandoned. Knowing you felt a certain way, and having to face the object of those feelings were two entirely different things. I also hadn't quite gotten a handle on said feelings. It made me uncomfortable.

"It's all right, Iris," Brennan's spoke what I would refer to as normally. "You're safe here. I won't bite."

I swiveled back to see him giving me a half-grin.

Some of the shyness and reserve I'd felt before walking in fell away. I walked towards him and sat in the chair closest to him. "You'd better hope I feel the same." I wondered if anyone had told him I'd bitten Drake, too.

He laughed, quietly. "I do indeed hope that. Being bitten is not on my list of further things to experience today." His face sobered. "I find that I owe you thanks," he said.

"For what?"

"For my life. I understand from Drake that you and he helped Taranath bring me back from my wounds."

"How do you feel now?"

He gave that half-grin again. "Not my best, but not dead, either."

It felt like the sun came out. "Did you just make a joke?"

"Oh, I doubt it. Not me, the Goblin King."

His eyes met mine, and we both laughed.

"So what happens now?" I asked. How is it I had no fear and only comfort? I didn't even worry about my mom or dad, my family—nothing. I sat with Brennan, and our shared laugh did more than the fairy Xanax, which said something.

What was happening here? Taranath was right. This time in Fae, things were different. *I* was different. I didn't feel any of the stress or anger or anything that I'd felt when I'd been with Brennan previously.

"You and I have some sort of tie. There is no other explanation for what happened today."

I cast my eyes down. "I know. My grandmother told me the same thing."

"She would know. I'm not sure it is the best thing for you, but you risked your life to come help me keep mine, so I shall keep you safe. You are, of course, welcome to return to your home at any time."

I couldn't look at him. "I don't think that's what I want." Leaving Fae, when I'd only just gotten here…no. Definitely not what I wanted.

Silence greeted my words.

"I don't think that's the best idea. However, Taranath seems to think otherwise, so you'll stay here."

I didn't care why. I just wanted to stay, and now I could. That was the only thing that mattered.

I found the courage to meet his eyes. They were focused on me with blazing intensity, and I nearly looked away. "I'm glad."

His brows went up. "Are you? I worry that something will happen that we cannot help or heal. You have to understand the risks."

I nodded. "I do."

Brennan tilted his head, not looking away from me.

"Oh, all right. I think I do. But…" I struggled to find the words that wouldn't give me away entirely. "I think this is the right thing. It *feels* right."

"That's all you have? A feeling?"

I shrugged. "That's it. I wish I had more. I prefer facts, but that's all I have at the moment."

He smiled, and it took my breath away. "Then we'll go on that. My facts differ from yours, but I, too, feel you are where you need to be for the time being. In spite of my worry, and concern."

Again with the immense feeling of relief. I wouldn't be sent away like an unwanted puppy.

"Thank you for not sending me back. And for keeping me safe."

"It is my pleasure, Iris."

I heard something in his voice I hadn't heard before.

"So…what do we do now?"

"Are you hungry? I find that coming back from the brink of death is hungry business."

I considered. "I could eat."

He got up and went into another room. I leaned forward, trying to see. He came back and sat down once more.

"Food will be here shortly."

"How do you do that? I didn't hear you talk to anyone."

"My close servants are never far. There's usually one in my chambers, in case I should have need of something."

That didn't explain a thing, but I could tell I wouldn't get any more from him.

"Who attacked you?"

His face darkened. Okay, maybe not the best conversational choice. I had to ask, though. I hadn't seen that. Only that he fell.

"I don't know. I will tell you that the man who did is the same man who sent Drake and I to your world."

"Oh! The uh…" I tried to remember how he'd described the bad guy. "Scarred! That's it. The guy had a scar on his face. Is that weird enough to stand out?"

Brennan nodded, his mouth twisting in a wry grin. "Or as you so aptly named him, Scarry McScarface."

I stared. "I did not. When did I ever say such a stupid thing?"

He laughed, and I felt something inside of me soar at the sound of it. "Indeed you did. When we first brought you to Fae, you were…"

Oh, that's right. "Drugged. One of you did something to me and made me go," I smiled sweetly. "Away with the fairies." That could not have been any more perfect.

The smile instantly disappeared. Okay, maybe needling him wasn't such a good idea but it was right there! I had to. I squared my shoulders and waited.

"No wings. Not fairies," He said politely. I saw a muscle jump in his jaw. Why did this bring out the jerk in him? It was funny.

He stared at the wall behind me, and I could feel the return of all kinds of tension. Okay, really. He needed to lighten up. I threw up my hands. "Ease up, Brennan! I am teasing you. No need to go to Defcon one when I do. I mean really," I smiled as he finally deigned to meet my eyes. "I can clearly see that you have no wings."

He rolled his eyes. "Do you laugh at everything?"

"Do you laugh at anything?"

He glared, and then sighed. "No, I don't laugh at much."

"That's pretty sad, Brennan."

"Why is it sad? Life is not often amusing." He looked down as he spoke.

"No, it's not. But that doesn't mean it's not amazing, Brennan." I stared at him. How could he not see that?

"You think that, even with all that you have dealt with?"

"What do you mean?"

"Your mother nearly died." He spoke as though this clinched things.

"But she didn't. If she had, I would have had to live with it."

Brennan leveled what I thought of as the Goblin King stink eye. "You were not so calm and matter-of-fact about that before we helped her."

I shrugged. "I had accepted it, although not really well, before I had a reason to hope. My crazy came from hoping."

Brennan didn't answer right away. "What would you have felt had you not met Drake and I? And Taranath? How did you handle knowing she would be gone?"

His expression suggested that maybe he asked about something more than my mom. I gave the question some thought. I couldn't explain why, but I knew I needed to get this right. What right meant, I didn't really know. "I didn't handle it for a while. When we came back to the States so I could go to college, we'd planned to live on the boat, and maybe I'd get an apartment. We hadn't gotten that far yet when Mom went to the doctor, and we found out about the cancer. That changed everything. And then," I remembered that trip where we laid it on the line, "We went out on the boat, and my mom said that she was pissed about how things had happened, but she wanted Dad and I to keep living after she was gone." I smiled at the memory of her wanting the *Not Dead Yet* tee shirt.

I glanced over.

"That's it? A trip out on a boat and you accepted it?"

I rolled my eyes. "No, that wasn't it. We talked, you know, communicated? Shared feelings? Opened up about how we all felt?"

He just looked at me.

I threw up my hands. "Don't you communicate, or talk with someone about how you really feel? Drake, maybe?"

He frowned. "What is there to talk about? How I feel generally doesn't make a difference in how things need to be addressed."

Brennan

Brennan couldn't make sense of Iris. It astounded him that so much of what she did seemed led by how she felt. That she placed so much importance on feelings. No wonder humans only lived to be one hundred years or less. Feelings could kill. Emotion, the kind that Iris had no problems with, did nothing other than make things messy. If everyone lived through it.

"What do you mean, Brennan? Are you saying you never take into account the way you feel about something when making a decision?"

"What is there to feel, Iris? You make a decision based on what is the best choice for you, your people. Those around you that you care about."

"You didn't answer me before. Don't you talk to anyone? Not even Drake?"

He thought about how Drake had confronted him on the castle walk, and how Drake forced him to think on things he'd rather not.

"Drake talks. I listen," He admitted grudgingly.

"You're lucky to have him," she sat back in her chair.

Brennan could agree with that. "I am. He's the most loyal of all those around me. That's why," He took advantage of the fact that she didn't seem combative as she had previously, "You will need to forgive him for threatening you. It was not personal, other than his concern for me."

She appeared to consider his words. Brennan found that he liked watching even something as mundane as her thinking. What was wrong with him? Everything she did had grace and charm for him. It made him feel good that she sat with him and seemed to enjoy his company.

"I'll think about it. How forgiving are you to people who put a knife to your throat?"

The expression on her face made him laugh. She glared, which made him laugh more. He calmed himself and said, "Point well taken. I'm very unforgiving. But those who have threatened me actually wanted to hurt me. Drake wanted to protect me, not hurt you. Intent matters."

"Humph," she said, frowning, "That's your opinion."

Why did her frown look so charming? He didn't want to look away. She enthralled him.

Enthralled him? The idea sat poorly with him. He couldn't afford to allow someone—anyone—to sidetrack him like this.

He stood. "Food will be here shortly. Please don't wait for me. I need to go and see Drake."

"But you said you'd stay with me!"

Brennan had to work to ignore the tone in her voice. She wanted to be with him. What he really wanted to do was sit back down and not leave for days.

"I'll be back when I can."

CHAPTER EIGHTEEN

Iris

What the hell? He just left? The door closed behind him. So yes, he just left.

I knew my mouth hung open. When he'd been sitting with me, talking like a normal guy, I felt warm. Comfortable. Safe. Cared for.

Just as I started to relax, and feel good, he kicked that feeling directly in the damn shin and rolled right on out.

I got up, pacing around the room. Why did he run from me? Because that is exactly what his leaving was. Running from me. Big damn baby.

Damn. My vocabulary was stuck. It was Brennan's fault. Damn man.

I walked to the window, crossing my arms around myself into a hug as I looked out over the castle grounds. Lawn? Garden? I didn't know what to call it. It looked like a combination of all the above. I could see a rose garden off to one side. From my previous time in this room, I knew that this window didn't open. I felt the urge to be outside, to let fresh air and sun clear my head.

I whirled around as the door opened. Maybe he'd decided to not be such a jerk.

I felt my shoulders sag as I saw Glynan, the little goblin woman I'd seen before, come in with a tray of food. She brought it over to a table, smiling at me as she set it down.

"Majesty says to please eat, and not wait for him."

"No joke," I muttered. "Heaven forbid he spend any more time with me."

"Sorry, miss?"

I shook my head as I walked to the tray. "Nothing. Thank you, Glynan. Oh, I am so glad you brought the bread and honey again!"

The smile broadened. "I'll tell Cook that you like it. She'll be pleased. This is fresh this morning."

I spread the honey on the bread and took a huge bite. "It's delicious," I got out. "Cook is amazing."

"Thank you, miss." She turned to leave.

"Wait!"

She stopped and I could tell she was surprised.

"How do I let someone know if I need something?"

"You just ask, miss."

"Like I ring a bell, or something?"

Glynan nodded. "Over there," She pointed at the doorway, "Next to the door. See the bell? Give it a jingle, and one of us will come directly."

Wow. Right out of *Gone With The Wind*. "Okay. Can I ask you if I can go outside after I eat?"

I could see the wrinkles form in her forehead with her frown. "I'm not sure, miss. You'd need to ask Majesty about it."

I waved a hand. "He said to make myself at home." Not quite what he said, but hey, he left. I was on my own.

"Where did you want to go?"

I pointed towards the window. "Into the rose garden I saw out there."

The wrinkles on her forehead eased. "Oh, that's the Queen's Garden. That's close to the castle. I think that would be okay. I'll need to get someone to go with you. Eat, miss, and we'll see what we can do. You're here for a bit, Majesty says."

I nodded, but I wondered what exactly Brennan had told the goblins. I'd love to have been a fly on the wall for that conversation. "I am, I guess. When can I go outside?"

"Well, I don't know, miss. I'll check with Majesty. Don't you worry none about it. Eat."

With that, she hurried out the door.

These goblins, from the king on down, were really good at getting out of Dodge when they didn't want to answer any questions.

***

Three days. Three days. It had been three days since Brennan had abruptly walked out of the lounge, leaving me to wonder what had happened.

I still wondered what had happened but he made it clear that something had happened. Whatever it was, it wasn't in my favor.

I'd seen Drake, and Glynan, and Taranath, but no Brennan. He practiced some serious avoidance. So much for keeping me with him, and safe. His idea of keeping me safe meant that Drake followed me everywhere other than the bathroom.

That didn't make me or Drake very happy.

Midday the day after I'd come back to Fae, where I sulked around my rooms—Brennan had given me a wonderful suite of rooms—and Drake lurked in the corners, I finally got mad, and turned on Drake.

"Since we're apparently stuck together, we might as well talk."

"There is nothing to say. You're here to be kept safe. I am doing the duty that my king commands, and keeping you safe." He stared over my head.

What had happened to the joking Drake of before? Did he still think I had something to do with Brennan being hurt? God. These guys.

"Well thank you ever so much for doing your duty. But it's going to continue to suck for us both if we don't clear the air. So go. Tell me why you're so mad at me still. Because I don't get it."

At my words, his gaze met mine. Ouch. Maybe I should have let him be a statue still. His eyes blazed hot and angry.

"I nearly lost my king, my brother. You are in the wrong place at the worst time, and it's happened more than once. I haven't seen anything that shows me you're not a threat to him."

"If I was a threat, wouldn't I tried to have get the hell out of this prison by now?"

"It's only been a day."

"It may as well be forever. If Brennan wants you to follow me like an angry pit bull, fine. I haven't tried to hurt him at all. I helped heal him. But if you don't want to accept that, fine. Can we get out of here for a while?"

His eyes narrowed. "Where is it you want to go?"

"I'd like to go sit outside. I'm dying, cooped up in here. I saw a garden, Glynan called it the Queen's Garden—can I go there?"

"Such a specific place."

"It's all I saw from Brennan's rooms."

He turned away from me, hands behind his back. I could tell he considered my request seriously. Even if he hated me, at least he listened. Maybe I could get him to listen a little more.

He faced me once more. "Very well. We will go outside. You will not leave the Queen's Garden, and you will come inside when I say you need to."

I put my hands on my hips. "Am I a prisoner here? Because it's starting to sound like it. That wasn't the deal."

"Do you wish to go outside or not?"

I hated to give in. "Yes," I got out.

"Then you will follow directions. You'll need to change."

Whatever I'd expected, that wasn't it. "What?"

"You're in your clothing from the Human Realm. You need to look fae. I'll have some clothing sent up. I don't want you to look any different. It will keep you safe. That is my concern, after all," He bowed, a mocking tone in his voice.

It took all my self-restraint not to yell at him. "That would be great. I appreciate your thoughtfulness."

His eyes narrowed again. I guess he'd not expected that from me. Good. *I will kill you with kindness.*

With that, he excused himself, and rustled me up some ladies' clothing.

The next morning after I ate, we went outside. I plopped myself on one of the benches and soaked up the sun. It felt like forever since I'd been outside. To someone who'd spent their life outside, the last two days had been difficult.

Drake hung around the edge of the garden, like the proverbial fly in the ointment. The garden was lovely. Roses of all shades bloomed, and they were larger than what I was used to seeing. The smell of them nearly overwhelmed me. I could hear birds in the distance, and after sitting a while, it sounded like bees were working in the flowers. I couldn't see them, but the hum of something was persistent in the background.

We stayed like that, me sitting, Drake lurking, for nearly an hour before I broke down.

"Come and sit down, please. You're like the specter at the feast."

"What does that mean?"

"It means you're hanging around the edge here, glaring and whatever, and ruining the day. Sit down. Yell at me if you want. I hate someone being angry at me and not just getting it out in the open about why they're angry. If I'm going to be here, I don't want to be fighting with you at all times."

"You're so sure you're going to be here for a while?"

But he'd come closer.

"Even if I'm not, is this pleasant? Because it's sure not fun for me."

Shading my eyes, I looked up at him. He still had his suspicious face on. I really hoped this worked, because my patience with him had worn thin.

He sighed. "Very well," And sat down on a bench across from me. "How are you feeling?"

"What do you mean?"

"Taranath said that the last time you were here, you were fading. Do you feel that way still?"

I thought about it. "I don't feel like running a marathon, but I don't feel like all I want to do is lay on a couch, either. That's how I felt before. I feel," I stopped. "It feels like when you've been sick, and you're finally getting better. Do you know what I mean?"

He shook his head. "I haven't been sick in a long time."

"Oh. Probably a fae thing, right? Never mind," I waved a hand. "How old are you, Drake?"

He looked surprised. "Brennan and I are about the same age. Mother and Father were not sure exactly how I was when I came here, but they guessed three years younger than Brennan."

"And how old is that?"

"Six hundred seventy-one."

I nearly fell off the bench. When I pulled myself back up, I could see that Drake sort of smiled. "What? How old? Is that you or Brennan?"

"Me. Brennan is six hundred and seventy-four."

I opened my mouth, then closed it. What do you say to that? "Um. Well, how do you live so long?"

He shrugged. "We just do. I don't know, really. Taranath could probably tell you."

"You're not treating me like a criminal. Does this mean you believe I'm not a threat?"

He leaned back, sighing as he did. "I don't know, Iris. I like you. I think you're good for Brennan." He held up a hand to forestall the question I started to ask. "I won't say anything more. It's not my place. But you're in the wrong place twice in a row, twice when Brennan was in great danger. I can't ignore that."

This was not going to be easy. "Did you ever think maybe I was supposed to be there?"

"Eh?"

"I mean, maybe I was supposed to meet you in the bathroom. And you can doubt me if you want, but talk to my grandmother and my parents. I felt it when Brennan got hurt. Like I'd been hit in the chest myself. Before that, I had no idea what was going on here. It scared the crap out of me, so much that I had to come back, even though coming back scared me too."

His head cocked, Drake studied me. "Do you give me your word that you speak the truth?"

I nodded. "I can't give you anything else."

I don't know what exactly it was that I said, but from that moment on, Drake relaxed with me.

Two days after that conversation, we were in the garden again.

"Drake?"

"Yes?"

"Where is Brennan, and why haven't I seen him in three days?"

Three days. It felt like an eternity.

He busied himself with looking at a rose. "I don't know, Iris. You'll need to ask Brennan that."

I got up, forcing him to look at me. "I would, if I ever saw him! I haven't seen him since the first night I got here, after he was hurt! He's avoiding me, the big baby!"

Drake looked shocked that I would refer to Brennan as such, but to hell with it. I didn't do well with this sit around, and play the nice lady part. Although the dress was nice. I loved fae clothing. Comfortable, kind of renfest-like, but comfortable.

"Why would you say that, Iris?"

"We had a pretty open conversation, and then apparently I asked too deep of a question for his royal highness and he stomped out. And sent you to hover over me." I scowled. "He knew you were mad at me. He knew, and still told you to sit on me."

"I have not sat on you."

"Never mind. That's not the point! The point is that he's avoiding me! If he's not going to talk to me or spend any time with me, he might as well send me home. I'd rather be with my parents if I can't..." I stopped. I didn't want to say that.

But Drake caught my slip up. "If you can't what?" He asked quietly.

"It doesn't matter. If I'm nothing more than a prisoner, I need to go home." I crossed my arms, walking away from him.

Drake didn't speak for a bit. Neither did I. What else was there to say?

"I'll go talk to him."

I whirled to face Drake. "You will? Thank you!"

"Don't thank me at this moment. I may not be successful and you may find yourself here tomorrow. But I shall speak with him, and convey your concerns."

"When?"

He stared at me, at my face that I knew had a hopeful expression, and sighed. "Oh, all right. I'll go find him now."

"Great! I'll—"

"You'll stay right here. I'll get one of the goblins to sit with you. I don't want to leave you alone."

"But—"

"Sit. Wait for someone to come and sit with you. That's my offer, or I don't speak with Brennan."

I glared. He returned my glare in full measure.

"Oh, all right. Go find my next sitter."

He grinned at me, pointing at the bench behind me.

I walked towards it, and before I sat down, looked over my shoulder to see him loping off to the castle.

I hoped he could talk some sense into Brennan.

Brennan

He watched as Drake left Iris in the garden. His anger flared like a fire. What was he thinking, leaving her alone? He'd told Drake to stay with her at all times.

Iris looked over her shoulder, and Brennan took a step back. The picture in front of him was the last thing he'd seen before everything had faded when Scarface attacked him. Iris, in fae clothing, looking over her shoulder. From this vantage point, it was almost as though she looked at him. He felt struck at seeing her as he'd seen her in his vision.

What did it mean? That he'd seen Iris as she was now? In his kingdom, dressed as fae, and happy.

With Drake.

The hot, sudden blast of jealousy that engulfed him entirely took him completely off guard.

Drake would never—he knew how Brennan felt—

A flash of something out of place in the garden caught his eye and stopped the building rage he felt.

He stepped closer to the window, looking for whatever it was.

There was Iris. Her dress and gown were a pale green. Pale like the spring, and suited her. He'd seen something dark.

Iris turned from where he could see her face, and he saw that she spoke to someone. A goblin, although he couldn't tell who it was. He squinted. Drake must have sent the goblin to Iris as he felt he needed to leave. Brennan knew he'd have words with Drake over that. Iris had been alone.

The goblin came closer to Iris, and Brennan watched as he—for it was a male—held out a tray he carried with a cup. He could see Iris smile at the goblin and reach for the cup. As she took it, the goblin bowed, and smiled up at her.

It was not the smile of someone happy to help her, but one of gleeful anticipation.

He watched as Iris lifted the cup to her lips and—

"No!" He cried from the window, already in motion. He pulled a stone from his pouch and raced out of the room to the door that led to the rose garden. He had to hurry. Only seconds before Iris drank and then—

He burst from the castle and ran along the path, stone in hand and raised waiting for only a glimpse of the goblin who'd brought her the drink. As he approached the center of the Queen's Garden where he'd last seen Iris, he saw that the goblin was no longer there, and he couldn't see Iris.

"Iris!" He shouted, running faster. He reached the center and nearly stepped onto Iris, lying in a crumpled heap next to a bench.

"Iris! Drake! *Drake!*"

Still clutching the stone, Brennan knelt and gathered Iris to him, cradling her in his arms as he lifted her and turned back to the castle.

"Brennan! What happened?" Drake nearly ran into him.

"You tell me, Drake! Why was Iris alone?" Brennan didn't break stride and Drake hurried to keep up with him.

"Taranath! Find the Court Mage now!" He shouted at several goblins who'd poked their heads out of the door. "And out of the way! I must get the lady to Taranath!"

Goblins scurried as he and Drake made their way through the corridor, heading for the mage's rooms.

"Iris wasn't alone," Drake said beside him as he kept up with Brennan's hurried pace "I sent Glynan out to her."

"Glynan did not go to her. A goblin I didn't recognize came out bearing a tray—"

"I sent Glynan with a cool drink for Iris."

"The goblin gave her the drink, and she collapsed." Brennan finally looked over at Drake. Drake's face showed his anguish plainly. "Find Glynan. Now."

With a nod, Drake reversed his direction, leaving Brennan to continue on to Taranath.

He burst through the mage's door. "Taranath! I need you!"

Taranath came gliding through from his study. "I am here, Your Majesty. What has happened?"

"I am guessing Iris has been poisoned," Brennan walked over to Taranath's examining table where he'd been only a few days prior.

He laid Iris down gently, and Taranath immediately moved over her, murmuring quietly. Brennan stepped back, knowing that Taranath worked best without anyone hovering.

It took all his strength, however, not to do something, anything. He couldn't look at Iris, lifeless and still.

"It is poison, but..."

"What?" Brennan snapped.

"This is interesting," Taranath said, leaning over Iris.

"What?" Brennan thought he'd go mad, waiting for the man to tell him what the poison was.

"They, whomever they are, have used a poison found in the Human Realm. It has been used to end life, and..."

"Yes?" Brennan forced himself to level his anger until Iris was out of danger. If she could be brought out of danger.

"Were she not part fae, she would have died, instantly." Taranath looked up at Brennan. "She was targeted with a poison deadly to humans. Her fae side saved her."

"She will live?"

Taranath nodded. "She will. But I must tend to her. Go, Your Majesty. Find the one who has done this. I need to be sure of what has been used on her."

Brennan moved closer to Iris, taking in how still and pale she was. Not the Iris of flashing eyes and constant motion. Not his Iris. His hand moved on its own and stroked her cheek, reveling in being able to touch her.

"Your Majesty, we need to find the poison," Taranath's gentle voice broke into this thoughts.

"Of course," Brennan drew himself up and whirled from the room.

He'd find the goblin and wring the truth from him if need be.

Iris

I struggled against...something. I didn't know what it was, couldn't tell. Everything was too dark, too heavy. I let myself slide into what seemed easiest. Let it all go.

Just as I began to relax, to stop fighting so hard for what, I didn't know, something pierced the darkness. I couldn't shut it out.

Gradually, light became visible to me, and I had to open my eyes.

The thing that had dragged me from my dark peace was Brennan. He was yelling. Holy hell, could he shout.

"Please..." I started. My voice came out in a hoarse whisper.

All conversation, even King Yelly Pants, stopped. I clutched at my head. Brennan also knew how to give a girl a headache.

"Iris!" He came to me and took my hand. "You're awake!"

"Did I have a choice? Do you realize how loud you are?" I sounded like a years-long chain smoker. God, what happened to me?

He stepped back at my words, surprise and then anger showing on his face. "Do I realize how loud I am? Do you realize how close you came to dying? Why would you take a drink from a goblin you didn't know?"

So much for being nice to invalids. I held my head with both hands now. "I don't know most of the goblins. I thought he was someone sent from the kitchens."

"Brennan—" Drake tried to intercede.

"No, Drake! I'll not hear it! You left her alone! I'm extremely displeased with you as well! I told you specifically Iris was never to be alone! For this very reason!"

He was close enough to me for me to grab his arm, and I did. He jumped at the touch of my hand on him. "Drake didn't mean for me to be hurt. It was an accident."

"This was no accident! This was a deliberate attempt on your life! One short moment of carelessness," He glared at Drake, whom, I was glad to see, stared back defiantly, "And you nearly died. The poison used would have killed you but for your fae side."

I laughed a little, which made Brennan's eyes nearly fall out of his head. "Guess it doesn't suck to only be part human."

"Your fae side barely saved you, Iris!"

"God, could you shout any louder?" I glared at him.

Brennan whipped around, forcing me to let go of him and turning his anger on Drake and Taranath. "Would you please leave us for a moment?"

Neither of them looked all that thrilled with his request, but, I guess since he's the king, they both shuffled from the room. Drake left last, closing the door behind him as he gave Brennan major stink eye. There was a lot of that going around here.

The two of them leaving meant that I got to be the focus of King Yelly Pants.

"You need to go back to the Human Realm! I cannot—" He turned away, and I saw his hands come up through his hair.

"I don't want to leave." I spoke quietly. I couldn't speak any louder. My head might fall off and bounce around the room. This was worse than when I snuck the Black Seal rum from the liquor locker on *Sorcha* and drank too much when I was sixteen. I had a terrible hangover and my parents made me get up at sunrise and do chores all morning, not caring that I threw up over the side four times.

He faced me once more. "You have to leave!" He shouted. "What will it take for you to understand you are not safe here? I can't protect you! Someone got to you in the heart of my castle, in my home! I can't keep you safe, Iris! Why can't you understand that?"

At that, half the glass bottles in the room shattered. It made me jump. Taranath was certainly going to be the loser from this whole affair. It was his potions and whatnot that had just exploded.

"Have you no sense of self-preservation?"

"I do."

He rolled his eyes at me. God, these fae were worse than girls. Lots of eye rolling.

"I do. But I don't want to leave Fae. I don't want to leave you, Brennan."

"You have to leave, Iris! If you don't," His voice dropped, and I could hear the anguish. A few more bottles shattered. "You have to go! Can you not see that I am close to hurting you? If someone else doesn't kill you, I will!"

I ignored them, and sat up from the pillows I was propped up on. I stretched out my hand to him. "Brennan." This was more than me being hurt. The anguish in his voice deepened to a knife of pain that cut me. I couldn't imagine what it did to him.

He looked at my hand, and then to my face. Slowly, as though moving through water, he took several steps towards me. Glass crunched under his feet. He took my hand carefully, as though I were a bomb that could go off at any moment.

"Anything could happen, Brennan. Anything at all. But is it worth it to see if this," I squeezed his hand, and covered it with my other hand, "Is something worth taking a risk for?"

"Not if you die before we...not if I hurt..." He stopped and looked away. I could see the struggle on his face.

"Brennan. I want to stay. With you."

His eyes met mine, and I saw, behind the anger, the fear. In the fear, I could tell he had the same spark of hope that I did. I looked at him, and gave him my hope. And my trust.

"I don't want to kill you, too, Iris," He spoke softly, no longer yelling.

Thank god.

I tugged on his hand, pulling him closer, and he let me. Then he stopped, and his free hand reached out, stroking my cheek. Before I could think any further, his hand slid behind my head and yanked me towards him.

I caught a glimpse of his face and his eyes were hot and ferocious.

Then he kissed me.

I'd kissed a few boys. Mostly as we traveled, never anything serious, or even where I'd see the boy again. Even if they'd been memorable, I didn't think anything in this realm or any other could measure up.

I could *feel* Brennan. His hope, his exhilaration at kissing me, *claiming* me. For himself. As his. He offered himself to me in that kiss.

I took it. I took him, and his crazy, bottle-exploding temper, and Yelly Pants tendencies, and I gave him all that back. And more.

He pulled me tight to him as I wound my arms around his neck, kissing him as my body went up in flames, and then flamed even hotter.

I'd never known that kissing someone could feel this way.

The door banged open and Brennan and I jumped so high that we nearly hit the ceiling.

Glynan burst in, her eyes wide.

"I asked that we not be disturbed!" Brennan snapped.

"I am sorry, Majesty, but the Lady Ailla is here! With her father! They wouldn't take no for an answer! They're on the way from the great hall now!"

Brennan

What on earth did Ailla mean, coming back again? After finding out that the old king's widow had lived in the Dragon Court for all these years and raised her children there, Brennan's suspicions were at an all-time high.

"Stall them. Now."

Glynan hurried from the room

Brennan rose, calling out for Drake silently as he did so. No time to send a goblin for him. "Iris, it will be best if you are not visible during their visit. I can't predict what they'll say, or why they felt they needed to come here in this hasty manner. Come here, and I'll take you back to the lounge. I don't want you far away from me." He gave her a look that made her blush.

She should be blushing. He felt that he'd fallen into a fire pit with no way out. Ailla could not have picked a worse time. Not to mention he really didn't want to think about his fiancée at all.

He scooped Iris into his arms, and felt the same thrill he'd felt kissing her when she wrapped her arms around him. *She must be able to see his mind,* he thought as she twined her arms around his neck and snuggled her head into his shoulder to gaze at him.

"Will you tell me what happens?" She had the look of a child being tossed out.

He grinned, although he felt no joy. "I shall do better. Since you are involved in this, I'll show you where you may listen. Remembering, however, that you might not care for what you hear."

Color bloomed in her cheeks, but her gaze stayed steady on him. "I understand."

"Then come." The fact that he needed to deal with a betrothal lay between them, on the ashes of what they'd just shared.

He strode out of Taranath's rooms, taking a back corridor normally used by the goblin servants. He didn't want to run into Ailla or her father, Eilor. Too many explanations. He made it back to his chambers and came into his bedchamber. He walked through the study, bringing Iris into the lounge. "Here. You'll be able to hear from this spot. I don't know whether you'll be able to see much, but as it will only be Ailla and her father Eilor, and Drake, and I, you'll be able to keep all parties straight."

He could feel Drake. The door in the study burst open.

"Bren?" Drake called out.

"Stay here. Stay silent." He touched Iris's cheek, and then moved quickly from the lounge, closing the door behind him.

"What is it? Where is Iris?"

"Safely hidden. Ailla and her father are here."

"What?" Drake had time to get out before the door from the corridor opened again. Glynan came in, curtsying as she did so.

"Majesty, his Majesty, the Dragon King and Lady Ailla."

She stepped backwards as the king and Ailla came into the room. Once they were in, Glynan carefully closed the door.

No one spoke. Brennan looked carefully at their faces. Nothing. They were skilled at hiding emotions.

"To what do I owe the honor of your visit?" He asked. "Will you be seated? Lord Drake and I were sitting down to order some refreshment. You are welcome to join us."

Drake moved closer to him. The air vibrated with a tension that Brennan couldn't decipher.

Then he saw it.

Ailla's nostrils flared.

"Why is she here?"

Brennan cleared his mind, allowing no thoughts of anything to cross it. "What are you talking about, Ailla?" He sat down in the chair he'd been sitting in before. Drake didn't sit, but moved to stand next to him.

Guarding him.

Alarming that Drake, too, felt the danger present.

"Word reached us that you are once again harboring a human," Eilor said. His voice had a deep, basso rumble.

Anytime he heard Eilor speak, Brennan wondered how much dragon was in the fae of that court.

"Harboring a human? As though it's a crime?" He kept his voice light, in contrast.

"You know it's not done." Ailla's eyes flashed at him.

"Well, there seem to be a great many things happening that aren't done. Such as not being truthful about members of your court." He kept his eyes on the table in front of him. He knew Drake watched the pair like a hawk on the hunt.

"What do you mean?" Ailla challenged.

"Why did you never tell me the old king's widow resided in your court? That she had a daughter from the old king? Or sons from a man in your court? Did you not think I might find such information interesting, at the very least?"

He glanced up as he spoke. Eilor kept his countenance, but Ailla flushed.

Ah ha, he thought. They had kept it hidden. Before this moment, he hadn't wanted to believe it was deliberate, in spite of his fears.

"I don't see why that matters. You are the rightful king, and have been for many years."

So smooth, Eilor. But I see through you. "It matters when the daughter of the former king and her lover attack me." Brennan saw no need for further niceties.

He watched carefully.

Ailla and her father both affected expressions of shock, but a moment later than if they had truly been surprised.

"I am grieved to hear that you have been attacked." Eilor said.

"Oh, I've been attacked more than once, as I am sure your daughter has informed you. Or perhaps you already knew?"

He felt Drake start next to him. He knew Drake didn't believe both father and daughter knew, and he also knew that such directness normally would not be the method he chose. Fae tended to subtler negotiations.

"You dare," breathed Ailla. "Having the human here has allowed you to forget all manners."

Back to Iris again. Why did Iris bother her so much?

You know why, his head answered. For the same reason it bothered him as well.

"The human has nothing to do with this. Experiencing an attack from someone with ties to your court twice in a span of days does. I do not wish to navigate through clever evasions. Why did you not tell me of this before?"

For the first time, Brennan saw a flicker in Eilor's eyes.

"I did not think it relevant."

"Did not think it relevant?" Brennan repeated slowly. "Were you aware of the negative feelings that the widow or her daughter might have harbored? The daughter, at least, definitely has them."

Ailla and Eilor glanced at one another. No more than half a second, but Brennan saw it. His heart sank. While he didn't love Ailla, he also didn't want to know that she took part in this...whatever it was.

"I allowed her to marry and retire to the Dwarf Realm. I've heard nothing of her since," Eilor rumbled.

"Well, lack of news doesn't mean lack of reason for concern. I am now very concerned." He allowed anger to creep in.

"Had you sent the human back, none of this would have happened!" Ailla burst out. "She has ruined everything!"

Silence greeted her words. Brennan almost wanted to shake his head to clear it, to be sure of what she'd said. Slowly, choosing his words carefully, because he couldn't fathom why Ailla had fixated on Iris, unless she knew somehow of his feelings, he said, "I don't see how having the human here ruins anything. She saved my life. I should think you grateful to someone, even a human," He looked up to see Ailla's face, "Who saved the life of your betrothed."

"Oh, please stop with your benevolent act!" Ailla shouted. "If you hadn't kept the stupid girl here, we'd be on the way to being married, and I would..." she stopped, realizing that her anger had led her to speak more freely than perhaps she wished to.

Eilor wouldn't look at his daughter, and Drake, next to him, took a step forward.

"My lady Ailla, I am sure you don't mean..." his voice trailed off as Ailla's eyes blazed even more brightly.

Brennan was startled as he looked up at Drake. There seemed to be almost a note of pleading in Drake's tone.

"I mean everything I say! Brennan, I tell you this now. You will send the human home and be done with meddling in that realm. Or I shall end our engagement!"

Fine! Brennan wanted to retort. He knew he needed to keep silent, if but for just a moment.

"Ailla, no need for haste," Eilor tried to calm her.

"No, Father, this has gone on long enough. Once, I could overlook. But to bring her back, and keep her here—"

How does she know that? I barely made the decision! Brennan thought. She could not be jealous. She didn't care for him in any romantic way. No more than he cared for her. He had no doubts of that. What drove this hatred of Iris?

"This goes too far. Well, Brennan, what say you?" Ailla faced him, hands on hips.

225

Brennan had laughed with Drake about seeing those of the Dragon Court lose their temper, but he now knew it to be no laughing matter. Ailla was most fearsome.

"I will be ordered by none, Ailla. Particularly not my intended who has been plotting against me." He made his words cold.

Ailla flushed more. "Then on your head be it, Brennan. You and your pathetic human! Remember that you brought this on yourself!" She whirled around and yanked the door open, slamming it with a resounding crash into the wall, and stalked out.

Eilor looked at Brennan with an unreadable expression. "It did not need to come to this, Brennan. I will…" he looked after his daughter. With another look to Brennan, and Drake, he left the room without another word.

Brennan knew Eilor lied. That he knew it would come to this, and while not pleased, Eilor was not surprised. The entire visit had the sense of something planned. Only Ailla's anger felt real, and Brennan thought it probably was. It made no sense, because her hatred of Iris bordered on irrational. Regardless, it was there, and he needed to be aware of it. Ailla would hurt Iris if she could. To avenge herself on Brennan, and because she wanted to hurt Iris. One more thing to worry over. Worse that his suspicions were correct, and there was some plot afoot. But what?

Brennan glanced at Drake again. Something shifted in his brother's face, and Brennan saw such a private, heartbroken expression that he lost whatever he'd been about to say.

"Brother?" He asked quietly.

As though a door closed, Drake's expression changed and he turned to Brennan. "I cannot believe they have been at work against us." The stern look brooked no further discussion.

"I feared it, but I didn't want to believe it." He looked down, the shock of it still reverberating.

"Iris!" He leapt up and threw open the lounge door.

She jumped back from the peephole in the corner.
He could see shock on her face as well.

"Well, guess that's one marriage shot to hell," she said.

Iris

I couldn't believe it. In an instant, Brennan no longer had a fiancée. I should be sad for him, but holy hell, she was one wicked bitch. I remembered his mother mentioning it at some point but I hadn't really thought of it. I ought to be mad at him. Kissing me like that while engaged. Then I thought about the fiancée. I didn't feel all that bad.

I could not be sad. Elation that he no longer had an obligation, and to such a nasty piece of work, raced through me.

What was that bit at the end, though? Drake sounded like someone had ripped out his heart and stomped on it. I wondered if Brennan even knew. Or the evil, traitorous bitch that had tried to hurt Brennan.

"Are you all right?" He asked, coming to kneel next to me.

"I'm fine. She's scary, your girl."

"My girl, as you say, no longer."

I dropped my voice. "I think someone is worse off than you are, though." I jerked my head towards the other room.

Brennan looked over his shoulder, and then comprehension showed. "You noted that?"

"How could you miss it?"

"I'd never seen such from him before."

"What?" How could he be so oblivious? "Is Drake that good at hiding his feelings? I don't get that impression, but I could be wrong. Short acquaintance and all."

At that moment, Drake strode in. One look at his face told me all I needed to know. I shook my head a little at Brennan, frowning as I did so. He got that, at least.

"Is she all right?"

I couldn't tell what he thought as he looked down at me and Brennan kneeling next to me. Maybe that I wasn't worth the loss of Ailla?

Who'd want such a scheming witch?

Drake, apparently.

I had to give him credit. He held it together.

Brennan took my hand in both of his, contemplating it. Then he met my eyes.

"You need to go back, Iris."

I jumped up, dropping his hand. "What? No! You said I could stay! That it was my choice! I choose to stay! I'm not going back!" How did we get here from practically kissing each other's face of only a short time ago?

Brennan stood slowly, and I could see that he no longer was the man I'd been with before crazy Ailla burst in, raining on a lot of damn parades.

"You must. For whatever reason, Ailla has fixated on you as the reason for my behavior. Given her actions, I'd say that she has no room to cast aspersions anywhere, but I don't think we're dealing with her at her most rational."

Drake crossed his arms with a snort.

I could still see the pain on him, and in spite of all the crap he'd said and done, I felt for him. His brother engaged to the woman he loved, and then the woman turns out to be batshit crazy. Not exactly a great place to be.

"Brennan's right. And not just due to the fact I want to get rid of you."

Oh dear. The bitter fairy had taken up residence in Drake.

"She's out for vengeance." Drake's voice was flat.

Oh god. I hurt for him. I hoped Brennan could see what had happened here.

"I agree," Brennan took my hand. "I wanted you to stay so that we could..." he stopped. "It doesn't matter. You must be safe, Iris."

I yanked my hand away. "It damn well does matter! I'm not going."

Brennan glanced at Drake, who turned on his heel and left.

"Where is he going? What are you up to?" I shouted at Brennan.

"Iris, I don't want you to leave, but if you stay here and Ailla hurts you, I won't be able to withstand the guilt. Go back to your parents. Enjoy your mother." He gave me a half-assed smile.

"How can I when I have this whatever," I threw out my arms, "Hanging around? Unfinished business sucks!"

"Once I have addressed the threat, maybe..." He stopped, shook his head. Walked towards the window. "You need to go back, Iris. Anything else would be extreme folly on both our parts."

Drake appeared at the door. "I have Taranath."

"Summon Mother," Brennan didn't turn from the window, only clasped his hands behind his back. Drake disappeared.

What the hell? I strode over to Brennan. "What is this? This stoic, sacrificing crap? I don't want to go, Brennan!"

He gave me the sweetest smile I'd ever seen and walked towards Taranath. "I want to send her back with Mother to ensure that she makes it home safely."

Drake came back in carrying a mirror, of all things. He handed it to Brennan.

"Mother," Brennan spoke to the mirror.

No one spoke, and then, "What is it, Brennan?"

"I need you."

I knew I stood on the edge of anger and hysteria that once again, I was being ordered about to where I didn't want to be, but I felt the urge to giggle, and put my hand over my mouth. First fairy Xanax, now fae mail. That's what the mirror thing was. Fae mail.

I would have expected Nerida to protest or say something, but all I heard from the mirror—fae mail—was, "I will be there momentarily."

Brennan thrust the mirror at Drake, who disappeared again.

Brennan took my hand and stepped to the window again. He lifted my hand up to his chest and held it close. I could feel the tears starting.

This was it. There wasn't anything I could say. I could feel him saying goodbye.

No! No no no no!

Drake appeared once more, Nerida behind him.

"What is Iris doing here?" She sounded surprised, and not in the good kind of way. How could she not have known I'd been here for almost a week?

"Going home." Brennan's tone allowed for no questions.

Nerida looked at him, and I saw her come to some sort of decision.

"Very well. Why do you need me?"

"I want you to make sure that Iris gets home to her family."

Nerida studied her son. Nodded twice. "Very well. Come, Iris." She walked into the study, expecting me to follow her.

I brought his hand close to me. Forced him to look at me, and put everything I had into my face. If my words wouldn't sway him, maybe seeing what this would do to me could.

He held my gaze, and a thousand words came to my lips, things I wanted to say, share.

I said nothing.

Neither did he.

"Good-bye, Iris. Be well. Live."

He dropped my hand. Stepped away from me. That was it? An hour ago, I could have sworn he stood at the edge of a declaration and now, he was all, *Be well?*

Drake, of all the people, put his hand on my back and gently led me to the door. I looked over my shoulder. Brennan stood highlighted by the window. His hands behind his back as he watched us. His face unreadable.

I walked through the door. My heart breaking.

Drake led me through the study into a wide open room. Did these rooms never end? I couldn't tell what sort of room this was. I didn't care. I'd never see it again. What did it matter?

"Come, Iris," Nerida reached out a hand for me.

Slowly, reluctantly, I made to take her hand.

A flash of light before me made me stumble. Had Nerida opened the portal early? I wasn't ready!

I saw them, struggling, then he fell.

He fell!

"Brennan!" I screamed.

Wrenching myself around, I shoved my way past Drake, through the lounge, and past a surprised Taranath. I heard shouting behind me, but I couldn't stop. I would be too late if I didn't keep going, going as fast as possible.

As I'd seen moments before, a figure rose up behind him, where he'd turned and leaned his hands on the window. Arm raised, the figure crept closer.

I could make it. The figure, so intent on Brennan, didn't hear me.

Oh shit! I saw the arm come down. I wasn't going to make it!

I sprang off my toes, aiming for somewhere at Brennan's back.

As I launched myself, I saw the arm coming down, down.

Oh, god! Please let me get to him.

Down it came, larger and larger, until the arm loomed over me.

Then nothing.

Brennan...

My thought faded to darkness.

Lisa Manifold

CHAPTER NINETEEN

Brennan

He hunched over the window as he heard Iris's scream. He knew she had to be hurting if she felt even half as much as he did. He wished the sound of her voice away. He couldn't go to her. If he did, his resolve would be lost.

If he did—

He fell into the window as something launched onto his back.

A wild cry that sounded like his name cut off abruptly.

Drake next to him, shouting something. He couldn't understand.

He turned his head, rubbing it where he'd hit the window.

Drake cut the head off a troll not two feet from him

"What—"

"Get Iris!" Shouted Nerida, skidding into the room. "Taranath! Brennan! Get her! Quickly!"

Brennan turned and saw that the thing that launched into him wasn't a thing. It had been Iris, and she lay in a heap.

He looked her over, and saw it at the same time Nerida did.

She gasped.

Taranath bent to Iris.

"It is a *shim* blade."

Drake muttered a curse that Nerida normally would have reprimanded him for.

But she didn't say a word. Her hands were still clasped over her mouth, looking in horror at Iris, on the floor, the blade through her right shoulder.

"Take her to my rooms," Taranath stood.

No one moved.

"Brennan, she needs my help." The words were gentle and stirred Brennan to move.

"She saved your life," Nerida whispered.

"How did a troll with a *shim* blade gain entrance?" Drake looked around. "How could this happen?"

Brennan picked up Iris, trying to be careful of the blade. He jostled her, and she moaned, but her eyes didn't open. The ugly, distinctive, black-wrapped blade that let everyone know it was a deadly *shim* moved in her shoulder as he lifted her.

"Drake," he barely recognized his own voice. "Find out where the troll came from. Mother, you come with me."

Nerida followed quietly. Drake strode from the room, his anger swirling around him like a cloak. Brennan would normally pity anyone who Drake found to be involved, but not today. Not now. Not after this.

The trio hurried through the corridors, brushing past the goblins they saw, speaking to not one, not even one another.

Brennan couldn't believe she'd leapt in front of the knife. How had she known? Had she been one second later, he would have died. Instantly.

Shim blades were lethal to the fae. He glanced down. He could see that Iris still breathed, so the fact that she was not entirely fae must have kept her from instant death.

Taranath threw open the door and gestured to the table where Brennan himself had lain only a short time ago.

"Lay her on her stomach. I will try to remove the blade."

"How is it she lives?" Whispered Nerida.

"She is not full fae."

"This will kill her fae side," Brennan stated flatly.

"Not necessarily," Taranath's hands flew in his cupboard, pulling bottles down as he searched for something. "Her fae side did not allow her human side to die. We must hold out hope that the same will be true of her human side."

"Is that not cruel?" Nerida asked.

"Life always wishes to continue," Taranath said.

Brennan ignored them and sank down next to Iris.

He held her hand and willed her to keep breathing.

Iris

"For the last time, I am fine!" I threw a pillow at Brennan. "Let me get up, please! I've been in this bed for ages!"

"Not until Taranath says you may," He sat next to me on the bed. "I don't want to take any further risk with you, Iris. I can't face your parents."

"That was very well played. Very sneaky, and completely unfair." I crossed my arms, and glared at him.

"I know. It's all true, too. Makes my victory all that much sweeter."

I couldn't argue the Mom card.

Taranath had something that allowed me to live. He had thrown together something in the moment, given me a whopping dose, and hoped for the best.

His gamble paid off. He told me later that he felt certain my two sides would work together to save me, but that he'd never been so nervous in his long life.

Brennan and Nerida had gone to visit my parents while I lay in a sort of coma, recovering. Apparently, they'd even pulled out the big guns and called my grandmother.

Both Brennan and Nerida looked the worse for wear in telling me all this. I gathered that between my parents and Mara, they'd both had their asses chewed.

I would have given a lot to have seen that.

The upshot of it? I was watched like a hawk, barely able to go to the bathroom by myself. That's a lot of joy right there.

Finally, Taranath declared I had turned a corner and could officially be declared as on the mend.

Today my impatience bubbled over. I wanted to go and see my parents. They didn't come to me for fear of what would happen to them. As best as I could tell, it had been three weeks since I'd come here. Mara had remained steadfast in her determination to stay in her adopted world. Nerida confided in me that my dad did a little of his own ass chewing in Mara's direction over that.

I got the impression that Nerida thoroughly enjoyed seeing someone else on the receiving end.

Wisely, I kept silent in such observations.

But today, I'd had enough.

"Call him in. I'm tired of being carried everywhere." Even though Brennan did all the carrying himself and my entire body eagerly awaited those moments.

Brennan seemed somewhat removed. As though my being hurt had built a wall between us. I didn't like it. I feared it would lead us to the same place we'd been before I'd been hurt. Before he finally let his guard down. Before he kissed me and my world shifted forever.

Hell, no. I didn't get stabbed for nothing.

As it turned out, we didn't need to call for Taranath. He came in, his face closed. Behind him came Drake, then Nerida. With her stood a man I hadn't seen before.

"Father!" Brennan stood up and went to embrace the man.

I took the moment to study him. Brennan had gotten his dark hair from Nerida. His father had long, blond hair, sharp features, and piercing eyes. Unlike Brennan, his eyes were dark.

He walked towards where I lay in bed. "This is the young woman who saved my son not once, but twice?"

Brennan nodded. "Father, please meet Iris Mattingly. Iris, my father, Jharak, king of all the Fae Realm."

Jharak took my hand and leaned over, kissing it lightly. He looked up and smiled at me. I started as I realized his eyes weren't dark. One was brown and one blue. They looked dark from a distance.

Interesting.

I didn't have time to ponder his father's appearance because Drake spoke.

"Brennan, we found out who sent the troll."

Brennan came alert in a way that I thought of as battle-Brennan. "And?"

Drake looked to his parents.

The faces of all three people other than Brennan spelled bad, bad news.

"We found a note, down in the kitchens, in one of the back storerooms. It was pinned to the wall with this."

Drake held up a small knife, the sort a child would have. Gold, with faceted jewels on the hilt.

Brennan frowned. "That blade…" He looked at his mother, then his father.

"Here is the note." Drake handed it over.

Brennan scanned it, and I watched as his face darkened. Anger, pain, anger again…what the hell did it say?

"He's alive?" The growl in the question made the king and queen cringe.

Brennan

This had to be a nightmare. If he waited, he'd wake up, and it would all go away.

He shut his eyes. Opened them.

He still held the note. It hadn't disappeared, and his parents still stood before him, looking guilty.

"How can this be?" He glared at both of them.

"What is it?" Asked Iris

Angrily, Brennan shoved the note towards her.

She took it, then looked up at him. "You'll need to translate."

"What?" Brennan turned to her, lost in his thoughts.

"I can't read Fae, remember?"

"Oh, yes. Of course. It's not much, but it tells it all. It says, *I will be hidden no longer.*" He forced his voice to stay steady.

"Who is it from?" Her face, her lovely face, the picture of innocence. How he hated to shatter it.

Although it could be argued that the *shim* knife had already done so, but in spite of that, Iris retained the clear, bright countenance that he…he shook his head again. He couldn't go there. Look what had happened when he allowed his thoughts to go in that direction before. Iris nearly died.

"It's signed, *Cian.*

"Who is that?" She asked.

"My brother." Now he did glare at his parents again.

"But…" Iris looked at his parents, and then Drake, and finally back to Brennan. "The one who died? How is that possible?"

"He's not dead." Nerida spoke.

"Why did you allow me to believe him dead?" Brennan demanded.

"Because he might as well have been!" Jharak had evidently had enough of being castigated by his son. I saw where Brennan got his impatience from. Or maybe it was a king thing.

Brennan stood. "Might as well have been and dead are two different things! I have spent my entire life feeling that I killed my brother! That because I could not control my magic, I ended his life!"

"Oh, no, Brennan! You didn't! He fell into a state, a non-waking state!" Nerida reached for him, but Brennan side-stepped her.

Only Iris and Drake could be trusted. And he had to send Iris home.

"Because of me. I saw his funeral," Brennan whispered. He sat down again. The weight of this felt too much.

Iris took his hands in hers. Her touch soothed him.

"No, you saw us removing him to a place where he might heal."

"Obviously he did heal," Brennan, feeling calmer, was able to look at his parents. Iris had that effect on him.

"He disappeared." Nerida whispered. "We haven't heard anything of him for many years. The keep where he stayed burned. We had no notion of what happened to those who cared for him. We mourned him."

"You didn't investigate?" Drake couldn't keep the surprise from his question.

"Of course we did!" Jharak snapped. "I myself went and sifted through the ruins. Our son was not there. We could only assume he died in the fire."

Nerida hung her head and wept.

"Even then, you couldn't tell me?" Brennan couldn't move past the fact that he'd spent his entire life in fear of what might happen if he lost control. Of allowing no one close to him so as to keep those around him safe.

It had all been a lie.

"Do you realize what you have done to me?" He focused on the coverlet on Iris's bed. "How this has shaped my life? In every respect? I nearly married a woman who plotted against me in order to keep myself distant, my emotions under control."

Ailla and her father, after leaving the Goblin castle, had returned to the Dragon Realm and sealed the borders. The rumors and threats that flew through the realms had everyone on edge.

Brennan had been trying to find a way to deal with the fact that Ailla conspired against him while being careful of how he knew Drake felt.

He and Iris had talked about it, one of the many things they talked about while she lay in bed recovering, again, from an injury sustained on his behalf. She'd thrown a pillow at him then, too, he remembered. Called him blind and stupid.

"How could you not know your brother loved her?"

Brennan had no answer. He'd never even thought such a thing possible, and thus, had never seen it.

Iris had rolled her eyes and flopped back into the bed.

"Thanks to Iris, you did not," Jharak said, as though that settled it all.

"Yes, thanks to Iris. Not thanks to my parents, who owe me honesty. In this, at the very least, you owed me honesty. Since you denied me that, our realms are in chaos. War talk flows from every corner of every realm. The Dragon Realm keeps out all those not of the realm, and refuses all delegations, even yours! Was this secret worth all that? We won't even get into what you have done to me, to Drake!"

Brennan found he rose from the bed again, shouting. He focused on Nerida. "You knew, did you not?"

Brennan had never seen his mother shrink before a question, but she did now. "I..." she began.

"You knew?" He shouted, done with the lies and not wanting to give her an inch. "When you attempted to scry him, and you saw him? You suspected and didn't think I had a right to know?"

Taranath chose this moment to glide between them.

"Your Majesties, if I may. Perhaps it would be better for their Majesties to return to the High Castle and leave us to plan here on our own."

Jharak glared, but then sighed. "Taranath speaks sense, as always. We did not intend to hurt you or Drake," he said to Brennan. "Or Iris. I am sorry that we have done so." He stopped. Started to speak, and then stopped again. He turned, and left the room.

"I am so sorry, Brennan," Nerida whispered, reaching a hand out towards Brennan.

He ignored her, and after a moment she let her hand drop.

Then she, too walked from the room.

CHAPTER TWENTY

Iris

I continued to heal. As I healed, I watched Brennan suffer more and more. I didn't feel like I could say anything over the next week after his parents had left. His focus on them made him momentarily forget about shipping me home. I was in no hurry to remind him.

He brooded. A *lot*. I felt sorry for him at first, because who wouldn't? His parents had done a number on him.

And Drake. Who rolled around the castle looking equally broody and miserable.

I couldn't help Drake. Not directly. I had to help Brennan, who then could maybe help Drake.

We sat in his lounge, as we had been doing each night, with a roaring fire warming and lighting the small room. I pretended to read (there were actually books in English), and he worked. I put aside my book and marched over to him.

"All right. Enough is enough, pal."

"What?" He looked up from the chair where he sat, going over household accounts. Through all this, he still kept up with his responsibilities.

"I'm tired of watching you drag your ass around here. So your parents lied to you? You're not the only one. Maybe in this world, but not all of them. So your brother is a psycho? We all have family problems. Your ex, well, she's kind of your problem, but since she kicked you to the curb, just put her in the enemy column and be done with it. You have problems. So what? Everyone does. You've moped around long enough. What are you going to do about it?"

He looked up at me, trying to act like me throwing a hissy in front of him was no big deal.

"What do you mean?"

"I mean it's time you acted like the grown-up you are and took control of all this shit! Knock off the crap, Brennan!"

Brennan

He stared at her, all pretense of indifference gone. He couldn't help it. She looked like a living candle, her light hair flickering brightly in the shadows of the lounge. Her anger made her magnificent.

"What...what are you staring at?" Her voice didn't sound steady.

He knew she wondered if she'd gone too far. "You, Iris. I'm staring at you."

"Why?"

"I cannot..." Brennan got up from his chair and turned away, tearing his eyes from her. He knew he should not go any nearer to her. Bad enough that he insisted on carrying her everywhere as she healed. Even here, in his rooms, while he worked. That he made himself touch her every day. He couldn't stand the thought of anyone else doing it. It pained him to a degree he hadn't thought possible, touching her and not kissing her, not touching her as he wanted. But he couldn't.

She was young, and she had a life elsewhere. One that didn't include him. The thought made his heart tighten.

"It is neither right nor fair that I burden you with all that comes with me, Iris," Brennan said to the bookcases, unable to look at her. "It's bad enough that I've trapped you here. I brought you here initially for my own selfish concerns, and because of that, you very well may be stranded here." He'd wanted to send her home but

Taranath had insisted she stay. Brennan feared the longer she stayed the harder it would for her to get back home. To escape all that would come to pass.

He could hear her walking closer to him. He steeled himself not to touch her, not to bury himself in the fragrance that rose off of her, not to wrap his hands in her hair and pull her to him. Never to let her go. *I will be strong,* Brennan thought. Ever since she'd come to him after he'd been wounded, ignoring her and how he felt about her grew more difficult.

Her small hands touched him, cupping around his waist and snaking around to his front. He stiffened as she leaned into him, laying her head in the middle of his back. A secret part of him thrilled at her touch, but he pushed that part down. It had no place here.

"I don't want to be anywhere else, Brennan."

He didn't turn to her, or take her in his arms as he wanted to. He forced himself to keep his arms at his sides, and his body stiff. He couldn't afford to encourage her in any fashion. "You need to go home, Iris. Back to your home. The only reason you're here is due to my selfish action. I should have never—"

"You should have never taken me. Yeah, yeah, I know. But you did. And now, I'm changed. Forever."

Her words both thrilled and saddened him. "It wasn't your choice."

Now she pushed herself away from him. He had no option but to face her. Her face reddened, she'd crossed her arms. When he met her eyes, her scowl greeted him.

"It wasn't my choice initially, no. But—"

"There is nothing else, Iris! I cannot involve you in the coming war. Because it is coming. You will be a target."

Her eyes flashed. "Why? I'm not really human anymore. I was, but not anymore. You said it yourself! I'm getting stronger! I can be an asset to you, Brennan!"

"It's not an asset when I have to worry for you constantly!"

"Would you have worried for Ailla?" Her tone lost all hostility.

"Of course not. She has many skills…" he stopped. The trap became clear. He'd walked right in.

"Why am I different, Brennan? I'm not as old as she is," she frowned, which made him hold back a laugh, "but I'm skilled in my own way. My human origin allows me to do things fae can't do. You know that. Taranath confirmed it. So why," She pinned him with her gaze, "Am I different?"

"You are different. I can't be certain of what will happen. I don't worry with fae—"

"I *am* fae!"

"Because I don't want anything to happen to you! Because if something happens to you, I couldn't forgive myself!" His voice echoed around the room. Shouting did that. *And if something happened to you, I don't think I could control myself*, he thought. *This time, someone really would die.* "Because I can't be responsible for thinking I've killed someone else I…" he stopped. "I care for."

Iris's mouth formed an *O*, and then slowly, as though time stood still, the corners of her mouth turned up.

"You care for me?" Her voice didn't rise above a whisper. The sound of it sent a chill through him that went straight to his groin. He forced himself to ignore it.

"I do. You know that."

"I do not. You've never actually said it. I know that I care for you, Brennan. I love you."

He whirled around, exploding into movement, looking for escape and finding the small room hemmed him in. If he didn't stand still her words wouldn't land, and she wouldn't be trapped here.

"You can't love me, Iris." He didn't look at her, because he knew he'd see the hurt on her face, and his resolve would be lost. "You are young, very young, and you don't know what you feel. This is…it's…" he searched for the words all while his head and his heart screamed at him to be quiet. "It will pass." He couldn't believe he'd gotten the lie out."

"No, Brennan, it won't." She came up behind him, and placed her hand on his arm.

A thrill ran through him at her touch. It felt as though she had lightening in her hand. He looked down at her, so small, still so human. So fragile, so vulnerable. So easily broken.

As she had once before, Iris seemed to know his mind. "You didn't kill your brother. You're not going to hurt me."

"How do you know that? I could not live with myself if I hurt you, too." Everything he feared ran through his mind. With the trouble with the Dragon Realm, with Cian still at large and no clues as to how he'd gotten into the castle, Brennan worried constantly.

"I love you. I am not the same girl you dragged through the bathroom. I'm something else, something different. And I love you. I always will. Denying it won't change that fact."

"Iris, you have your whole life ahead of you. One free of conflict, one where being fae in the Human Realm will be to your benefit. You don't need to choose the chaos that is erupting here. I can't guarantee your safety—I can't guarantee anything!" Frustration made him run both hands through his hair, avoiding the soft hands still on his face

She stood on her toes, pulling his face towards her at the same time. "I don't care. I love you. I would rather live with you in chaos than live a peaceful life without you." She pulled him closer and kissed him.

Brennan felt his world explode. She loved him. She'd said it—not only once, but twice. *She loved him.*

This, right here, this kiss—this had been the reason for keeping away from her. He pulled back but she yanked him to her again and kissed him harder.

Iris

Why was he fighting this? I gave up trying to be sweet and loving, and kissed him like I wanted nothing more than to fall into him and never come up for air. I felt as though kissing him didn't bring him close enough to me.

More than that, I wanted him to stop being such an ass and stop fighting what everyone around us had seen for ages. I hadn't wanted to admit it because I was sure he didn't feel the same. How could he? The Goblin King and me, plain ol' Iris Mattingly. It made no sense. Then, he'd tried to send me away. I'd saved his life again. Why did he still fight this?

Really.

When I kissed him, it made all the sense in the world. The feeling I'd had before that everything was right in the world intensified as we kissed. This was right. I was meant to be with him.

I just needed to get him to see it. He didn't have a choice any longer. Neither did I. I could not give him up, leave him. I had no intention of doing so. I no longer could imagine life without him. In the short time we'd been together, he'd become the center of my world. This was it. I couldn't let him go. I feared that I truly might die if he sent me away.

"Brennan, don't push me away. I am here with you. I won't leave you. I will be with you, at your side, no matter what. But you have to let me in." I held his face in my hands, forcing him to look at me.

"We are meant to be. We've been meant to be since we met. All this other stuff—that's all it is. Stuff. We can get through this. And we will."

I stared hard at him, willing him to see what I saw, to listen and hear what I said.

Shit. I couldn't tell what he thought. He had the neutral face on.

Brennan

She looked at him with trust, with surety, with...love. With love. Her face, still open and pure as it had been from the first. In spite of all the intrigue, the fact that both of them had nearly died—she still looked at him with the open face of love.

He gathered her to him and buried his face in her neck.

For the first time in six hundred plus years, Brennan felt that he had come home.

CHAPTER TWENTY-ONE

Iris

"Are you ready?" Brennan asked me. He smiled as he spoke.

Almost as much as I'd been smiling.

Ever since that night after his parents had dropped their bombshell, the two of us were together nearly all the time. I had rooms next to his and spent the entire day with him. Not only for safety reasons. I still felt weak, and Taranath hadn't declared me healed until yesterday.

Ailla, his brother, Dhysara—were still out there. The entire realm still teetered on the brink of war. We still didn't know the true motives of all the parties involved.

Which still sucked.

Balancing that out, Brennan had tossed out all of his objections to our being together. Today, we were traveling to see my parents. To tell them that I would be staying here. Unlike my grandmother, I had every intention of moving between my two worlds. After all, I belonged to both.

"I am so ready."

He gathered me to him, kissing me gently on the lips. "As am I."

We still had a lot to deal with. My parents were not going to be happy. He *still* wasn't speaking to his parents. Our few arguments had been regarding their actions. I kept trying to defend them, but wow, it was hard. I found it hard to forgive them as well. The thing that kept me trying was that I knew, in my heart, if Brennan and his parents remained estranged, Cian and Ailla would win.

You could say I fought for my life and my future.

"Let's go, then."

"I love you," we said at the same time.

He opened a portal, and we stepped through.

Together.

EPILOGUE

The room darkened as the light from the portal faded. The only sounds were from far away, from other parts of the castle. Then the fireplace flared into life, lit by an unseen hand.

A man stepped into the light of the now merrily crackling fire.

"You are right to be worried, Brennan. Your time is ending, little brother," the man sneered.

The room went dark as he blocked the fireplace, leaving only the smallest amount of light in the room.

A whisper of movement and the fireplace died as though doused in water.

The quiet of the night returned.

ABOUT THE AUTHOR

Lisa Manifold is fortunate to live in the amazing state of Colorado with her husband, two kids, two dogs, and one offended cat. She enjoys skiing and carting kids and dogs to wherever they need to go, and she adores "treasure hunting" at local thrift stores. Her other hobbies include costuming within her favorite fandoms and periods. Lisa is very (probably overly) involved with her regional writers' organization, Rocky Mountain Fiction Writers. To her great surprise and delight, Lisa has been nominated as a finalist for the RMFW 2016 Independent Writer of the Year award. She is the author of the Sisters Of The Curse series, based on the Grimm Brothers fairy tale The Twelve Dancing Princesses. Her new series, The Heart Of The Djinn, is a trilogy that shows what happens when a free-lancing djinn does his own thing. Three Wishes, the first book in The Heart Of The Djinn series is out now. Book two, Forgotten Wishes, will be out soon! Finally, Brennan, the Goblin King will be making his debut in the Realm trilogy in early summer. You can find her on
Twitter @Lmmanifold
Facebook
https://www.facebook.com/authorlisamanifold
Or her blog https://www.lisamanifold.com

Made in the USA
Middletown, DE
12 June 2016